A GEORDIE UP THE GANGES

THE JOURNEY OF A LIFETIME - THAT MIGHT JUST SAVE HER LIFE

NELL COOK

For John, who understood why I needed to go on that journey.
And for my girls Mam, Joanne and Freyja; my best friends.

For permission requests please contact the author at elaine@nellcookauthor.com

ISBN 978-1-9161724-0-1

"Maybe the journey isn't so much about becoming anything.

Maybe it's about un-becoming everything that isn't really you, so that you can be who you were meant to be in the first place."

Paulo Coelho

CONTENTS

Chapter 1	1
Chapter 2	3
Chapter 3	10
Chapter 4	24
Chapter 5	37
Chapter 6	52
Chapter 7	60
Chapter 8	65
Chapter 9	72
Chapter 10	88
Chapter 11	94
Chapter 12	102
Chapter 13	109
Chapter 14	116
Chapter 15	126
Chapter 16	131
Chapter 17	135
Chapter 18	141
Chapter 19	143
Chapter 20	148
Chapter 21	154
Chapter 22	162
Chapter 23	171
Chapter 24	179
Chapter 25	186
Chapter 26	199
Chapter 27	212
Chapter 28	224
Chapter 29	233
Chapter 30	242
Chapter 31	251
Chapter 32	260

Chapter 33	273
Chapter 34	278
Epilogue	281
Chapter 35	287
Chapter 36	293
About the Author	297
Interview with Nell	299
Acknowledgments	303

1

Am I going to die?

No, no, NO. I can't die yet. There are so many things I haven't done. Swimming with dolphins; witnessing the northern lights; getting a tattoo; skinny-dipping in the Med; sharing a passionate night in a hotel with a stranger.

Must have got my test results mixed up with someone else. Yes, that's it. There's bound to be more than one Jennifer Barnes living in Newcastle.

On the morning the Consultant declared I was in serious trouble, the overriding sensation which engulfed me, piercing my heart with a sword of ice, was one of regret.

You see, the Consultant had just smashed me over the head with a hammer.

It hit me side-on and my brain ricocheted off the inside wall of my skull. Why the hell was the Consultant using the word *cancer*? I'd looked up my symptoms on the net. That persistent nagging pain which radiated from my abdomen around to my back. It was obvious. I had kidney stones. The Consultant carried on talking, 'You'll need surgery to remove your right kidney. Kidney cancer of this type can spread to other parts of the body, and we need to carry out more investigations to check there's no further disease elsewhere.'

I twisted to look at Martin. A ghostly pallor shrouded my husband's face. His grip on my hand tightened as the Consultant continued.

'You're lucky that the cancer seems at the moment to be restricted to just your right kidney. We'll have to remove it, but many people live successfully with only one kidney.'

Lucky? If I'm lucky why the hell did I get kidney cancer in the first place?

The Consultant apologised for giving me such bad news. He shook my hand and sent me towards the x-ray department for urgent chest and lung scans.

It was my fiftieth birthday. When I'd walked through the clinic door earlier I was hoping Martin had noted my thinly disguised hints. I'd seen an amazing and very expensive new telephoto lens for my DSLR camera which I just had to have for my birthday. I'd lusted over that piece of kit for months.

Now, all I desired with every fibre of my being, was a brand new kidney.

2

Martin wanted to talk about it but I froze him out. 'You can't bury your head in the sand, Jen,' he yelled after me as I rushed through our front door, a hint of authority underlining his words. It was the morning after the diagnosis and, like me, he was on the edge of hysteria. Battling hard to retain a grip on my sanity I had to carry on as normal, so I headed off for my Thursday early-morning yoga class.

* * *

A THICK, freezing fog had descended on a subdued Tyneside. This was the season of chapped lips, numbed faces and tingling fingers and toes. I drove over the Tyne Bridge from Newcastle into Gateshead and the misty cityscape, its blurry edges and indistinct, washed-out shapes receded in my rear-view mirror. My body jerked as the car tyres thumped over concrete seams. The fog was thickest surrounding the bridge. Scant, fuzzy light from the Victorian-style street lanterns created an optical illusion, throwing the shadows of the bridge's steel support beams into inscrutable, sinister shapes. The flutter of wind from the open window carried with it a chilly dew which settled on my face and made me shiver. I needed to feel connected, hear another person's voice, so I fiddled with the controls, trying to tune into Metro Radio. The moody river below rolled towards the freedom of the North Sea, determined to escape the confines of the mist sliding over its surface. I started as the muffled horn from an invisible boat further downstream punctured the air.

I'd grown up playing on the banks of this river, it ran through my blood and I loved it. A memory flashed before my eyes. 'Howaaay. Last one in's a geet big soft shite.' A bunch of excited ten-year-old kids galloped towards the edge of the wooden quayside on a warm summer day. I was the first one to jump over the side into the fast-moving water, and bloody hell was it freezing, but I didn't care – I'd won. I was a tomboy, and no one dared call me a soft shite in those days.

* * *

THE YOGA CLASS WAS BUSY, and I chose a mat in the second row. The floor skimming, bottle-green velvet curtains shut out the ambient light and shielded against the winter chill. Melodic Indian chanting played in the background and infused the atmosphere with a calm, mystical aura. A sweet smell, clinging, ancient and dusty filled the air. I recognised the aromatic odour of incense and, looking around, found its source. The white luminous smoke swirled from the glowing tip of the tawny stick and danced up to the ceiling. The lighting was dim and there were twenty other people, of diverse ages, shapes and sizes spaced around on their various coloured mats. A few were warming up, others lay flat on their backs, eyes closed. Some chatted in hushed tones.

Our teacher Emma sat cross-legged on her mat in front of the students. In her hand she held two little cymbal-shaped tingsha prayer bells. The thin, pure tone as she struck one against the other announced that class had begun.

'Ooooommmmm.' The sound radiating from Emma floated around the room. It echoed deep, rich and primordial.

I followed Emma's instructions lying flat on my back, arms and legs extended, eyes closed. Her voice grew soft and calming as she invited us to let go of thoughts from earlier in the day and relax our breathing. I lay there struggling to tune in to my breath moving in and out of my body. For two months now I'd been throwing myself into yoga with a passion. Seeking I didn't know what. Why oh why could I not stop my monkey mind from banging on with those perplexing questions? Oh God. Not now, in the middle of my yoga class. Here we go again. Is there more to life than this? Why am I here? I'm discontent. My life has stagnated. I want happiness and contentment. I want to know I'm making the most of my time. I had an ever-deepening fear I'd leave this world with a heart and a mind full of regrets. And now that was a distinct possibility.

I stretched into the downward dog pose. There I found myself with my body in the shape of an upside-down 'V', my hands and feet on the floor and my butt reaching for the sky. 'Now, concentrate on your breathing, experience the flow of the breath moving in and out of the body and gaze towards the navel,' said Emma. My wrists ached and my legs shook with the exertion as Emma adjusted my spine, assisting me to flatten my back just a few centimetres more. Obviously it was a man who'd invented yoga. How can you gaze at your bloody navel when your boobs are swinging in front of your face?

'That's great, Jen, this pose helps to energise and rejuvenate us. Now, turn your thoughts inward and concentrate on your body.'

But that wasn't happening. My mind was determined to torture me with the recent niggling disagreements I'd had with Martin. My mind headed off down the path of re-living the painful row I'd had with my best friend Pat which had ended our friendship. It was the quarrel with Pat which had prompted me to try yoga. I'd lost a friend, and I grieved. Maybe yoga could help me make sense of my life and the road I had to take.

'Our next pose will be bhujangasana, or cobra pose,' said Emma, offering me a lifeline back to the present. 'A backbend to stretch our muscles and increase flexibility.'

Flat on my stomach with hands on the mat under my shoulders and with arms flexed, I pressed hard through my palms when instructed. I straightened my arms and raised my head and torso until my back arched. My hips and legs remained connected to the floor. I pushed into the ribbing of the pea-green, springy yoga mat as my fingers and palms gripped the surface.

Time stopped. My senses heightened. Now there was only me in the room. The wind outside a murmur. As I focussed my attention on my breath, something shifted in my mind. I could see my breath. I watched in wonderment as it flowed strong and pure on its journey from my nostrils into my trachea. It inflated my lungs then moved back out of my body the way it had arrived. Cool as it entered, and warm as it streamed out of me. I was seeing and feeling the sensations as my breath fluttered, pressing on the inside of my windpipe as it moved in and out. And then it appeared. A tremendous emotional surge. Followed by a hot, stinging sensation behind my eyelids. Get a bloody grip of yourself, Jen. Squeeze your eyes together as tight as you can. But it was no use. My chin quivered as tears forced their way out between my eyelashes.

Oh, the shame.

I relaxed my elbows and lowered my torso back to the mat to hide my face within the safe, dark confines of my folded arms. Try to stop your shoulders from shaking, don't make a noise, Oh God I hope no one can hear me. But there was no fooling Emma. She placed a gentle hand on my arm. 'Don't worry Jen,' she whispered, 'you're experiencing an emotional release, backbends have this effect on people. Your subconscious mind is processing issues rooted deep within, unresolved issues that don't rise to the surface of your consciousness. They can become stuck inside, often you aren't aware of their presence so they never get resolved.' I nodded in acknowledgment, my face still buried in my arms.

Our final posture was cat-cow pose, and I assumed the position on hands and knees.

'You should look like a cat arching its back,' said Emma. 'Now move into cow pose. Inhale. Drop your belly towards the mat. Lift your chin and chest and move your head upwards to gaze towards the ceiling.'

I raised my eyes slowly to stare into the psychedelic patterned lycra-clad backside of the woman on all fours on the mat in front of me. It was a small room and our mats were too close together to feel comfortable in that pose. As we moved back to cat posture, I forgot the proximity of the posterior as my eyes clouded over. From a sinister corner of my mind a predatory voice sunk its claws into my consciousness. *Am I going to die?* In an instant, blackness enveloped me. All around was dark. I saw nothing. Heard nothing. The black stretched on into infinity. It was heavy, pushing down on me from all sides. It was all there was. I stood on the edge of an abyss looking down into a deep, bleak unfathomable nothingness. My awareness hovered on the brink between sanity and madness. A sensation of terror overwhelmed me. Is this it for me? Am I only to be granted fifty years in this life? Is my time over? My thumping heart didn't drown out the voice in my head. I transitioned into cow pose, slowly lifting my head.

Phhffrrttt! Oh My God. She farted. My eyes were level with the psychedelic, protruding backside now pointing straight at my nose. It loomed only inches away. The woman in front of me had only gone and farted right in my face. It was loud and everyone heard it. There was a moment of embarrassed silence before Emma chirped, 'better out than in,' and everyone giggled.

I was furious. How bloody inconsiderate, blowing off like that in someone's face. But people backfire in yoga classes all the time, Jen. It's purely a physical reaction. Howay man, don't take it personally. It wasn't aimed at you. Actually, yes, it was. Right in my face. I wrinkled my nose, anticipating the malodour that was about to invade my personal space, and fought the compulsion to get up from my mat and storm from the room.

It was at that moment the lightning bolt hit me. Hang on a minute. That fart isn't an insult. Can't you see? It's actually the answer. That one goji-berry infused moment of absolute release struck me with sudden insight. That butt trumpet is the herald urging you to let go. Yes, that's it, you have to let go and take action. You mustn't hold things inside any longer. I gagged as sulphur-laden gas assaulted my nostrils but accepted it with grace. That bottom burp was the catalyst I'd been searching for. It told me I shouldn't run away. I should face my situation head-on and fight. I should burst forth. I should blast off.

I actually felt a little gratitude towards the lady who had let one rip.

3

After that yoga class, I parked on the Gateshead side of the Tyne, stretched my beanie hat over my chestnut brown, mid-length bobbed hair and headed on a brisk walk along the quayside. The mirrored facade of the billowing steel, glass and aluminium Sage concert hall reflected the aerobatics of hardy seagulls. They whirled above my head, gliding on spirals of wind pockets. The freezing early morning fog was lifting, making way for the smells which reminded me of childhood adventures here; algae clinging to wet wood, rusty metal, tar, and briny sea water.

The river was high, running fast, carrying with it swirling debris and feathers from birds which had long-since deserted the North-Eastern chill for warmer climes. A niggling trepidation flickered in my abdomen. A fear of the unknown.

The salt carried on the breeze settled on my lips as traffic thundered on the Tyne Bridge overhead, the city coming to life as commuters travelled to work and shoppers headed into the Toon to spend their hard-earned pay. The riverside was empty but for one lone dog-walker. He stopped blowing into his hands just long enough to greet me in true Geordie fashion as he passed by. 'Alreet pet?' he asked.

'Aye. Aaam canny pet. Yee alreet?'

'Aye pet. Aaam canny.'

I flopped down onto my favourite bench. As the murky, swollen water rolled by, my mind was somewhere else entirely. Yoga Convention, two weeks earlier. Stall holders were enticing me to buy their wares, shoving leaflet after leaflet into my hand which I in turn shoved unceremoniously into my bag, not wishing to offend. I'd no intention of investing in a piece of yoga-inspired jewellery which had been lovingly made in India; I didn't need a beechwood meditation stool; I steadfastly refused to use a neti pot to squirt salty water up my nostrils to cleanse my sinuses; and I wasn't interested in a recipe book instructing in the twenty ways one could concoct a nutritious meal out of sodding mung beans.

A pamphlet was thrust towards me. 'Now, you look like the kind of woman who would love an adventure.'

A matchstick ignited in my mind and fizzed into life. 'Ganges Voyager.'

The leaflet lyrically described the curving River Ganges in India; mystical yogis conducting ancient ceremonies in ornate temples; medieval cities crammed with devotees submerging themselves in the river; Royal Bengal Tigers; sultry sari-clad ladies swirling in a kaleidoscope of colour; a breath-taking sunrise.

Soon I could be dead and I don't even know who I am. A vision of a gravestone hovered before my eyes. *Here lies Jennifer Barnes. A stranger to herself.*

I sprang from the bench as though a cattle prod had poked my backside.

* * *

'YOU DID WHAT?'

Priti squinted at me across the top of her monitor. Our desks faced each other in the corner of the hospital's large open-plan finance department. She was twenty years younger than me with long black hair that shone so much that in bright light it looked inky blue. The tiny diamond stud in the side of her nose glinted playfully as the sun from the window bounced off it.

In her broad Geordie accent she asked, 'Eeeh, what's brought all this on, like?'

'Working with you all these years has finally cracked me up,' I said, as the corners of her eyes creased in mirth.

I carried on typing my e-mail.

'And just what does Martin say about this?'

'He's behind me all the way. Wants me to get the wanderlust out of my system.'

'Wey aye man, he'll probably be glad to have the telly remote to himself. But you can't just jet off to India. You need to make sure you're fit and healthy first. Everyone knows middle-aged women need to take more care with their health. Don't forget you're at a funny age.'

Anyone else would have been insulted, but I knew Priti's heart was in the right place.

'Well, thanks for that Priti, I really needed reminding I'm not as young as I used to be.' The ringing of her telephone cut off her retort.

She finished her phone conversation and asked, 'Have you seen that advertisement in the *Chronicle* for the job as a Photographer on the cruise ships?'

I had.

'When I saw it I thought of you. Why don't you apply?

You're always saying you're bored with accountancy and you could put your obsession with photography to good use.'

A shiver of excitement had pulsed up my spine when I'd spotted the advert for Photographer on the cruise liners sailing out of the Port of Tyne starting in the summer. It was two weeks onboard, and two weeks off. Martin had no objections to me being away from home for two weeks at a time. He'd smiled and said, 'absence makes the heart grow fonder.'

I imagined myself doing a job I loved. But what was the point? Someone better than me was bound to apply.

'What? And leave you here crunching numbers all on your own?' I said.

'Seriously Jen, that job would be perfect for you. And the best bit? The interview date is just after you get back from your whirlwind trip to India.'

* * *

SHE WAS RIGHT. It was a whirlwind. I had less than two weeks to learn about India, buy everything I needed and sort out my visa, vaccinations and find specialist travel insurance for those with a cancer diagnosis. I pulled my laptop onto my knee and got comfortable on the sofa.

* * *

THREE HOURS later and I'd only scratched the surface of the search results. What on earth was a shewee? I clicked on the link at the end of a video nasty showing a particularly gross montage of those hole-in-the-ground type toilets. "The portable urinating device for women. Allows you to use the loo standing up. For when you just have to go", read the advertising blurb. Within minutes I'd purchased the bright pink deluxe version, with eight-inch extension tube. But how was I going to ensure the safety of my money? There were so many accounts of people who'd been robbed. Pick-pocket-proof-knickers, of course. Little shorts with a zipped pocket at thigh level on each side at the front. "Much more comfortable than a money belt," the seller boasted. Perfect. It would be a brave man who tried to get his hand down the front of my trousers to get at my cash. I bought a neoprene camera cover to protect the new telephoto lens Martin had bought me for my birthday; a chain and padlock to secure my luggage to my bed on the sleeper trains; and an electronic door wedge that let off an ear-splitting alarm should some fool attempt to open my hotel door at night.

Delighted with my purchases, I closed down my laptop, excitement fluttering in my abdomen.

* * *

THE WOMAN SEATED NEXT to me chatted to her neighbour in the chair to her left. Sections of her hair wrapped in silver foils bobbed up and down as she spoke. The heavy bass lines and syncopated beat of funky music merged with buzzing hairdryers and general chitchat.

The mirror reflected my hairdresser standing behind my chair. I'd been a customer of Rick's for twenty-one years. Today, he held a section of my wet hair between the first and second fingers of his left hand and grasped his scissors aloft in his right. Pausing mid-snip, he had a thoughtful look on his face.

'Why don't you set up a blog? It would be a great way to keep in touch with your family and friends when you're out there. You could even upload your photos. It would be a record of your adventures to look back on when you're old and grey.'

'Wey howay man – me? Set up a blog? I wouldn't know where to start.'

Blogging seemed to be an activity of the younger scene. I was internet savvy, but blogging? That was another level. Rick clipped the overgrown ends off the clump of hair and picked out another neat section.

'You could find out how to set it up on the internet,' he carried on cutting as he spoke. 'If you check out how to set a blog up now, you'll have it done before you leave. Then when you're away, you can keep everybody updated.'

'It would give you something to do at night instead of your knitting and crocheting,' he said with a smile and a wink.

I had to admit, it was a canny idea.

* * *

'NAMASTE, AAPKAA NAAM KYAA HAI?'

'Namaste, meraa naam Jen hai,' I replied to the track.

'Have you learned to say *please give me a bottle of Newcastle Brown Ale?* yet?'

'No, but I've mastered the phrase for *can you advise how I can murder my husband when I get home?*' My well-aimed cushion flew across the lounge, bounced off Martin's head, hit the wall and landed on the floor.

'Well, you never know when you might need a few simple words or phrases, Jen. These thirty minutes a day may prove invaluable.' He went on in his broadest accent. 'Anyhoo, nee bugger'll be able te understand ye if ye rattle on te them in Geordie, like.'

* * *

After much angst, gnashing of teeth, swearing and pulling out of hair, I unravelled the mysteries of setting up a blogging website through internet research. I called my blog A Geordie Up The Ganges and with one week to departure I published my first entry to the world, entitled “And So It Begins”.

On my website’s About Me page I kept it brief.

I want excitement.

I want to experience life.

I want to learn about me.

* * *

‘Martin, my plastic willy has arrived,’ I shouted up the stairs in excitement.

The postman who was just turning to retrace his steps down our driveway twisted to peer at me through the half-closed door. I grinned and pushed it closed.

‘This should help me navigate those hole-in-the-ground toilets,’ I continued. I attached the tube section to the funnel and held it up, turning it round in mid-air for Martin to see.

‘Hmm. The box advises practicing in the bath at home before using it outdoors. I don’t have time for that now. I’ll just have to fly by the seat of my pants and give it a go when I’m out there. It can’t be that difficult to use.’

‘Wey aye, you’ll just have to go with the flow, Jen.’

Groaning, I lobbed my little pink wonder onto the growing stockpile of items marked *India*.

* * *

The following day the same postman handed over my second delivery with a smirk, before heading off to deliver a package next door. I couldn't wait to try on my knickers. As I dashed upstairs to the bedroom, I ripped open the packaging to reveal three pairs of light grey underwear which I had dubbed my "security knickers". I pulled a pair on, stuffed my passport and credit cards into the specially designed zipped pockets, and strutted off to find Martin. I raced down the stairs wearing only my thick woollen winter jumper and my new knickers. He was in the dining room at the front of the house with the door from the hallway closed.

I was in a frivolous mood.

I pressed down on the handle, knowing my performance would be private. The voile at the window would be protection enough in case anyone was passing.

I belted out the "Stripper" song at the top of my voice whilst I gyrated through the door.

To my horror, Martin was standing at the window with the voile pulled to one side. I froze for an instant before spinning and running full pelt back through the door in the direction of the hallway. There was someone passing at the precise moment I appeared dancing and singing suggestively in front of Martin. He heard my singing and had an extensive view of the interior of our dining room.

It was the postman, on his way back to his van.

* * *

Once I'd displaced my shame with a manic sorting and packing session, editing the family-sized pack of ten toilet rolls down to one, taking the tea bags out then sneaking them back in again (how could a Brit go on holiday without her tea bags?), my thoughts turned to my fellow travelling companions. Did I mention that I was about to embark on a journey with seven strangers?

I had already concluded what my strategy would be if my chemistry conflicted with another's. At fifty years old I knew my personality traits pretty well and one thing was a certainty. I could not fake congeniality and I was resolute I would allow no-one to ruin this once-in-a-lifetime experience. If there was anyone I didn't gel with, I'd stay as far away from them as the group travel situation would permit.

Adrenaline warmed my abdomen, and the hairs prickled on the back of my neck. What was that sensation? I'd known it many times. This time the answer came. It was wariness. Mistrust. I resigned myself to the fact that although I shied away from group situations, this time I couldn't avoid it. I wanted to go to India, and it was necessary to go as part of a group. No group, no India.

* * *

PING.

A Geordie Up The Ganges flared to life. I had ten followers. And what's more, some had left messages.

> *Hey, have a great time in India. The blog looks awesome. Told ya you could do it Jen. Goforrit. Rick.*

> *Hi, You don't know me but I've signed up to follow you. Hoping to pick up some tips. I'm off to India too in a few weeks. Lucy.*

> *Gonna be quiet in the office without you. I'm with you in spirit all the way. Have a great adventure. Love Priti x*

I hit the publish button just as Martin announced it was time to leave for Heathrow.

<u>Friday, 26th February, Newcastle-Upon-Tyne</u>

Bye, bye Geordieland.

At last the time has come to embark on the first leg of this journey, and this will be my final blog from Newcastle. I've come to the end of the research, speculation, worrying, fantasising and woolgathering. The wait is over, the spadework complete and this is where my adventure begins.

Flight socks, check.

Travel sickness tablets, check.

Earplugs, check.

Travel pillow, check.

Kitchen sink, check.

Well, you never know do you?

I can't contain my excitement.

Wish me luck,

Jen x

* * *

FIVE HOURS after leaving our front door in Newcastle, we followed the signs for Heathrow Airport's Terminal 4 Departures, and found our way to the vast glass-fronted building which housed the departures check-in desks. 'Away ye go and have a fantastic adventure love,' said Martin, pulling me into a hug before he turned and strode away. Just before he disappeared from view he turned, waved and shouted, 'look after yourself.' I waved a final goodbye and then he was gone.

I suddenly felt very alone.

I looked around at all the people stood in snaking

queues at the numerous check-in desks. Others strolled around, staring up at the glimmering neon signs above each queue beckoning travellers towards their destination. Some huddled in small groups chatting, luggage at their feet. Others talked into their mobile phones and some leaned or squatted on the floor with their backs against the glass wall, reading newspapers and books. There was a frequent, cheery bing-bong from the public address system. A faceless woman with a plum in her mouth cautioned passengers not to leave their baggage unattended.

I found my queue and joined the end of the meandering line at desk number three. The neon sign above advised that the departure of flight number 9W121 to New Delhi was due to leave on time at 8.50 pm.

Once in line I scoured every piece of baggage before I studied the other passengers. Transform Your World Travel had provided the Ganges Voyager travellers with a triangular plastic, cedar-green luggage label resembling a tree. I hoped that I might identify my fellow voyagers and introduce myself.

Disappointed not to spot any familiar tree triangles, I settled down to observe the efficiency of the checking-in process and appraise the other passengers in the queue. I enjoyed people-watching in such situations and speculated about the lives of those I observed. Strangers made furtive glances, assessing each other in the line. Some were bold enough to look their fellow travellers up and down, ready with a smile if the person of their interest caught them red-handed in their evaluations. I noticed another desk for the Delhi flight with a sign above stating Online Check-in Passengers Only. There were only two people stood in that line whilst I was still near the end of my present queue. I had checked in online and reserved my seat on the plane on the previous evening, so I made a quick decision to swap queues.

The man turned to look at me as I dropped my luggage with a thud on the floor behind him. Our eyes met. He didn't respond to my smile but looked me up and down, taking in everything about me and my luggage. Undeterred, I maintained a friendly smiling demeanour. 'Is this the queue for passengers who've already checked in and booked their seats online?'

A stony-faced 'yes' and I was left to grimace at the man's back. I held my breath and allowed my eyes to drift towards his luggage, hoping this person was not one of the group of individuals who was about to share my grand adventure.

Dressed in a checked shirt and jeans, he towered above the woman standing next to him. He looked about early sixties in age with luxurious greying hair groomed to perfection. His eyes darted back and forth as he rubbed at his aquiline nose. He held himself tall and proud and had it not been for his frown I would have described him as a handsome and distinguished man. But the corners of his mouth were turned down in what I imagined was a permanent scowl. He radiated an expression that implied someone had dared let loose a smelly fart in his presence.

My attention turned to the woman with him. She too wore a checked shirt and jeans but that was where the similarities ended. Where he was tall and slim, she was short and chubby. Her mousy hair scraped away from her forehead sat high on the back of her head in a ponytail. Huge round cornflower blue eyes squinted as she flapped a fan furiously in front of her face in a vain attempt to cool her shiny pink complexion. The cheeks above her generous plump lips expanded as she huffed and puffed. She looked weary. On edge. Not surprising being married to that miserable sod.

The desk clerk interrupted my reverie as he called the couple forward to check in their baggage. My curiosity piqued, I strained to listen as they answered the questions posed about who had packed their bags. I couldn't hear the words but my impression of the conversation taking place at the desk, was that it seemed ill-tempered. The man became animated and heaved their cases onto the conveyor belt. He snatched the boarding cards and passports from the clerk and with his wife scampering behind him, loped off to disappear amongst the Heathrow crowds.

Next it was my turn. The crimson-faced, exasperated desk clerk beckoned me forward. It was obvious I'd just encountered one of life's ass wipes. As I would never see the sour-faced man and his wife again, I soon forgot about the short but disagreeable experience.

I found the bar, took a selfie with my glass raised in cheers and uploaded the image to my blog.

Friday, 26th February, Heathrow Airport, London

Yes, I've hit the drink already folks. With time to kill before the departure gate opens, there's nothing else for it but to indulge in a large glass of red. My next blog will come to you from New Delhi. I hope you enjoy coming along with me on my adventure. Love Jen x

Ping. A message from my colleague Kev, the office joker, popped onto the screen.

Cheers Jen, I hope you've packed your wellies, with all those king cobras waiting to strike unsuspecting Geordies, it's the only safe way to travel in India!

I liked blogging. It was fun. The overhead screen flashed with information about the flight to New Delhi. With no time to fire off a sarcastic reply to Kev, I rammed my laptop into my bag, drained my glass, and scurried off towards departure gate two.

* * *

THE THROBBING deep inside my ears indicated the cabin air pressure had dropped. Flight number 9W121 was descending towards New Delhi. As the minutes passed, the pulsating heat in my ears grew worse. Five minutes later the pain was at its peak and my only option was acceptance. All the swallowing, yawning and sucking of boiled sweets was futile. I tried pressing the area beneath my ear with my thumb and holding my nose whilst attempting to breathe out. None of this reduced the hurting one jot. Time for my coping strategies again. Over the years I'd become adept at burying thoughts drenched in pain, and I was able to redirect my focus away from the throbbing heat. After another ten minutes the ache abated, then faded away as the plane approached the runway.

The plane's wheels contacted the tarmac with a smooth landing. I was on Indian soil at last.

4

Once we disembarked from the plane, the crowd headed as one towards Arrivals in the modern terminal three of Indira Gandhi International Airport. The sign above our heads greeted us with "Welcome to India". The white letters shimmered with a silver glint from the radiant sun beaming through the windows, and I felt a delicious shiver of anticipation.

As we entered the main concourse on our way to baggage reclaim, my gait slowed as I gazed agog at the spectacle before me. A huge metallic sculpture adorned the whole length of the facade above the check-in desks. Jutting from the wall, covered with hundreds of great shining copper discs, were nine enormous silver hand sculptures in various poses.

I'd learned about these expressive hand gestures, or mudras, from Emma at my yoga class. Abandoning my quest to be one of the first at the baggage carousel, something compelled me to pause and gaze. I'd read that many of these hand motions form an intrinsic part of Indian classical dance, visual arts and yoga. I recalled Emma telling me, 'It's believed mudras channel natural forces, and aid spiritual and mental well-being by enhancing the flow of energies through the body.'

I recognised pranayama mudra. The expression which symbolises good health, equilibrium, well-being and life force. I had used those hand and finger positions in class when we'd practiced nadi shodhana pranayama, to alternate and regulate the breath through our nostrils. I'd been amazed when controlling breathing in that way had produced a calming effect.

The metallic surfaces of the concave copper coloured discs produced abstract rippling reflections, which gave the impression they were living, breathing creatures. Creatures which depicted fragmented scenes of life, playing out on mercurial screens. Here was a secular representation of India, symbolising all of her people without adherence to any specific religion. It perfectly defined the Indian values I'd read and heard about, displaying a warm welcome to all. I'd travelled over four thousand miles to a country I hadn't visited before. Yet here was a depiction which was familiar and comforting. It felt like coming home.

I stopped hurrying and felt perfectly peaceful when I reached the baggage carousel, to discover it heaved with the usual scrum.

The man in front of me stretched his left arm out in front of him. Sensing he would need space, I took a step backward. The top half of his body moved forward, and he heaved a huge black suitcase from the belt and swivelled his body to face me. We moved in unison. I stepped to the side to let him through, then glided into the space he had vacated. At last I had a front-row view.

My green soft bag with its identifiable bright red strapping wobbled its way towards me. It was approaching from the left-hand side and when it was within reach I strengthened my legs, reached for the handle, and hoisted it. The weight pulled my body forwards, and I lost my footing, staggered to the side and collided with my neighbour.

Just as I was about to instigate a domino effect tumble on the people to my left, a long, graceful green sleeved arm veered in from the right. The mysterious saviour grabbed the other handle on my bag and pulled. Together, the green arm and I swung the bag around. With one fell swoop it hit the floor with a resounding thwack behind the gaggle of people.

'Thanks very much, pet. I was just about to create havoc within an hour of arriving in India.' I smiled at the lady who had come to my aid.

'Don't mention it. Jolly chaotic, isn't it?' She spoke with the cut-glass accent of a toff.

She glanced at my bag. 'I see you're with Transform Your World Travel. You're not joining the Ganges Voyager tour by any chance, are you?'

'Indeed I am.'

'Oh how jolly marvellous.' She beamed a sincere, friendly smile. 'Me too. It's awfully splendid to meet you. I'm Alexandra Lennox.'

We shook hands. 'Wey hello, Alexandra. It's lovely to meet you too. I'm Jennifer Barnes, everyone calls me Jen. I'll hang out at the back while you wait for your luggage to appear. I'm here to help if you need me!'

She marched forward into the centre of the scrum and I observed her from the side. She towered head and shoulders above everyone else. With her shock of bright ginger hair, choppy fringe, pale freckled face and glossy red lipstick, she shone like a beacon in a murky sky. She stood her ground in the melee, dispatching the guy who tried to shove her to one side with a withering look. She turned and glanced at me, the laughter lines around her forest-green eyes crinkling as she smiled.

She stepped forward. I moved closer and as she swung around, her luggage in one hand, I grabbed the other handle and together we landed her bag next to mine with a thud.

'Great teamwork,' I said as we whooped and gave each other a high-five.

We headed in the direction of the Currency Exchange desk pulling our bags behind us.

'Is that a North-Eastern accent I detect, Jen? It's jolly nice.'

'Wey aye man.' I emphasised my Geordie twang. 'Have you ever been to Newcastle?'

'No, but I positively love Ant and Dec.' She winked at me. I was warming to her, she had a sense of humour.

'Where are you from?' I held my breath, expecting her to say Buckingham Palace.

'I'm from Windsor.' It was near enough. 'Have you ever been there?' she asked.

'No, but I really love the Queen.' I winked.

We giggled and, as she giggled even harder, she snorted. That was infectious and made me laugh even more. We laughed at each other laughing. Our merriment echoed around the corridor.

As we walked, we told each other a little about ourselves. She was a fiction editor. Divorced with no children and single for the last fifteen years. She hadn't been to India before but this was her sixtieth birthday year, and she wanted to mark it with an unusual experience.

I shared a few basic details about myself – omitting of course my recent news and the real reason for my trip.

Although we'd hit it off, I didn't want anyone to be uncomfortable around me, and certainly couldn't bear to have her feel sorry for me.

Whatever happened in India, one thing was certain. My secret would stay locked inside until I got home.

We joined the shortest of the four snaking queues at the Currency Exchange desks.

As India operated a closed currency, it meant that we couldn't change our British pounds for Indian rupees before arrival in the country. The trip notes from Transform Your World Travel had advised travellers to exchange a few pounds into rupees at the airport, to get us through the first day. We could then change a larger amount of money in Delhi for a better exchange rate.

I'd read many horror stories on the internet of skilled Indian pickpockets and was glad my credit cards, passport and cash would be stashed in the zipped pockets of my security knickers. I'd counted out forty pounds in five and ten-pound notes and slotted them deep into the pockets before leaving home.

People chatted amongst themselves as the queues shortened. This section of the airport was spacious and airy with sunrays streaming in through the high windows. 'I need to retrieve my cash from my knickers now,' I said. I inhaled and tugged at the belt of my combat pants, struggling to force my hand in and down to the space just above my crotch. Alexandra looked on, mystified.

Why had I fastened the belt too tight to get my hand in, and down far enough to open the zipper on the little pocket holding my cash? After a few attempts there was nothing for it but to unbuckle the belt. At last it was open and the buckle end dangled down the front of my right leg. Next I unbuttoned the waist on my trousers, pulled the zipper on the fly open an inch and jammed my hand down far enough to reach the zip. People in the immediate vicinity were taking notice. With my arm thrust into the front of my dangerously loose trousers, I fiddled with the tiny zip which I could only open an agonising centimetre by centimetre.

'Och lassie, can I be of any assistance to help ye search for whatever ye'r looking for?'

Swivelling around, my hand still thrust down the front of my trousers, I peered into mischievous, heavy-lidded eyes of electric blue. There was a hint of turbulence in their depths. Feigning outrage, my gaze settled on the wizecracker's lopsided cocky grin. My breath caught. That smile reminded me of the schoolgirl crush I'd had on my English teacher.

Finally, the zip was open. 'Hey presto.' With a theatrical 'Ta-da' I yanked the notes out of my knickers with a flourish.

'That's a strange part of yer body te use as a money box, hen.'

As the joker spoke, he held up the familiar green tree luggage label. Alexandra and I spoke in unison. 'Ganges Voyager?'

'Och, aye. Fraser MacLean, lady-killer and ace personal trainer at your service.' His broad Scottish accent boomed around the hall.

His sandy coloured hair shaved close to his head, and half-inch scar above his right eyebrow, added emphasis to his roguish appearance. A cropped beard covered a powerful chin and jawline. He resembled a British Bulldog, short and stocky, his muscular body evident in jeans and tight black t-shirt. He thrust a tattooed arm, which proclaimed his love for Glasgow Rangers, towards us, and Alexandra and I introduced ourselves.

The desk clerk beckoned me forward.

I handed over the notes to the cashier while paying attention to the exchange-rate board on the wall behind him. The advice on the net had been to exercise vigilance during these transactions to avoid being short-changed. The cashier took my notes and held out his other hand towards me. What the hell did he want now?

'Passport, madam.'

Damnit.

I undid the belt on my trousers again as a long queue formed behind me. Oh God, I couldn't get it out. I rooted around in my knickers trying to extract my passport. Hot and bothered, I handed it over the counter. Twenty, forty, sixty, keep your concentration on the cashier's hands. He counted the unfamiliar rupee notes out on the desk in front of me. I focused as he planted each note on top of the other until he reached three thousand, three hundred and sixty rupees. A quick calculation in my head confirmed that I'd received the correct sum of money. I picked up the cash and strode away from the desk.

'Madam, madam, oh madaaam.'

What did he want now? I spun round to see the cashier holding up my passport, waggling it back and forward. Shocked at my sloppiness, my face burned. The seconds it took to walk back and retrieve it as everyone looked on seemed like hours.

I consigned my passport and most of the cash to the depths of my knickers, putting a few hundred rupee notes into the zipped pocket of my shirt. I grabbed my luggage bag and trundled it to where Fraser and Alexandra stood waiting for me. They hadn't seen the exchange, and I was too embarrassed to enlighten them on my air-headed encounter. Minutes later we exited through the airport door into the bright, hot sunshine where our Group Leader and a further five strangers awaited.

Fraser spotted the sign first and my gaze followed his outstretched arm. My head weaved from side to side striving to identify the Transform Your World Travel sign, in between the crowds milling around and the endless stream of traffic. We negotiated a course across to the other side of the road and dragged our cases behind us, heading for the arm stretched up in the air.

An Indian guy around fifty years old strode towards us, leaving behind him a small group of people. 'Hello, I'm Vijay Harish, your Tour Guide. Welcome to India,' his beaming smile played in his eyes and accentuated the dimples in his round cheeks as he shook our hands. He had a face that inspired trust and a comfortable body made for hugs. He presented a safe and reliable image of Transform Your World Travel, dressed in a crisp white shirt, camel-coloured slacks and brown sandals. His jet black hair was thick and shiny, brushed back from his forehead and cut into the nape of his neck.

'We're just waiting for two more people who will join us. Then the coach will be coming to transport us to the hotel.' He mopped perspiration from his forehead with a pristine white handkerchief.

From where we stood I had a perfect vantage point of the arrivals door, and the people emerging from it. There were still two members of our group not yet accounted for, and my eyes were glued to the door.

And then I saw them.

They appeared through the glass sliding doors pulling their cases behind them. A tall, slim guy with a down-turned mouth. A short plump woman, her mousy hair tied up in a ponytail. My breath slowed as I spun my wedding ring on my finger. Her head weaved from side to side looking for someone or something specific through the crowds. Where are they? I can't see them. There she is. Her ponytailed head was bobbing across the road which separated our meeting point from the main airport building. There they are again in the middle of that crowd. Chagrin rose in my throat as they headed towards Vijay's raised arm. Go away. Go away. My desperate desire for these people to change direction away from where we were gathered was fruitless. They stood in front of our group leader, shaking his hand.

'Hello, we're Derek and Betty Adamson.' His voice boomed.

How long is the Indian jail sentence for throwing a person from a speeding sleeper train? My deliberations on how to commit the perfect murder were interrupted when I recalled the advice I'd read about protecting myself from mosquito bites in India. I fiddled around in the plastic bag for the spray I'd bought at Heathrow. The brand I'd chosen included one hundred percent Deet, the recommended active ingredient used to protect against mosquitos. I wasn't taking any chances. I sprayed the exposed parts of my arms, neck and chest then sprayed the palm of my hands and rubbed the solution all over my face.

At last our group was complete, and the coach arrived.

It was hot. I hoisted my main luggage bag into the holding compartment of the coach and swung my day bag onto my shoulder. I fiddled with the plastic bag containing my purchases from Heathrow, looking for a bottle of water, and climbed the steps into the coach. After hauling myself into my seat with a 'phew,' I wiped the sweat from my face with my hands. It was a relief to be out of the sun and in the air-conditioned interior of our coach.

Alexandra slid into the seat next to me. I dropped my day bag onto the floor in between my feet and rummaged in the plastic carrier bag for a tissue.

As I withdrew my right hand from the bag, I recoiled with surprise.

'What the hell?' I held both of my hands palms upwards in astonishment.

They were stained bright blue. Alexandra heard my exclamation and turned to look at my upturned palms. For a second or two we both stared incomprehensibly at my hands. Then in a flash I realised my mistake.

'It's the plastic bag Alexandra, the bloody plastic bag.'

I held up the plastic bag with its now smeared blue and white design and I knew in an instant what had happened. The user reviews on the net about mosquito repellent had warned, sprays which included the ingredient Deet may be corrosive and dissolving to plastics. Most of the blue ink from the company logo on the bag was now on my hands.

I rubbed my hands on the tissue but the ink had dried and I couldn't wipe it away.

In the next second, I remembered I'd wiped my face with my hands as I took my seat. Not daring to ask, I turned my face to Alexandra. She returned my look and her grimace gave me the answer I was dreading.

Saying nothing, she handed me the small travel mirror from her rucksack. I raised it and looked in horror at myself.

There reflected at me, covering both sides of my face, were two large streaks of bright blue ink smeared hard-and-fast from cheek to jowl.

As I scrubbed at my face with a wet wipe, Vijay spoke to us through the coach microphone. It would be a short drive to our hotel. He explained the coach could not drop us off outside the door as the roads in that area were too narrow for the driver to navigate. We'd have a short walk, just ten minutes down two streets. New Delhi flashed by street by street, but I was too busy scrubbing at my face to pay much attention. The blue streaks were fading to reveal my now stinging, lobster-coloured skin underneath. The others either chatted or became lost in the unfamiliar scenes whizzing by.

It wasn't long before the coach came to a stop and I clambered down its steps onto the dry, dusty street. Within seconds I was transported from a world of cool, orderly peace into a hot, swirling cacophony of noise. The intensity was a shock to the system, and it disoriented me. We stood in single file at the side of a road which had no pavement. Vijay led from the front.

'Follow me. Please be keeping to the side and always be watching out for the traffic.'

He held his red clipboard in the air and we stepped one after the other into pandemonium.

We were hemmed in as we proceeded. On one side it was whacky races. Cars ranging from old bangers to well-cared-for taxis; horse-drawn carts; motorbikes; automatic tuk tuks; bicycle-powered tuk tuks; coaches; lorries and bicycles flashed by so close that my clothes flapped in the hot draught. On the opposite side was row after row of flimsy dwellings and huts made from sheets of polythene attached to trees and lampposts. The clamour was deafening. The impatient and constant toot-toot competed with squeaking bodywork as vehicles bounced over bumps in the road. Shouting in a foreign tongue bombarded my ears from all directions. There was screeching of breaks and slamming of doors. The throngs of people heaved, running and skipping, deftly dodging traffic and swelling the masses at each side of the road.

My stress levels rose a notch.

Bloody hell. That was too close for comfort. A green and yellow automatic tuk tuk sped past, its wing mirror skimming my shirt sleeve.

My hand, hot and sweaty, shook with the effort of clutching the handle of my luggage. As I dragged it, the wheels bounced over the uneven hard, dusty ground. My tongue was wedged to the roof of my mouth and the walls of my throat stuck together each time I tried to swallow. I was desperate for a drink of water, but maintained my concentration on Alexandra in front of me as we made our way closer to the hotel.

As we trundled past groups of people assembled in huddles, they stared. It wasn't threatening, they were very curious about the group of westerners who had clearly just arrived in their city. A barefoot child about seven years old appeared by Alexandra's side. Her tiny, dirty legs skipped below her faded blue dress as she sought to keep up with Alexandra's striding gait. As she tapped on Alexandra's arm, her other hand extended and palm open, she repeated over and over, 'Money please lady, for baby shoes.'

After a few minutes Vijay left the front of the line, walked back to us and gently shoo-shooed the child away.

'It's best not to be giving money to beggars on the street. You can't be donating to everyone and only it is encouraging them to see it as a way of life, instead of attending school or looking for work.'

He strode back to the head of the line, yelling, 'Almost there now.'

At last we reached the hotel. My nerves were jangling, I was sweating and felt light-headed. I exchanged a glance of bewilderment with Alexandra when Vijay said, 'It's being very quiet today because it's Sunday.'

We congregated in the deliciously cool reception as Vijay distributed our room keys. He asked us to meet in two hours to begin our first sight-seeing tour of the city.

I struggled through the door to my room, dragging my large luggage bag over the threshold. My day pack was slung over my shoulder, my camera dangled around my neck and the plastic bag, now devoid of its blue ink, swung from my wrist. The door banged shut behind me. I slung my bags to the carpeted floor with a huge effort. A double bed with high dark oak headboard and matching bedside tables dominated the room. Opposite the bed was a dressing table in matching oak with a huge mirror. It was clean and comfortable. I opened the bathroom door. A proper loo. No need to scramble around in my luggage for my shewee here.

I collapsed gratefully onto the bed. Now, as I sat there alone staring at myself in the mirror, I wondered what I'd done.

5

I climbed on board the minibus searching for two unoccupied seats together. I preferred not to sit beside anyone. There was a spare seat next to a young woman with lilac-coloured hair. As I walked down the aisle, she patted the seat next to her, and with reluctance I had no option but to take it. She introduced herself as Summer Payne and her bangles chuckled as we shook hands. Her name typified her look – carefree, warm, blooming.

'My parents were hippies, and we travelled the world when I was young,' she said. 'Mum said they chose my name because it symbolises happiness.'

She had a joyful, relaxed vibe surrounding her. Her parents had named her well. She looked at home in India dressed in multi-coloured harem pants. Black eyeliner emphasised her almond-shaped brown eyes, shining with an inscrutable intelligence. A nose ring and stud just above her lip added to her ethnic appearance. I guessed that she was a yoga teacher when I noticed the chakra tattoos on her feet and arms. Her smoky voice had the same soothing quality as the faint smell of incense which clung to her clothing.

On our first sightseeing outing we were to visit the Red Fort, followed by the Jama Masjid Mosque. I was keen to get my adventure underway, and couldn't figure out why our vehicle was stationary outside the hotel door with the motor running. I looked around the minibus and discovered the reason. There were two people missing. Derek and Betty.

Fifteen minutes later they appeared, strolling towards the minibus. Derek looked like he had all the time in the world as he smoothed back his hair and adjusted his sky-blue baseball cap. Betty looked distracted as she flapped her fan in front of her face. I hoped they weren't going to make a habit of this, but told myself not to be too hasty to judge. I'd make an effort to get to know them at the group meal that night.

I settled into my seat next to Summer. This time I could give my full attention to the activity in the Delhi streets flashing by. The scenes from the coach were staggering. I'd read of the culture shock that awaited people on their initial visit to India. Nothing anyone had written, or any scene from television, could have prepared me for my incredulity as I witnessed daily life in Delhi first-hand.

There wasn't an inch of space on the crowded streets teeming with people. Some were well dressed. The clean and modern younger male generation in trendy jeans and shirts. Women and girls in shalwar kameez or saris, shimmering in a kaleidoscope of colours. Then, at the other end of the scale, were families living in grinding poverty, huddled in groups on the pavements, their meagre belongings surrounding them. There were huge contrasts everywhere. One minute, here was a man dressed in rags sleeping in the dirt; the next a beautiful young woman draped in luxurious silk.

Did I see a man urinating up against a wall? No, surely not. But as we cruised past street after street, there were others. Men were peeing in broad daylight and crowded areas. And still that constant toot-toot. The proliferation of traffic on the roads swallowed up any remaining available space. This whirligig world stirred up memories of the chaotic and unsettling mindset I'd experienced at the time of my diagnosis. A knot of fear throbbed in my abdomen. I clasped my arms around my body in an attempt to soothe myself. I was vulnerable. A tiny, scared person in this swirling, out-of-control vortex.

We passed mile upon mile of stands and markets, selling a multitude of goods to thousands upon thousands of customers and browsers. There were indoor bazaars and outdoor shops on the hard earthen floor with their wares piled high on blankets. Clothes, food, equipment of every kind. The list was endless. The sellers utilised every accessible space. Clothing hung on coat hangers dangling from tree branches, or nails hammered into disintegrating walls of buildings. Every single one crumbling and shedding its once fresh-painted plastered facade of red, blue, green or yellow.

Monkeys scampered up decaying walls, vaulted between trees and swung on overhead wires stretching between dilapidated buildings.

I had fallen asleep and woken on another planet.

* * *

LEAVING THE FRENZIED STREETS BEHIND, we arrived at the Red Fort.

Before we stepped from the minibus, Vijay gave us a potted history. He explained that Emperor Shah Jahan had ordered the construction which was completed in 1639. It had been the main residence of the emperors of the Mughal dynasty for two hundred years. We would be free to wander around the fort and its museums, but were required to return in two hours to allow us time at our next stop. The Jama Masjid Mosque.

The patchy grass surrounding the architectural wonder amplified the saturation of the imposing red sandstone walls. Iridescent green birds filled the air, swooping from the encircling trees. The peace and quiet was a world away from the frantic scenes I'd witnessed from the coach, and a welcome reprieve from the intensity. The air was heavy with the scent of parched grass and sweltering tarmac as we made our way to the Lahori Gate. Alexandra, Fraser, Summer and myself chatted as we strolled.

'That's a rather professional looking camera Jen, are you into photography?' Alexandra pointed to my camera strung around my neck.

'It's just a hobby, but I'm very passionate about it.' I lifted the camera to allow her a closer look.

The others had walked on a few steps. I concentrated on dialling the correct settings into the camera, as usual losing myself in the technical aspects of aperture, shutter speed and depth of field. I called out for them to turn round and took a shot. The telephoto lens captured the scene perfectly. The resulting image showed three smiling faces with the fort correctly exposed in the background.

'Golly, that's a marvellous shot, you must be our official group photographer, Jen,' said Alexandra.

But I knew it wasn't a marvellous shot. It was an okay shot. I couldn't pinpoint it, but something was missing. Oh yes, the exposure and composition were spot on, but the image left me cold.

'I'm nowhere near good enough for that.' I dropped the camera into my bag.

'Don't put yourself down, Jen. You should jolly well have confidence in your abilities.'

Alexandra was right. I always doubted myself.

We joined the security queue at the entrance. Each person had to show the interiors of any bags they were carrying. Then it was a quick frisking around the arms, down the sides of the body finishing with the legs. The security officer had herded the others through the gate, and they watched as I approached the scary looking policewoman carrying out the frisking.

I opened my bag. She poked around the insides with a wooden stick moving the contents around, checking the interior. Placing my bag on the floor, I raised my arms and stood with my legs apart. She began by rubbing her hands along each arm. Then she frisked each side of my upper body before rubbing her hands down each of my legs. The next seconds happened in a flash. Instead of ushering me towards the others, she grabbed me between my legs and squeezed. Before I could react, she had reached down picked up my bag, shoved it into my hands and pushed me forward and through the gate.

I was aghast. My eyes blinked rapidly. I didn't know where to look. I could still feel the pressure on that private place in between my legs. It tingled with nauseating heat. One glance at the others confirmed that they'd seen. Alexandra looked as shocked as I was, her eyes wide, her hand covering her mouth. Summer bit her bottom lip and shook her head slowly, struggling to hide a smile. Fraser guffawed with delight.

I felt queasy. 'Have you seen her grab anyone else like that?'

The others shook their heads.

'Och Lassie, didn't ye know? News travels fast in India. She's heard which orifice ye stash yer cash in.'

Alexandra and I convulsed into laughter. Summer looked at me, mystified.

'I'll tell you later, Summer pet,' I said as we strode off to investigate the fort.

* * *

THE AREA inside the fort was busy with people of many nationalities wandering around, marvelling at the splendour on show.

'May I tag along with you, Jen? It would be jolly nice.' Alexandra fell into step beside me.

My attempt to extricate myself from the group unnoticed had failed. I was on a mission. At stake was a two-hour photo-fest where I could lose myself behind my lens, and there was no time for small talk.

'Yes, of course, that would be lovely, should we head over to the Hall of Audience first?' I said. I forced a smile, hoping my expression wasn't a giveaway.

Gorgeous light bathed the Hall of Audience where the Mughal Emperor used to receive courtiers and state guests. Beams of sunshine shone through its columns and illuminated the engraved and gilded curving arches within. A perfect photo opportunity. Excitement filled me as I adjusted the settings on the camera and took my shot. Alexandra peered over my shoulder at the image on the back screen.

'Utterly splendid. I'd adore it if I possessed skills to take photos like that. Would you give me a few tips, Jen?'

'Well, I'm no professional but I'll teach you what I know if you like.'

I removed the strap from round my neck and passed it over Alexandra's head.

'Now, you take a shot. No, don't stick your elbows out, bring them into your sides, frame your subject and squeeze the shutter smoothly.'

I recognised the look of pleasure on Alexandra's face as she viewed her shot. That ephemeral instant she'd captured of shafts of sunbeams streaming through ancient pillars. I knew how the satisfying precision of the electronic chunk and double click of the shutter danced in her ear. I was so delighted to see how enrapt she was, I forgot my shyness.

We moved around the fort seeking out photogenic scenes together. The eager student and enthusiastic teacher. My awkwardness forgotten, I revelled in imparting my knowledge. I surprised myself with just how much I knew on the subject of photography. The hours of internet research, the trial and error based self-education, it was all pouring out of me.

We were so engrossed in each other's company, we had no perception of time until we bumped into Summer and Fraser, who alerted us that in fifteen minutes we needed to be back at the minibus.

'That was marvellous Jen, you're a bloody good teacher.' Alexandra took one last shot before handing over the camera.

'You've got an eye for a good composition, Alexandra,' I said as we reviewed the shots she'd captured on the back of the camera. I was elated as warmth spread throughout my body. I was so passionate about photography and it seemed I'd introduced someone else to its wonders.

We hurried back to the minibus not wanting to be late and arrived with ten minutes to spare. Alexandra bounced up the steps two at a time and sat next to the young guy called Charlie who I'd yet to meet. I didn't want to get onto the bus just yet, though. I'd spied a photo opportunity.

Sat on the steps outside the fort was someone clad in the garb of a holy man. His gigantic frame was draped in shimmering white which contrasted against his dark, shining nut-brown skin. His long brown dreadlocks and beard of black and grey transitioned into bright ginger at the ends. He was a perfect subject. I worked fast, attaching the long lens to the camera. I wanted that shot. I wasn't comfortable photographing strangers, but he wasn't looking in my direction, I could grab a side shot of him without being detected. My heartbeat quickened. I seized my chance, raised the camera to my eyes with caution, extended the lens to its full length and pressed the shutter. Just at that exact second he turned his head towards me.

My heart leapt. Could I have insulted him?

He smiled. I breathed a sigh of relief and held the camera up asking permission to continue. He beckoned me towards him and struck a pose to show I could take more photos. It seemed I was lucky as he enjoyed having his photo taken, posing, smiling and laughing for me, displaying red stained teeth to match the ends of his beard. I worked fast without speaking. Snap, snap, snap. I concentrated on getting my settings right to ensure correct exposure and composition. Afterwards, I thanked him, clasping my hands in prayer position, bowing 'Namaste.'

'Namaste,' he replied.

I made a beeline for two empty seats on the minibus.

The guy with the Welsh accent strolled up the aisle and dropped into the seat beside me.

After another ten-minute wait for Derek and Betty to board, we set off to the Jama Masjid Mosque.

* * *

'Hello, I'm Ivan Llewellyn.'

We shook hands.

'That's a lovely Welsh accent, where are you from?' I'd visited North Wales in the past to photograph in Snowdonia.

'I'm from Pontypridd, in the valleys I am,' said Ivan with a hint of pride in his voice.

My anxiety at having to fit in and make conversation with strangers waned as Ivan talked about the beautiful scenery of South Wales. I told how I loved the panoramas of the Northumberland coastline. His intelligent blue eyes shone from behind his glasses when he spoke of home. Medium height and sturdy, I guessed he was around seventy years old. His head was bald with the last vestiges of grey hair at the sides cut short.

'What brings you to India?' I asked.

He held aloft a chunky guidebook. 'History. I'm as fascinated with the past as you are with your camera.' I detected a playful glint in his eyes as he talked.

He spoke of his years of teaching history at high school. His wife had died six years ago, and he was determined to see as much of the world as possible before his kids put him in a rest home. There was that spirited sparkle again. We pored over the pictures in his guidebook as he filled me in with a brief history of the mosque.

'The Jama Masjid's one of the largest mosques in India.

Shah Jahan ordered the building. They started construction in 1644. It's got three great gates, four towers and two huge minarets made of red sandstone and white marble. Do you know, they can get twenty-five thousand people in the courtyard?' he said in his sing-song accent.

On the journey he narrated the history of the mosque and I gave him my full attention. The enthusiasm in his voice was compelling as he brought the story to life. His talent for teaching was unmistakable.

'Thanks for sharing your knowledge, Ivan. It makes the visit so much more interesting.' We climbed the steps to the entrance to relinquish our shoes and cover ourselves in the robes the security guards provided.

It was clammy hot with a cloudless sky. Visitors to the mosque spoke in hushed tones, men worshiped in the prayer hall and families sat in clusters in the courtyard. There was a familiar rolling, throaty coo, coo from the droves of pigeons huddled together on the rounded domes. As Alexandra and I wandered around the courtyard picking our way through pigeon poo, she became the focus of attention. First one group of young Indian men, then others approached asking politely if they could have their photograph taken with her. At one point a queue formed, everyone waiting patiently for their opportunity to take a selfie with the tall, impressive flame-haired foreigner. Occasionally someone would ask for a photo with me, but their fascination was with Alexandra.

'I felt rather like a film star, it was utterly marvellous,' she joked as we hurried down the steps at the end of our visit.

* * *

We had time for a quick change of clothes before meeting in the hotel reception to head out for our evening meal. I peered at myself in the mirror, grimaced at my unkempt hair, shrugged my shoulders and closed the door behind me.

I'd learned earlier that Charlie's surname was Mason. He was thirty-two, and he laughed, commenting, 'That's cool,' when I joked that he was the baby of the group. His handsome face was topped with short brown tousled, gelled spiked hair. Dark chocolate doe eyes gave him an innocent look and even with his mid-length rough tawny beard, women would feel the need to mother him. He was from Manchester and, after studying for his Philosophy degree, found working in a charity for the homeless was his dream job.

We were a diverse bunch, I mused as we waited for Derek and Betty to appear before setting off on the short walk to the restaurant.

* * *

The melodious reverberation of the sitar mingled with lively Hindi chit-chat and the air hung heavy with a medley of spicy aromas. Waiters dressed in lily-white tunics clinched at the waist with a deep red sash, jotted down orders, pointing to menus as they advised customers on the restaurant's specials of the day. Muted lighting from lotus flower pendant lamps, suspended low over tables, cast a soft glow over the room. Our maitre d' led us to our table. He lit tea lights in crystal votive holders, bringing flickering crochet patterns to life. The shadows danced on the ivory tablecloth, adding to the mellow vibe. A gigantic tapestry in a riot of colour, depicting a god in a chariot pulled by seven alabaster white horses, covered one wall. In answer to Charlie's question, Vijay spoke as we took our seats at the table.

'This is Lord Surya, the Hindu god of the sun. He is considered the creator of the universe and the source of all life. He is bringing light and warmth to the world when he travels across the sky each day. His golden chariot is being driven by Aruna who is the personification of the reddish glow of the rising sun.'

I took my seat next to Derek, who didn't acknowledge me. I scrambled for words. 'We bumped into each other at Heathrow, didn't we?'

'No, I don't believe we did.'

An Oscar-winning performance. If I didn't know better, I would have believed him. 'Oh, I must be mistaken.'

Betty tugged at her earlobe, cleared her throat and stared into the chilly void that vibrated between us. I polished the cutlery with my napkin, folded it back into its fan shape and shrunk into my chair folding my arms.

Studying the menu was a welcome relief from the uncomfortable pause that followed. While in India I was determined to feed my foodie adventurous streak. My enthusiasm for the unexpected faltered as I glimpsed a few of the more exotic dishes lurking amongst the choice of tempting curries, tikkas and tandooris. I found it easy to resist the temptation to discover the speciality from Assam, Eri Polu; silkworm pupae described as a colourful, melt in the mouth delicacy. The north-eastern Doh Khlieh didn't tickle my tastebuds either; I didn't mind pork and onion salad but the garnish of steamed pig brain didn't make my mouth water. My stomach clenched as I imagined popping the tasty morsel of Chaprah onto my tongue; that yummy chutney of red ants and their eggs from the state of Chattisgarh. I was almost thankful that, as I'd developed a bad case of heartburn from a greasy kebab at lunchtime, I had to be careful with what I ate.

'What low-fat options do you have on the menu please?' I turned to the waiter.

Before the waiter could reply, Derek let out a theatrical groan. 'I think you'll find they don't cook Slimming World meals here.' Betty whipped her fan into motion, her eyes downcast.

'No Derek, I'm not being awkward. I've got heartburn so want to steer clear of food that might make it worse.' This had the makings of an uncomfortable evening.

'Ye canna avoid getting indigestion sitting next te Derek hen,' Fraser shouted from the other end of the table, and everyone laughed awkwardly.

On the advice of the waiter I ordered the yellow dahl, rice and a chapati.

I clenched my jaw to prevent my mouth falling open when Betty told me they had settled in the Cotswolds after years of moving around the UK with Derek's job as a hotel manager. My cheeks quivered, straining under the effort to maintain a polite smile, as I imagined Derek dealing with dietary requirements and customer complaints with his customary grace.

'Derek's just taken early retirement. We've always wanted to see India, so here we are.'

'What did you order, Derek?' I asked.

'Erm, it was chicken, erm...,' his attention drifted off elsewhere as his words trailed off rudely.

I shrank in my chair and folded inward the way a hedgehog does to protect itself. This is one couple I'll not be spending much time with here. Gulping my yellow dahl would not help my heartburn, but it was worth it to get this meal finished quickly.

'We're all going te the bar for a nightcap Jen. Are ye coming?' asked Fraser on our walk back to the hotel.

'Uh, oh no thanks. I'm shattered. Need an early night,' I answered.

* * *

Back at the hotel I forgot about Derek and Betty and, taking no chances, sprayed too much mosquito repellent into the room. I slipped in between the cool bedsheets, coughing over and over trying to clear my irritated airways. I fired up my laptop and logged onto A Geordie Up The Ganges. What? I did a double take. Yes, I've read it correctly. My follower numbers have tripled. I've now got thirty people keeping me company on my adventure.

Ping.

> *You must be in India now love. Hope you're trying out your Hindi speaking skills. The locals don't stand a cat in hells chance of understanding you otherwise with that broad Geordie accent. Also, you'll need to speak the Queens English to your travelling companions as Google Translate doesn't include Geordie in its languages. Enjoy India. Miss and love you. Martin x*

I squirmed deeper under the bedclothes, looking forward to creating my first blog from India.

Ten minutes later I stared at a blank screen, unable to articulate the events of my day. How could this be after a full day of sightseeing and the hundreds of photos I'd taken? Scrolling through my images on the camera didn't fire me with enthusiasm either. What was missing?

Saturday, 27th February, New Delhi.

Hello from India family and friends, and welcome to my new subscribers. You're following me from such far-flung places as Brazil, USA, Australia and Russia, to name just a few. I'm delighted to have you along and I hope you enjoy the journey with me. A couple of strange things happened today. First, I was lost for words and anyone who knows me can confirm this is indeed a miracle. But the sensory overload I experienced on my first day in Delhi struck me dumb. And second I had a very close encounter with a female security guard. Let me explain.

I TAPPED into the laptop with a brief overview of the day's events, included a list and general description of the places I'd been to and uploaded a few snapshots. My article was short and sweet, but at least everyone would know I was safe and sound.

I logged off, and within seconds I was asleep.

6

Fraser tilted his head backwards and let out a sigh. 'Och, where are those two this time?'

'Glad I'm not the only one to notice,' I said without raising my head from Ivan's guidebook. The juddering from the engine reverberated through my abdomen.

Seven pairs of eyes followed the couple as they climbed aboard the minibus, strolled nonchalantly up the aisle and took their seats at the back, acknowledging no-one.

'The weather's rather lovely today, isn't it?' chirped Alexandra.

'I see two troublesome clouds on the horizon I do,' said Ivan.

It seemed Vijay had noted Derek and Betty's tardiness too. He took his opportunity to request punctuality at our meeting points as he spoke through the minibus mic, informing us of the timetable for that day. Our first visit was to the Birla Mandir, one of the largest Hindu temples in Delhi.

'The devotees have dedicated the temple to Laxmi, the

goddess of prosperity and Narayana, the preserver,' Ivan said, as he and I thumbed through his guidebook together.

'I like the idea of praying to the goddess of prosperity. I could do with some of that,' I said, pointing to the picture of Laxmi.

'And I could do with being preserved a bit longer,' said Ivan, turning the page to a depiction of Narayana.

We deposited our shoes in a locker before entering the temple. It was early in the day, the temple was quiet and I welcomed the opportunity to wander introspectively amongst the carvings, depictions and icons. I opened the guidebook I'd bought at the entrance. A random quote from the ancient texts jumped off the page. "Do not make thy life a continual sadness and sorrow." I could relate to that one.

Summer knelt in front of a magnificent statue of Lord Ganesh, the elephant-headed god, destroyer of evils and obstacles. Her eyes closed, prayer beads bobbing as they moved in her hands, her lips moving as she chanted to herself. She looked so serene. Perhaps if I asked Summer to teach me to meditate, it might help to clear my mind, although the notion of retreating into silent reflection scared me. I was reluctant to face the naked truth, frightened of what I'd find there.

I glanced to my side and caught Fraser watching me from across the hall. He quickly looked away.

* * *

As I CLIMBED the steps of the minibus at the end of the visit, I felt relaxed. For the first time since our arrival, Derek and Betty boarded the vehicle on schedule. Bright blue skies promising a mild day in Delhi had faded to a pale grey. It drizzled as we arrived at the Gurdwara Bangla Sahib, one of the most prominent Sikh houses of worship in the city.

The morning heat had given way to cooler air. The on-off drizzle wet the ground and created little rivulets in street gutters. Puddles formed in holes and hollows in the road. Sprinkles of rain cooled my face and glistened in my hair like diamond shavings. I licked my lips, enjoying the cool fresh taste instead of the saltiness I had become accustomed to since my arrival in India. The earthy, musty pong of rotting garbage left too long in the street prickled in my nostrils. My footsteps squelched and beat the ground in time with the strains of music, singing and chanting floating in the air. This was a country of wild contradictions. The pungent aroma of excrement floated in the air mingling with sweet melody; monotone skies were a backdrop to an artist's palette of eye-watering hues in turbans and saris of every colour imaginable; the heart-breaking smiling faces of people whose only possessions in the world were the clothes on their backs. It was fascinating. All of life was here. I was falling in love with India.

As we rounded the next corner, my mouth fell open as the lily-white marble building came into view. Its golden dome punctured the sky like a gigantic ball of sunshine, spreading light on everything around. We gave our shoes in at the entrance and covered our heads with our hats and scarves.

'You should get jolly marvellous shots here, Jen. The architecture's just so photogenic. I've never seen so many styles and colourful turbans in all my days,' said Alexandra.

She linked her arm through mine as we tiptoed through the small footbath before entering the complex. Once on the other side, she steered me towards the main building.

I was learning Alexandra had a bossy streak. How could

I put this without hurting her feelings? 'I'll see you later, Alexandra. You wouldn't want me for company. I'm going to lose myself behind my lens today.' I unlinked our arms and, without turning to look at her, strode away feeling mean.

There was a large pond surrounded on three sides by graceful arched colonnades to the right of the building. Devotees believed it contained holy water, known as amrit. A constant stream of people stood on the steps at the water's edge, splashing their heads and hands. Heightened emotion shone on faces glittering with a million crystal droplets. The cascading amrit looked like morning dew dripping from eyelids, noses and chins. Devotional renditions filled the air with constant repetition of rhythmic chanting. It had a hypnotic resonance. The spiritual atmosphere was palpable. The glassy water on the opposite side of the square pond reflected the pristine colonnades. Serene and watchful like the ancient gurus welcoming everyone to their holy space, it was a photographer's dream.

Not for the first time, I thanked God for my camera. I could shelter behind my lens and forget everything.

* * *

HUNDREDS OF PHOTOS LATER, it was time to meet up with the rest of the group by the dining hall to start a tour of the kitchens. I found myself stood next to Derek who asked pleasantly, 'Did you get good shots?'

Shocked by his sudden politeness, I flicked through the images on the back of my camera showing him what I'd captured to purrs of approval. The positive energy of the place must have woven its magic on him! I smothered a giggle as we gathered round to listen to Vijay.

'All work being carried out at the temple is by Sikh

volunteers. It's a great honour to be chosen to provide services to all peoples who visit the Gurdwara,' he said. 'We're going to visit the kitchens where the volunteers are making the food to be offered to anyone who is needing or wanting it. Irrespective of creed or colour.' Vijay finished talking just as the sound of chanting filled the air. Outside the dining hall, waiting for their turn to enter, were groups of people sitting cross-legged in neat rows. As they waited, they chanted melodiously Sat Nam, Sat Nam, Sat Nam, over and over. 'Sat Nam is the devotional chant to their one and only true God,' Vijay explained as he ushered us through the doors into the kitchens.

The massive kitchens were a hive of activity, stacked high with the food donations volunteers would transform into meals for thousands of people every day. The subdued lighting, hot air filled with the pungent aroma of curry and scorched walls and ceiling added to the medieval atmosphere. Volunteers of all ages stirred huge copper pots filled with different curries. More gigantic pots sat on fired stoves, the flames encouraging the exotic mixtures inside to bubble, and push their individual aroma up and out to blend and mingle. In the central area of the kitchen, people sat on small benches in groups rolling dough, making chapatis and nan bread. The skill and teamwork on show was mesmerising. One lady patted the dough, rolled it out, spent a few seconds passing it from hand to hand. Then when it was the right size and shape, she tossed it onto a hot plate. A young man using a metal rod flipped the bread over two or three times before another man collected the chapati, now ready for serving. Every so often there was the singing sound of metal against metal as huge stirring ladles scraped the sides of pots. This was followed by the soft clunk as helpers splashed curry onto plates ready for serving.

We strolled around taking our photos and the good-natured people working there didn't mind one bit the group of western tourists snapping away with their cameras. They stopped and posed, smiling, willing to please. All the while the sound of faint hypnotic, spiritual devotional chanting floated towards the dining room and kitchen from the main building.

Connecting with the goodness in people whose desire it is to help other human beings in such an unselfish and loving way reached somewhere deep inside me.

'Are you okay Jen, is there something on your mind?' Alexandra put her arm around my shoulder.

All I could do was nod and offer that very British answer. 'I'm fine Alexandra, thanks.'

* * *

MY SINUSES DETONATED as I hit the wall of aromas.

Vijay shouted above the clamour as we clustered around him, eyes watering and covering our noses and mouths to avoid breathing in the stinging chilli powder. 'Khari Baoli is being Asia's largest and oldest wholesale spice market. Over four hundred years ago it was created by one of the wives of Shah Jahan.' He coughed into his handkerchief as he spoke.

A low wooden cart laden with bulging sacks pulled by a lumbering white bullock rumbled by. Two guardians followed up the rear, hands pressed against the load to steady the wobbling, precious cargo. An army of porters carried burlap sacks on their heads to waiting carts. They heaved down their load with a grunt sending more intoxicating dust into the atmosphere, and scurried back for another. 'Watch your belongings guys,' warned Fraser as we wound our way through one of the overcrowded, narrow alleyways radiating from the main thoroughfare. I stumbled on the uneven dirt pathway and clutched my day bag into my stomach amid the relentless jostling, bumping and shoving.

A vendor called out to us, 'Come buy my spices; cardamom, cumin, ginger, chilli. The finest in all of Asia.'

From the opposite direction, 'Quality dried fruits. Best price in the market especially for you.' A thousand voices competed for dominance.

A merchant sat on the floor with only his head and shoulders visible above the huge sacks surrounding him. Each open-topped sack displayed a miniature mountain of spices, herbs, nuts or dried fruits in a psychedelic spectrum of colours. A customer took a pinch of spice from the tangerine mini-mountain, rubbed it between thumb and forefinger, sniffed it and nodded his intention to buy.

We continued pushing our way through the crowds, past rows of benches creaking under the weight of mounds of assorted spices; many with strange names I'd never heard before. The deeper we ventured into the labyrinth of alleyways the heavier became the air. At last Vijay led us up a dingy stairway to emerge coughing and sneezing into bright sunlight. I gulped at the fresh breeze; the taste of a million spices coated the inside of my mouth and stuck to my teeth.

We stood on the parapet on the roof of the ancient, time-worn building and looked down on the hectic market below. The streets of Old Delhi were spread out before us.

'Here you have Fatehpuri Masjid Mosque,' said Vijay, pointing towards the red sandstone structure with its fluted dome and sky piercing, slender minarets. 'And over here, the turrets and bastions of the Red Fort.'

We amused ourselves watching the antics of the resident monkeys scampering up and down the facades of every building in sight. Mothers with babies clinging to their backs leapt from window ledges, landing with ease on the balconies of adjoining buildings; youngsters grappled, grunting and squeaking trying to assert their dominance in play fights; elders squatted on walls surveying the troop with a regal air.

'Look they're stealing the washing from that line,' Charlie shouted as two juvenile monkeys fought over a man's vest. We erupted into laughter as the winner leapt to victory, waving his prize in the air like a flag.

We headed back the way we'd come and emerged into a bustling open courtyard where we encircled the chai wallah. He lifted his metal pan from the flame of his stove and swirled the simmering milky masala liquid in hypnotic circles, before clanging the pot back onto the heat. The scent of warm vanilla cream with underlying notes of cinnamon, cardamom, ginger and nutmeg floated in the air. A movement flashed in the corner of my eye. A shadowy shape. Dashing forward. Claw-like hand extended.

'Ivan,' I screamed. 'Your bag!'

7

With the speed of a striking cobra, Ivan spun his body around to face the thief and grabbed the hand as it reached for his bag. With a flick of his hand he bent the robber's wrist; twisted his arm against the joint and turned in a circle, with the robber forced to follow or risk a broken arm. The face of the attacker contorted in pain. Then with a second twist of his wrist Ivan reversed direction. The villain screamed as Ivan forced him to the floor in another painful arm lock. The bedraggled man grasped the futility of an attempted escape, stopped struggling and lapsed into indecipherable howls of pain. Ivan looked down upon the offender, his face an alabaster portrait of controlled anger.

A policeman strode through the throng which had gathered pushing the spectators back, shouting and waving his baton.

'You can release him now Ivan,' said Vijay. 'You can be assured the authorities will deal with him.'

The vagabond was led away through the crush. Ivan

retrieved his bag, slung it over his shoulder, looked at each of us with our mouths agape and shrugged his shoulders.

'Years of Aikido training as a youngster in the valleys can come in useful sometimes it can.'

* * *

As the minibus pulled into the hotel car park Fraser said, 'Och, I need a drink after all the excitement today. Come on everyone, let's have a nightcap in the bar before bed.'

I jumped down the steps, 'Not for me thanks Fraser, it's been a long day and I'm dead on my feet. Goodnight all, see you in the morning.'

Before climbing into bed, I grabbed the opportunity to log in to A Geordie Up The Ganges, impatient to update my subscribers about the amazing sights and sounds of the city.

Ping.

Fifty-six followers.

I uploaded a few more snapshots and ended my report with a brief description of our final stop-off of the day.

Sunday, February 28th, New Delhi.

After the excitement of the spice market a visit to Raj Ghat was very welcome. The Mahatma Gandhi memorial, in the heart of Delhi, is a peaceful oasis of calm. At the spot where an assassin killed Mahatma Gandhi in 1948, an eternal flame burns on a simple black marble platform adorned with displays of marigold flowers.

Tomorrow we will celebrate the arrival of spring as we attend the ancient Hindu Holi festival. The celebration signifies the victory of good over evil. One of the many legends surrounding the origin of the festivities is that of Lord Vishnu. There was a demon king called Hiranyakashipu who wanted everyone in his kingdom to worship only him. His son Prahalad refused and worshiped Lord Vishnu instead. Hiranyakashipu decided to kill Prahalad and commanded his sister Holika, who was immune to fire, to sit on a pyre with Prahalad on her lap. But their plan failed as Prahalad recited the name of Vishnu throughout for protection, and it was Holika who burned to death.

Bewilderment washes over me as I reflect on today's events. One moment I'm laughing as a monkey leaps from a parapet dressed in a man's vest; and the next I'm aghast as I witness a soft-spoken, Welsh grandfather shape-shift into a lightning-fast, deadly ninja.

* * *

THE AIR WAS ELECTRIC. Excited revellers bounced in unison, as deafening Bollywood music blasted from mammoth speakers mounted on the stage in the middle of the jam-packed field. We'd all followed Vijay's advice when he told us, 'dress in clothes you don't mind getting trashed and cover your hair and skin in baby oil. It will be easier to wash off the powder later. Keep sunglasses on at all times to protect your eyes and leave valuables and electronics in your room.'

A rainbow of neon powdered paint, flung from thousands of hands turned the air into a swirling artist palette. Splat! The balloon exploded on my chest spraying shimmering purple water which covered my face and found its way into my laughing mouth. 'Ye look like Tinky Winky from the Teletubbies,' shouted Fraser, his words just audible above the earsplitting roar.

'You're as red as a rose, Fraser,' shouted Summer.

'Aye, a rose between two thorns,' Fraser countered. His

arms wrapped tight around mine and Summer's waists as the three of us clung to each other, bouncing to the techno beat.

Unadulterated joy shone from every face in the swarming crowd. Friends and strangers splattered, smeared and puffed dazzling hues of paint, covering each other from head to toe.

This was a time for people to become children again. In my hand was a ball of lustrous tangerine powder paint. Derek's eyes were shining with joy. Did I dare? He was in a good mood today, and why not? This is Holi. He laughed, ran after me and repaid the compliment, smearing my face with a metallic shade of turquoise.

A group of dancers took to the stage in gleaming snow-white Bollywood dance costumes. They launched into a high-impact routine accompanied by a driving drumbeat. Puffs of powder mushroomed over their heads, flung from plates held by people at the side of the stage. Within minutes, virgin white had morphed into pulsating psychedelia.

Vijay watched us from the sidelines, smiling at our playful antics. But he wasn't getting away scot-free. 'Come on everyone. Vijay looks too clean,' shouted Alexandra, and we bore down on him, smearing his face with so much powder paint, he looked like a multi-coloured lollipop.

The celebration had been an ice-breaker, and we stood in a circle, arms around each other, swaying to the beat. Over our heads sailed a ball of luminescent green paint. It splattered full in my face and clouded my vision. I gagged on the slimy globules in my mouth, and spat them out. Everyone roared with laughter. For an infinitesimal space of time a disturbing memory stirred and tried to break into the light. Determined not to let anything ruin this moment, I pushed the thought back down into the dark depths where it belonged.

'Anyone up for a quick drink before we leave for the sleeper train?' asked Fraser, as we wound through the paint spattered streets on the route back to the hotel.

'That would be great,' I said. 'I'm in.'

Monday, March 1st, New Delhi

...So, we finished the celebration with a taste of traditional gujiya, a yummy deep-fried dumpling filled with condensed milk and dried fruits. I hope you've enjoyed reading my account of Holi. It's a festival, parade, concert and paint war all rolled into one. My friend Summer said it's also known as "The Festival of Love" which is the perfect description for such a joyful celebration. I'm falling in love with this country.

It's time to leave Delhi now. As I head off for our next destination with purple teeth, I hope you'll come along with me to Haridwar and the Maha Kumbh Mela. Vijay has described the Kumbh as the biggest festival on earth. A mass Hindu pilgrimage attended by hundreds of millions of people.

8

'Chai, chai, chaieee,' the chai wallah chanted as he weaved his way through the narrow aisle of the Delhi to Haridwar sleeper train. Steam rose from the spout of the large stainless steel teapot as the stream of milky masala tea splashed into the plastic cup I was holding.

'Mmmmm, it's heavenly.' I craned my neck to look up at Alexandra as she sat on her bunk above mine, sipping her cup of masala chai.

'It's positively glorious.' She reclined on her bed, her eyes half closed taking another sip.

'A perfect night-cap to lead us into the land of nod. Cheers, Alexandra.' I raised my cup.

She raised her own cup in response. 'Cheers my dear, here's to a jolly good night's sleep.'

We'd said goodbye to the city of Delhi two hours before – but only after waiting yet another fifteen minutes for Derek and Betty to board the bus.

'This is becoming too much of a habit,' I'd grumbled to Alexandra.

'Don't you know we've got a train to catch?' The irritation in Ivan's voice had seemed to fluster Betty. Her hands flapped as she boarded behind Derek, shoving him up the steps.

Darkness had fallen, and the drizzle had gotten heavier by the time we'd arrived at the station. Vijay had scurried around organising porters to load our baggage onto carts. These guys amazed me. In their bright red jackets and turbans for protection, they carried two huge bags on their heads as if they were carrying a flimsy basket containing bread. They'd lugged our bags onto the train and helped us find our carriage. Although Vijay had given them a decent tip from the group kitty we'd put together for gratuities, I slipped a few more rupees to my porter. He'd taken the extra care to help me locate my bunk and deposit my luggage beneath it. He was thankful, and we honoured each other with the now familiar 'Namaste', bowing our heads, hands in prayer position.

'Say cheese.'

Our helpers had looked at me nonplussed as they posed for photos. What was Hindi for smile? I hadn't learned that one. They cottoned on when I exaggerated a grin and pulled the corners of my lips upwards with each forefinger. I knew I'd looked comical when everyone laughed.

As advised, we chained our baggage to the sides of our bunks. I felt a pang of guilt at this security measure but told myself better safe than sorry. Now, settled onto our comfortable bunks sipping chai, I surveyed what was to be our overnight sleeping quarters for the next nine hours.

Repeated down one side of the whole length of the narrow train aisle were two bunks, one top and one bottom. Opposite each set of two bunks were a further four bunks facing perpendicular, also set up as two sets of bunk beds. During the day the brown leather beds folded up into seating. Now, in readiness for the overnight journey, there were two clean crisp white sheets, a pillow and brown blanket atop each one. Each bed had matching curtains on the window and aisle side to allow for privacy. The dark red and brown hues of the fabric contrasted with the pale yellow walls, brown leather beds and dimmed lighting to induce a relaxing atmosphere.

The gentle vibrations of the engine rippled through my body as the train idled at the station. I welcomed the slight waft of cool air from the large metal fan rotating in the ceiling above our six-bed section. Outside my window people sat on the floor of the platform in huddles, surrounded by their luggage, blankets covered their shoulders to ward off the cold, damp evening. Summer, Charlie, Derek and Betty occupied the beds alongside Alexandra and myself. In the section adjoining ours were Vijay, Ivan and Fraser. Travellers occupied every bunk, and I listened to the quiet chatter in strange languages as people prepared their bedding for the night ahead. I tried in vain to recognise a few words from the Hindi I'd taught myself. The only opportunity I'd had to try out my new language skill was to say to my very helpful porter, 'Danyevad' – thank you.

The Station Master announced departure with a long whistle and the train trundled forward. We were on our way to Haridwar.

'C'mon ye two,' Fraser shouted to Derek and Charlie. 'Leave the lassies to blether on aboot hair and makeup. We guys need to talk aboot something much more important like ummm, football.'

Charlie and Derek rose to join the other men in the next

compartment. Betty jumped from her bunk like she had a spring attached to her backside.

'Hold on Derek, wait for me.'

My wide eyes met Alexandra's who said, 'Golly, you don't want to listen to that lot rattle on about the beastly off-side rule, Betty. Stay with us for some intelligent conversation.'

Betty hesitated, watching Derek disappear around to the next compartment. She flicked her fan and flapped as if she was trying to blow herself away. Summer took her hand and guided her back down to sitting.

I fiddled around in my luggage. What the hell just happened there? She's so controlled by him. Frightened to leave his side. Oh God, was I seeing Martin and me in the future?

'I've got something to show you girls,' I said

'Good golly, what on earth is that?' Alexandra sat upwards, swinging her legs over the edge of her bunk.

I held up the special piece of equipment I'd purchased for just this scenario. Our carriage had squat toilets. It was time to try it out.

'It's a shewee,' said Summer. 'A must-have for any girl who attends festivals with those grotty portaloos.'

'I call it my little pink wonder.' I attached the eight-inch extension tube to the small funnel-shaped section and twirled it round for the girls to marvel at.

'How does it work?' asked Betty.

'To be honest, I've never tried it.'

'It looks rather like a small version of something a mechanic would use to fill a car engine with oil,' said Alexandra. She climbed down the metal ladder from the top bunk to take a closer look.

I slipped the shewee into my trouser pocket.

'Well, now's as good a time as any to give it a go. Wish me

luck!' I swayed with the motion of the train as I made my way to the toilet three carriages down.

The toilet comprised a stainless steel basin installed in the floor with a hole in the middle, and footrests on each side. A metal jug hanging on a chain clattered against the wall and tolled like a bell in time with the swaying carriage. Wrapped behind a hand rail on the opposite wall was a small shower head on a white hose. I placed my feet on the footrests, struggling to gain my balance and my body rocked back and forth, side to side in harmony with the shifting carriage. The rhythmic, ear-splitting clattering metal wheels rotating on the track blared through the hole leading in from the outside.

I put all my effort into strengthening my legs to gain stability and unzipped my fly. Now Jen, gently does it. I guided the funnel section through the open zipper. Pulled down the top of my knickers and positioned the shewee in between my legs as the drawing on the instruction leaflet had shown. With the extension tube in place, I was ready. With one hand I held on to the rail in a vain attempt to stop myself from constantly swaying. I pointed the shewee spout down to the hole with the other, relaxed and allowed a steady flow to begin.

Exactly at that moment, the carriage lurched violently to one side. To prevent myself from falling, I rapidly brought the hand holding the shewee to the wall to steady myself. The contents of the funnel spilled out. The impact of my hand hitting the wall forced the shewee from my grip. In slow motion it flew through the air before it clanged down onto the metal basin, bounced twice then disappeared down the hole.

'Bloody hell,' I cursed as I stared at the dark soaking wet

patch stretching the whole length down the right leg of my beige combat pants.

My body swayed in harmony with the motion as I made my way back through the three carriages to my bunk. With one hand I steadied myself and with the other I held my fleece jumper in front of my legs.

'Oh, jolly good, you're back. Well, how did you get on?' Alexandra asked. She had sat on the bottom bunk in between Summer and Betty. They all looked up at me, curiosity on their faces. I maintained a straight face as I inched my jumper to one side.

'Oh, lordy me.' Betty's hand flew to her mouth.

'Bugger Jen, it seems you need rather more practice,' said Alexandra with a snigger.

* * *

After a quick change of trousers, it was time to settle down for sleep. My body rocked in time with the chug-thud, chud-thud, chug-thud of the wheels turning and the carriage swaying. Each time I woke from my fitful sleep as we pulled into a station, the scene was the same. Through rain-streaked windows I watched as hundreds of people huddled together in groups around fires on the platforms. Blankets wrapped around them. Light from the flames illuminating their faces. I was grateful for the warmth of my sleeping bag, my comfy travel pillow and even the squat toilet.

As I lay there with time to think, my mind reverted to my illness and a now familiar blackness descended. Determined to push the darkness away, I brought the faces of my family to the fore and looked at each one in turn. One by one I studied every tiny feature of each face I loved so much.

I smiled back at each beloved face and pressed my fingers into my eyes to stop the threatening tears, feeling relieved no-one could see me. I must keep my secret safe at all costs. The black cloud lifted. I fell asleep again and before long Vijay woke me, announcing that we'd be at Haridwar train station in half an hour.

9

After checking into our hotel we had two hours spare, before meeting for our visit to the bathing ghats at Haridwar, and the Kumbh Mela. It would be our first sight of the River Ganges. But now it was time to log in and update A Geordie Up The Ganges. What sights I'd seen in Delhi. My images must be out of this world. How on earth would I decide which ones to upload? But my disappointment increased with each image I viewed.

This one's boring. That one's flat. This one at the amrit pool in the Sikh Gurdwara may as well have been taken at the fishpond in my local park. Every one has a distant quality to it. As if there was an invisible brick wall between the scene and the viewer. Why? Why? Why? Wey howay man, there's no point in crying. Is that ganna make you shoot better images?

Ping.

Ninety-three followers.

Hi love, hope you're having a fantastic time. Looks like you enjoyed your visit to Delhi. The photos are great and I can see you've made a new friend; with his white robes and red beard he must be a Sunderland supporter. You should take more photos of people, not just the architecture. I keep looking at your empty chair and wondering where you are and what you're doing. I can sleep easier in my bed now though, knowing you'll be safe with Ivan around. Missing you. Love Martin xx

I'm Billy Scott, Martin's best mate. I can't praise Jen highly enough. What a brave woman, leaving a comfortable lifestyle to go on an unknown adventure, however... I know her husband.

Hi, Martin here. Well, knowing who I hang around with, Billy, I'm surprised Jen doesn't go more often.

Hi Jen, I've been reading your blog and loving your Geordie sense of humour. I too am embarking on a "find myself trip" soon, and I'm relieved to find I'm not the only woman out there who feels this need. My whole family think I'm mad but are happy to let me go and get it out of my system. Following your adventure is adding to my excitement. Best wishes, Amanda x

I second what Martin said about the photography. More people photos please. You need them for your portfolio. Miss you at work. Love Priti xx

I had just enough time to check my private message inbox.

Do you know what your husband is up to while you're in India? Love from Your Marra.

My body froze. My hand flew to my mouth. What the hell? Who would send me such a nasty message? What's the username? "Marra". That's the Geordie word for "friend". This is no friend of mine. It's obviously some saddo with nothing better to do. Delete it.

I put the mean words out of my mind and, uplifted by the warm messages of support and growth in follower numbers, I picked out the best of a bad bunch of images to upload. Only enough time to check in briefly before meeting the group.

Tuesday, 2nd March, Haridwar

Hello family and friends. Welcome to my new followers, glad to have you along.

We're on the move all the time and had it not been for my pack of malaria tablets with its labels, I wouldn't know what day it was.

Here are a few pics of the wonderful volunteers working in the kitchens at the Sikh Gurdwara in Delhi.

Thanks for the likes and shares. Please leave a comment below to tell me a little about yourselves. It would be wonderful to get to know you and it would keep me grounded, for which I'd be eternally grateful.

Must dash now, will get back to you soon xx

I pressed publish, closed the laptop and headed downstairs to the waiting minibus. Boarding, I gave a cheery smile to Derek. He sat in the front seat alone, scowling. Urgh, it was mister nasty today by the looks of it. Where was Betty? That's why he had a face like a slapped arse. She'd escaped him for a while. I dropped into the space next to Fraser. This time it was only Betty who kept us waiting.

'I have a very serious announcement to make,' Derek's voice bellowed. Everyone stopped to stare in his direction. 'Someone on this bus is a thief.'

There was a stunned silence. Ivan was first to gather himself. 'Hey boyo, you better have damn good proof before you go accusing anyone of that.'

'My wallet has gone missing. Someone here has stolen it.' He pointed at each of us as he spoke.

I glanced at Fraser. A vein at the side of his eye pulsed. His ear lobes shone like a bright red traffic light. Through taut lips he spoke with a deep carefully controlled tone. 'Naebody here's a thief, Derek. Check yer belongings, mate. Ye'll probably find yer wallet hidden amongst yer skiddies.'

'When did you last see it, Derek? Are you sure you didn't leave it on the sleeper train? It was jolly chaotic at the station, and the pickpockets here are rather bloody professional at what they do,' said Alexandra.

Just as Derek took a breath to reply, Betty thumped up the minibus steps. She took one glance at the angry faces turned towards her. Her body froze, and a flush crept across her cheeks.

'Derek?' she asked.

A look of horror spread over her face as Summer spoke in the calmest of tones. 'Derek's lost his wallet. He thinks one of us here has stolen it.'

Betty regained composure quickly and forced a laugh which she followed up with a fake smile. Reaching into her shoulder bag, she pulled out a brown leather wallet. 'Here it is, darling. I'm so sorry I didn't tell you it was in my bag the whole time.'

Derek glared at her and flung himself into his seat in indignation.

'I'm so sorry everyone but this is all my fault. Derek didn't mean to cause offence. I'm an idiot for not telling him I had his wallet.'

'She's in for it now,' I whispered to Fraser as the bus

pulled out of the car park into the worst traffic mayhem I'd ever seen in my life. The congestion in Delhi had been heavy, but the clogging of the roads here was ten times worse because of the sheer number of people heading for the Kumbh. It seemed the whole of India was on the move. People determined to arrive at the place where the Ganges emerges from the Himalaya, there to bathe in the holy water. There wasn't an inch of space between vehicles, and no discernible lane separation on the road. Although there was a constant honk-honking of horns, everyone stayed calm. They were on their way to the Maha Kumbh Mela.

The drama was over and the crackling atmosphere on the bus subsided. My body swayed, jolted and jumped reacting to the uneven roads, chock full of traffic. And all the time the heat from the proximity of Fraser's body burned. My knee tingled at the point where it stroked his by accident. His hand brushed against my forearm as he turned a page of his book. My skin quivered from the contact. This was my chance to furtively study this enigmatic man. There was an air of danger about him, rippling below the surface. He must have sensed I was watching him and looked up from his book straight into my eyes. His gaze was unflinching. Penetrating. I had to say something. 'Erm, what brought you to India, Fraser?'

Before he could answer, there was a flash of silver at the window.

I gasped, agog at my first sight of Haridwar. The Ganges snaked ahead of us, at the centre of a scene straight out of an epic movie about a faraway land. Vijay had told us the steps on each side of the river were called ghats. Today they were a heaving blanket of living, breathing humanity. Colourful buildings, temples and a clock tower punctured the skyline. For as far as the eye could see, the area was a mass of millions of people. Overlooking the spectacle was a majestic one-hundred-foot statue of Lord Shiva, the destroyer of evil. A cobra encircled his neck representing past, present and future and the trident in his hand depicted will, action and wisdom.

It had been twelve years since the last Kumbh at Haridwar and the vibe and excitement crackled in the air. Somehow our driver snaked through impossible gaps in the jam-packed traffic. As we approached the site of the festival the buzzing, humming mass grew larger. On the long dusty road to the entrance, a red truck pulling an open trailer filled with twelve wraithlike nagas sped past. Their brown bodies covered in white ash gleamed in the sunlight. Some with dreadlocks down to their waists and others with their hair tied up in buns. Dressed in loincloths, they waved in delight at us through the minibus window.

We were to visit Har-Ki-Pauri ghat later in the day to watch the bathing rituals. This most revered ghat was also known as the Steps of Shiva, where Hindus believed Lord Vishnu had left his giant footprint on a rock. According to legend, Vijay told us, Lord Shiva created the river here when he sent the Ganges cascading down from his locks of hair.

'Haridwar is being one of the seven holiest places to Hindus. We are believing that moksha, which is the liberation of the soul from the cycle of birth, death and re-birth, can be achieved here. This is the end of all suffering.'

I waved back at the gaggle of excited children who shouted 'hello' as they trotted alongside our crawling vehicle. How wonderful to believe that pain, heartache and suffering will one day end. I envied those with such deep faith. Would my own pain ever end?

Vijay filled us in on the festival's age-old history.

'The story, it is going back to the time when the gods

used to be living on earth. A curse had weakened them, and they could not be resisting demons who caused havoc in the world.'

'The word "Kumbh", actually it is meaning urn. Lord Brahma he advised the gods to churn out the nectar of immortality with the help of the demons and hold it in an urn. The gods decided against sharing the nectar with the demons, who were then chasing them for twelve days. During the chase, nectar is falling from the urn at four different locations and these locations are where we hold the Mela today.

Charlie, seated next to Summer on the back seat shouted, 'How do they decide which dates to hold the Kumbh, Vijay?'

'Aha. You see. The festival it is being held on dates from the zodiac positions of Jupiter, the sun and the moon. This is when the sacred rivers are said to be turning into nectar.

'We Hindus are believing that those who are submerging themselves in the holy water during the Kumbh, are blessed by the divine for eternity. They are being cleansed of all of their sins.'

We gathered our belongings to join the multitudes on foot as Vijay came to the end of his talk.

'Today is being a very auspicious bathing day. It's called Maha Shivratri Pratham Shahi Snan or, The first Royal Bath. Many sadhus they are coming here to bathe in Mother Ganga.'

We made our way across the bridge and were swallowed up by the hordes. The millions of people stretched further than I could see to the south. I turned to look northward and was greeted by a similar sight. Stretching away into the distance, people flowed forever onward like the Ganges. I looked towards the east where the human sea swirled around obstacles, people streaming forward as if invisible hands pulled them onward towards the water's edge. To the west the swell of humanity rolled forward like an endless multi-coloured ocean.

The road we were to traverse towards the bathing ghats teemed with people. The sound of chanting swelled the collective reverence as orange and yellow draped holy men, women dressed in vivid coloured saris and beggars in rags intermingled. 'Hare Krishna, Hare Krishna, Krishna Krishna, Hare Hare.' The tuneful mantra settled in my mind. Summer joined me as we sang along. We passed a makeshift tent, a tarpaulin tied to the trunk of a tree, where a naga sat preaching to devotees as he smoked a huge cannabis joint. He had covered himself from head to toe in white ash which contrasted with his red loincloth, dread-locks and beard, giving him a ghostly appearance.

I snapped a few frames off with different settings, hoping to get one well-exposed image.

As we twisted and turned through the crowds a dirty-faced little girl of around nine or ten focused on me. Taking two steps to my every one, she stuck by my side for the whole length of our winding route towards the ghats. She tapped my arm with pleas of 'Chapatie, chapatie, chapatie.' Vijay's words about not giving to beggars rang in my ears. But the child's pleas were louder.

How could I ignore this little girl dressed in rags?

'Thank you, lady.' The child grabbed the money, melted my heart with her beaming face, and skipped away on her filthy feet to disappear into the crowds.

We arrived at the entrance when suddenly Alexandra sprinted to the side of the road and vomited. I held her hair while she heaved. After fifteen minutes she could hold herself upright.

'Bloody hell Alexandra, you look like one of them nagas, your face is lily white.' I took out my handkerchief, poured water onto it and handed it over for her to wipe her face. 'I think you've got Delhi Belly. Didn't you buy some of them spicy dough balls from that street vendor outside the hotel this morning?'

She nodded before retching again.

'Do you think you can carry on?' I passed her a bottle of water. She took a few loud gulps, then nodded.

'Yes I think so, I feel dizzy but we're only here for one day and I'm jolly well determined not to miss this.'

The sun blazed down from a bright blue cloudless sky. It was midday, and the heat was oppressive.

I glanced skywards. 'Okay, have you brought your hat with you?' She shook her head.

I removed mine and plonked it onto her head. 'Here, you need it more than me.'

'Oh no Jen, that sun is a demon today. I can't take your hat from you.'

'I insist, Alexandra. Don't worry about me. I'll be fine.'

'Well, okay, but I'll just borrow it for an hour, then you can have it back.'

'Only if you feel better, now drink more water.'

'Listen everyone.' We crowded around Vijay as he spoke. 'There are millions of people visiting today. We'll walk in single file. You must be keeping your concentration on the person in front of you. Watch your belongings. Most important of all, enjoy the spectacle you are about to witness.'

We arranged ourselves into a line behind Vijay, his scarlet baseball cap jiggled on top of a pole which he held high in the air. I positioned Alexandra in front of me with Charlie behind me and we strode into the throng.

The scene was a riot of colour from beautiful saris worn

by women from all over India; sunny oranges, daffodil yellows and wine shades of burgundy. Iridescent liquid blues. Poppy and ruby reds. Forest, jade and bottle greens. Yogis, holy men and sadhus often draped themselves in saffron or cinnabar red. Only naga sadhus had no desire for the colourful garments of this world, the ash which smeared their bodies the only cover they needed. 'Are there any female nagas?' I asked Vijay.

'Yes Jen.' He pointed to a knot of shaven headed women, draped in yellow cloth. 'A woman who wishes to become a naga sadhu must abandon her family. She must renounce the materialistic world and practice celibacy. After shaving her head, the head bath must be done in the Ganges. Then she becomes a naga sannyasi, and equal to male naga sadhus.'

The air was heavy with the smell of incense. The temple bells chimed. One musical strike exploding into life as another faded, filling the atmosphere with an undulating cadence of joyous, unrestrained celebration.

A group of drummers dressed in psychedelic silk kaftans hammered out a rhythmic beat on the traditional Indian dholki hand drums hung around their necks. A naked prancing sadhu accompanied them. His only adornment was his rudraksha necklace made from the seeds of the trees which grow in the Himalaya. To the beat of the drums he skipped and jumped, expressing total joy of life. Around his ash-smeared body and over his head he swung an ornamental sword with abandon. We stopped to watch, and a tightly packed crowd gathered. Dust flew into the sultry air when the sadhu's feet stomped the hard earth, and mingled with the aromas of stale spices, curry and sweat.

The sadhu thrust his hips forward, turning round on the spot proudly displaying his nakedness to the crowd. The sword flashed around his head. No-one expected what happened next. He grabbed at his jiggling manhood and stretched it like a huge elastic band. Alexandra and I exchanged shocked looks, both of us struggling to conceal our amusement.

'Och, that's making my eyes water,' shouted Fraser above the drumbeat.

With one final stretch to elongate his member to its limit, there was a collective gasp as he wrapped his manhood around the blade of the sword.

Everyone clapped in encouragement and with each thrust of his hips the sadhu executed one more turn of the sword. From somewhere behind us, Betty strained her voice so Derek could hear her above the drumming.

'What's he doing, Derek? I can't see,' she yelled.

'He's wrapping his penis around a sword,' shouted Derek at the top of his voice.

'What did you say? He's clapping in happiness to the Lord?'

'No, Betty. He's wrapping his penis around a sword!'

The sadhu jigged and bounced like a jumping jack on Guy Fawkes night. When he had twisted the length of his penis to its limit, he passed the sword with his manhood still wrapped around it through his bent legs. Then he brought the blade up behind his buttocks, holding onto each end of the sword with his hands behind his back. The drumming increased in volume and speed and the crowd clapped and cheered harder. He stopped prancing and bent his knees to allow another holy man to position himself behind and place his hands on his shoulders. The second sadhu pulled himself up into position with a foot on each end of the blade. Then the sadhu straightened his legs and, with his accomplice clinging onto his shoulders, launched into a very impressive pogo dance.

The crowd went berserk.

When the drumming crescendo faded, the sadhu unwrapped his manhood from around the blade, gave it two gentle tugs and bounced away to delight his next audience.

'The reason the sadhu is not wearing clothing and is covering himself in ashes,' announced Vijay above the noise, 'is to signify to God that he is being above the need for material desires. He only is wishing for spiritual satisfaction. The purpose of the demonstration you have just witnessed is not to be just shocking and delighting. It is being part of the sadhu's spiritual journey. The sadhu, he was transcending his pain, taking him closer to his God.'

We rearranged ourselves and continued squeezing our way through the sea of people.

I marvelled at the serene energy emanating from the crowd, the palpable sense of purpose. There was a feeling in the air I could only describe as cosmic. A deep, sacred spirituality of oneness that was totally alien to my western notions of individualism. It was bewitching. And yet I did feel a bit different today. There was something bubbling under my skin, vibrating inside me, deep in my stomach. Was it because I was here within this gigantic outpouring of humanity? Part of it. Not on the outside, but included.

I retreated behind my camera and grabbed a shot of the row upon row of yellow, orange and blue A-shaped tents stretching into the distance. Each tent contained a sadhu or naga. We squeezed our way through knots of people and greeted the holy men we passed. Surrounded with pictures of gurus and spiritual paraphernalia, they responded with 'Namaste,' their hands in prayer position. Sat or standing on rugs or blankets, they were naked apart from beads or fresh flower garlands and head dresses. Their white ghostly faces painted with zig-zags, stripes or swirls of vibrant colours. Devotees, whom they blessed, surrounded them and they daubed their foreheads with a round dot of dye. Steam rose from pots of water sat on small fires and metal plates held donations of money. At each tent we passed we were greeted with the smiling, happy, welcoming faces of these holy men, who had given up all worldly goods to live a spiritual life.

'Does he ever put his arm down, Vijay?' I asked

We'd paused at the tent of a sadhu whose right arm was held up in the air. It resembled a petrified withered branch, the uncut fingernails curled like apple peelings and dug into his palm.

'No, he is keeping his arm up in the air constantly for thirty-eight years now. It's thought he is raising his arm all those years ago in opposition to all the fighting going on in the world. So he is raising his arm to advocate peace and harmony.'

We twisted our way through the jammed crowds. Dizzying clouds of dust rose from the floor and covered my trainers. I could feel it in my nostrils and on my fingers. It settled on my lips and I could taste it when I took a swig from my water bottle. The cloying air stole the edges of my breath, the sun beat down from the cloudless azure blue sky and the top of my head was ablaze. I hadn't taken my eyes off Alexandra's back for a second, apart from glancing behind me to smile at Charlie who put his thumbs up each time.

'How are you doing, Alexandra?' I shouted. She turned to look at me with a smile. 'Wey aye, that's great pet, you've got colour back in your cheeks.'

Thousands of hoardings of all shapes, sizes and colours

dominated the landscape, depicting gurus, sacred messages or advertising written in Hindi script. Every so often a procession would drown out the devotions blasting out from hundreds of loudspeakers as groups of devotees paraded, blowing huge horns or conch shells. They sang, shrieked with laughter and cavorted, swaying their arms with abandonment in the air. Some clashed cymbals together whilst others held effigies of gods on their heads as they hopped and skipped. Massive, hulking white oxen with necklaces and bells strung around their necks pulled decorated festival floats draped in elaborate fabrics. Riding on the floats white-clad swamis saluted everyone, waving their arms back and forth.

Aromas of incense, marijuana, spicy food and dusty earth swirled in the air, taking turns to dominate. We watched processions, greeted holy men and women in their tents and engaged with those around us. We were the only westerners there and people were often keen to acknowledge us. One sari-clad lady in a family group made eye contact with me and I raised my hands in prayer position and greeted her with 'Namaste.' That delighted her. Both groups stopped and even though neither of us could speak each other's language, she introduced me to all of her huge family. I introduced her to my travelling friends. She kept hugging me and I pleased her when I repeated in Hindi the words she'd taught me for 'God is great'. After posing for photographs, we said goodbye. They were so joyous, gracious and friendly and a feeling of heat radiated throughout my chest at the friendship with them all, however short-lived.

'This festival is a leveller. No-one gives a toss about who's rich; who's poor; what someone's wearing or what they look like. Isn't it a fantastic feeling to connect with strangers in such a joyous way? I've got a warm, glowing tingling,' I said to Summer.

'We're all connected Jen, we're all one,' she replied.

A buried memory stirred and subsided before it could spring to life. It whispered, *There was a time when you believed that, Jen. A long time ago.*

'Will you teach me to meditate, Summer?'

Her face beamed in reply, and we hugged, agreeing we'd make time at our next stop in Rishikesh – yoga capital of the world.

On our way to eat our meal we passed a row of children dressed and posing as gods and goddesses, hoping to charm a few rupees from the passers-by. I craned my neck to look inside as one lady inched up the lid of her small wicker basket. I reeled back in shock as the head of a large light brown snake glided up, its pink tongue flickering at the air. Yet more naked nagas stood at the doors of their tents, their ash covered crown jewels in full view to all. Dirty-faced children in dusty, ragged clothes sat on blankets on the ground eating food from cardboard plates with their fingers. They held out their hands as we passed. 'Rupees, please. Rupees, please.'

There was one sad-faced child with no food, sat at the back of the gaggle on his own. He looked in my direction with unseeing eyes. I picked my way through the other children to get to him. He stared ahead as I took his hand and pressed the twenty rupee note into his palm. First Alexandra followed suit, then Fraser and then the others. I glanced back as we walked on, and my heart leapt to see his face creased with a huge grin.

Sellers laid their wares on blankets on the ground. One lady sold pipes for smoking hashish; another displayed little metal pots filled with rich coloured powders for mixing into a face and body paste; another offered spiritual and ethnic beads and bracelets. Even the policemen, who leaned on their long batons with their rifles slung over their shoulders surveying the activity, were in good humour. I gave ten rupees to a holy man with only one eye, no teeth and a trailing, straggling grey beard which reached to the middle of his chest. He daubed the space between my eyes with scarlet paste and wished me a long and happy life.

We squirmed our way through a crowd listening to a swami giving a lesson and I stopped dead in complete shock at the sight that faced me. Prostrate on the ground was a line of tortured souls struck down by leprosy. Dirty brown, ragged woollen blankets covered most. Some of their affected limbs were wrapped in filthy bandages. Often the mangled parts were exposed, showing where the disease had eaten away skin and muscle, leaving a green and black stump where fingers, hands or feet had once been. They lay in the dust in the heat of the midday sun moaning and shaking. I wondered how life could be so cruel and what a hell upon earth such an existence must be. I tried to imagine what could be in the minds of the piteous people lying there in rags and tears coursed down my face.

10

The authorities had provided a free meal for anyone who wanted it at the immense tent city a short distance from the main bathing area of Har Ki Pauri ghat. The vast encampment of row upon row of temporary canvas accommodation included tents for cooking, taps for washing clothes, and shower and toilet cubicles. Palls of smoke drifted up towards the empty blue sky as people went about the hustle and bustle of their daily chores. Children ran shrieking with excitement around their temporary playground, dust swirling around their bare feet as they played tag. The everyday chatter was drowned out by the constant music and chanting from the tannoy blasting out at ear-splitting decibel levels. All the while there was a relentless stream of pilgrims coming and going, carrying bundles of clothes and other belongings necessary for a visit to the Kumbh.

'For some, attending the Kumbh is involving an epic journey from towns and villages all over India,' said Vijay. 'Some are walking incredible distances and some are travelling on trains and buses for many hours. Every devotee is having the same goal to achieve, they all are wanting the same thing. Moksha. To be released from reincarnation. Now come, enjoy the hospitality of the Kumbh.'

We queued at the long tables holding huge metal pots full of curries, rice, vegetables and fried side dishes.

'These are to be thanking you for coming to our Kumbh,' said the man serving the food. He smiled and heaped fresh fried crispy samosas from a karai of crackling hot oil onto my plate

I sank my teeth into the crisp, golden brown, blistered triangular crust, releasing the aroma of cinnamon and cloves. The shell crunched, initially resisted, then crumbled in my mouth, allowing the spicy flavour bomb to burst onto my tongue. The potato chunks were tender but still retained a satisfying amount of bite. The peas, onion and carrot, coated in the sweet heat of ginger and chillies initiated a pleasing glow at the back of my throat as I swallowed.

'They're very moreish,' said Betty, speaking in between mouthfuls of food.

I was glad she was finally getting to eat her own food after waiting on Derek hand and foot. He'd plopped himself down to sit on the floor while Betty stood in the queue, chose his food for him and ran back and forth with his cup of chai and cutlery.

We sat cross-legged in a circle, thankful to rest our legs. The organisers had covered the sitting area in fresh straw which crunched under our feet, releasing a sweet, earthy dry grass smell into the air. Knots of people assembled in huddles, joined in enthusiastic singing and chanting as they spread out saris of every colour imaginable on the straw. All the while spiritual music floating from the tannoy enhanced the sacred mood.

Fraser was quiet and looked sad, almost sullen. 'Missing the Clyde?' I said, jolting him out of his reverie.

'Uh, eh, sorry I was miles away hen.'

Summer and Charlie sat close together, their knees touching. 'Aren't you having anything to eat, Alexandra?' asked Summer.

Alexandra's answer was cut off with a retching of her body. She was looking a whole lot better though, and dropped my hat back onto my head. 'Thanks for being a rather marvellous friend. I think I'd have jolly well passed out if it hadn't been for your hat.'

'Are you sure you don't need it any more?' I asked, relieved. The fierce midday sun had relented. It was late afternoon now, but my skull had been on fire over the last hour. I took a long drink of water. My mouth tingled with a pleasing heat. 'Howay lasses, let's find the loos.'

'Do you need a toilet break, Derek?' asked Betty.

'Howay man Betty, let the blokes find their own way to the loos.'

* * *

THE TOILETS WERE CHALLENGING. Ceramic holes set in concrete blocks with two bricks for the feet.

'How are you managing, Jen?' shouted Alexandra from the adjoining canvas cubicle.

The bricks wobbled under my feet and my thighs burned as I squatted, trying to hit the target and avoid falling backwards at the same time. 'I'm having penis envy, Alexandra. I want my plastic willy back.' The vision of my shewee disappearing down the hole on the sleeper train and the sound of Alexandra snorting from next door, very nearly caused a disaster as my giggling threatened to upend me in the dust.

'The secret is to keep your balance and squat slowly,' shouted Betty from my other side.

'You sound like an expert, Betty. Do you have many squat toilets in the Cotswolds, then?' came Summer's voice from a cubicle somewhere to my left.

There was a scraping of bricks. 'Oh, oh, ooooh.' It was Betty shouting. Then came an almighty clatter as the canvas walls shook with earthquake tremors resembling a nine point five reading on the Richter scale.

'Good golly, are you okay Betty?' Alexandra sounded panicky.

'No, I've fallen off the bricks. I can't get back up. I've twisted my ankle. I'm stuck on the floor.'

Within seconds all three of us were outside the door of Betty's compartment listening to her grunting with the effort of trying to get herself to her feet.

'Listen Betty, we're going to have to come in and help you. Is that okay?' shouted Summer through the canvas door flap.

'Yes, I can't get up.' Her voice broke.

'Here we come, Betty,' I said.

She lay on her side on the floor by the concrete block cradling her ankle. One brick was lodged in the ceramic hole while the other had been flung to the corner of the cubicle. Her jogging bottoms were around her ankles and on display was the biggest full moon I'd ever witnessed. 'Eeeh Betty pet, howay let's get you up. Something's winking at us hinny.'

Between the three of us we heaved her to her feet, helped pull her knickers and joggers back up, and held her while she gingerly tested putting her weight on her ankle.

'There doesn't seem to be any harm done,' said Betty as we stood in a circle in the tight space, laughing with relief.

'Are ye okay, hen?' Fraser ran towards us, concern etched onto his face at the sight of Betty limping.

'I'm fine Fraser thanks, just a slight twisted ankle that's all,' she answered, as she hobbled over to where Derek sat. Not a shred of concern showed on his face.

* * *

TIME TO FALL into line again to make our way to Har Ki Pauri ghat. We were to watch the procession of holy men who would head to the water's edge to be first to bathe. The crowds had swollen, and I found myself at the back of our line. This time, behind Derek.

It was slow going. We swerved our way through tight groups of people, everyone was on their way to the water's edge for their opportunity to wipe out the sins of their past. Sat inside a voluminous white tent was a sadhu, dressed in apricot coloured robes. Strands of gaudy beads danced on his chest, he had long silver dreadlocked hair and had painted his forehead with stripes of crimson and burnt orange. He sat on a colossal candy red velvet throne trimmed with intricate gold metalwork. Devotees sat at his feet. They hung onto his every word.

He was obviously a teacher of great magnitude. This could be that one unforgettable, representative image of the Kumbh I was searching for. If I could capture the emotion, that was. I sunk to my knees just as the sadhu turned to look at me. He nodded his approval, and I checked the settings, changed the shutter speed, and took ten quick shots. 'Namaste.' He nodded again, and I turned back to the line.

Shit, where was Derek's baseball cap? I couldn't see it. I

was surrounded by strangers. Telling myself to calm down, I looked for Alexandra's ginger hair, then listened for a Glaswegian accent. But the crowds were so dense, the conversation a roar. It hit me then how small I was in the crowd, how lost and vulnerable.

'Vijay. Vijay!' I screamed.

People looked back at me blankly. Detached. They didn't look so friendly now.

'Have you seen a group of white people? I've lost my friends.'

The air was so muggy and hot. The dust even thicker than earlier. I thought back to the report I'd read from the last Kumbh when there was a massive stampede and loads of people died.

I had to think logically. They were headed to the water. But where was that? I'd learned the Hindi direction words back at home and remembered the word for river.

'Jo jis tarah se nadee hai?'

He understood. He pointed to the left. 'Namaste.'

I pushed against the sari-clad wall of bodies trying to prise open a tiny gap. The hit of spicy body odour filled my nostrils. Why wouldn't they let me through? A revolving kaleidoscope of fuzzy colour clouded my eyesight. I pulled at my shirt collar, it was too tight. This baking heat. I can't bear it. It's getting hotter, hotter. I'm going to throw up. A curtain of darkness closed inwards from the edges of my vision, like a tunnel stretching out ahead of me. My knees trembled. I've sprouted earmuffs, the tannoy's all muffled. Oh God, I'm going to—

11

I was jolted out of a black hole. *Wait, what am I doing here? What happened? What's going on?* The stench of marijuana enveloped me. Even before I opened my eyes, I knew I was lying in a tent. My stomach quivered, stimulated by a potent, high-voltage chanting from close quarters. I fought the compulsion to scream and squinted through one eyelid. The shock of the sight that greeted me forced an involuntary gasp from my throat. *They didn't hear you. Keep still. Don't let them know you're awake.* The terrifying realisation struck me. I was in the corner of a tent of a group of Aghori, the most extreme and feared of all religious sects in India. And worse, they were practicing black magic. A ritual I'd watched a group of Aghoris perform on a video I'd seen during my research.

In the dim light I could make out the shadowy forms of four naked, ash-smeared sadhus. They sat cross-legged around a hearth drinking from human skulls. Firelight flickered across their wizened faces, long matted hair and beards. One man lit a huge chillum and, cupping the pipe to his mouth, drew in five quick breaths. He exhaled a dense, swirling plume of smoke and with head raised to the ceiling roared an intonation before passing the pipe to his neighbour. The acrid stench reached my nostrils and irritated my throat. I needed to cough but gripped by the need for self-preservation I steeled my nerves and lay motionless. Crippled with fear.

In their midst a candle flame burned atop a human skull. One of the men held a smoking taper to the nasal opening and smoke puffed from the eye sockets like steam from a train. The whiff of alcohol rose in the air as his neighbour poured from a bottle, soaking the skull and dousing the flame. The elder Aghori clapped his withered hands, a succession of hand gestures followed accompanied by a series of ghoulish intonations making my skin crawl. As they beat the top of the skull with their fists and the chanting grew louder, the rhythmic thump echoed in my body.

Oh God help me, how am I going to get out of here alive. Is it true that Aghoris cover themselves with the ash from cremation pyres? That video said they eat human flesh and stool and even drink urine. They stood as one and stomped the ground in time with their intonations. The dust assaulted my nostrils. I took one huge breath, and a sneeze erupted from me that shook the walls of the tent. In that instant all four sadhus stopped mid-stomp and turned to stare in my direction. I froze.

'Oh, you are awake.' A gnarled vision in saffron robes and flowing silver hair materialised from the darkness.

I jumped to my feet and regretted it as the world swirled around me.

'No, no, you must take it easy. Come sit down until you've recovered. Don't be scared. We mean you no harm.'

'H-h-how did I get here? W-where am I?' I pressed the cool napkin she offered me against my throbbing forehead.

'You passed out at my feet. I brought you here to care for you. Did you come here with friends?'

'Y-yes. I lost them in the crowd. Please can you help me find them?'

'Of course we will help, but first you must drink this. It will make you feel better.' She handed me a steaming mug.

Relieved that the contents didn't smell of urine I took a tiny sip while the Aghoris looked on, heads bent to one side, curiosity etched on each face.

'Don't worry it's only herbal water. It has basil, mint, cumin, clove and coriander. It will diminish your fatigue.'

'I feel better already,' I said, draining the mug. 'I think I'm ready to go find my friends now. They were headed to the ghats.' The men didn't look quite as frightening with bright sunlight streaming through the open tent flap.

Encircled by the Aghoris and led by the lady in saffron we cut through the throng like a hot knife through butter. These sadhus were feared and no-one stood in their way. Thirty minutes later we neared the place where the crowds thickened and the water flowed. I surveyed the scene in every direction.

There it was. The bright red baseball cap jiggling on top of the bamboo pole.

'Jen, Jen. Can you hear me?' Vijay's wonderful deep Indian tones floated above the ether towards me.

'I'm here, Vijay.' I grabbed my hat from my head, waved it in the air wildly and jumped as high as my five-foot-five frame would allow.

The crimson cap bobbed towards me. At last Vijay materialised from the crush of people. I fell into his arms.

'These people looked after me, Vijay, and brought me here.'

Unable to hide his shock Vijay, bowed deep, 'Namaste'.

'I'm eternally grateful. Namaste.' I bowed.

'Namaste,' came the replies, and they headed back the way we'd come, the crowds parting before them.

'Did you come to any harm, Jen?' Concern etched Vijay's face.

'They were very kind Vijay and I've learned one huge lesson. I'll think twice before judging a book by its cover in future.'

Vijay smiled. 'Come with me please Jen, everyone's waiting for you. The procession of the sadhus will pass by soon.' We stepped forward and were swallowed by the crowds again.

'Bloody hell Jen, you gave us a jolly good fright. We thought we'd lost you forever.' Alexandra grabbed me in a bear hug followed by Fraser then Summer.

'Sorry everyone.' I was shamefaced.

'No harm done, at least Vijay found you,' Ivan said kindly.

Betty rubbed my arm. I glimpsed Derek watching me through narrowed eyelids as we waited for the sadhus to begin their bathing ritual.

* * *

WE'D MADE it to the steps and had a clear view of the proceedings. Devotees were amassed on both sides of the river, the ghats packed solid with pilgrims waiting for their turn to bathe.

'There are thousands of them,' said Alexandra as the hordes of naked ash-smeared holy men galloped headlong into the water. In their hands they waved tridents, spears and swords. Wild-eyed and dreadlocked, they charged ahead calling out mantras. They hit the water like an exploding bomb. The brown water churned with the masses who jumped, shrieked, cavorted and splashed the river with their hands flinging water in every direction as they chanted. They submerged themselves then rocketed back up out of the water like Poseidon emerging from the deep. Holy men swung their heads backward, their long dreadlocked hair creating arcs of sun-glistening water above them.

Then it was time for the devotees and pilgrims to take their dip. They hurled themselves into the holy river, some splashed water over their heads and faces, whilst others immersed their whole bodies. The women entered the water fully dressed. The sun shone through silk saris setting the gold and silver threads alight and they glinted like liquid splashes of electricity. Their hands were raised in prayer position as they chanted mantras, rapt in concentration. They emerged with wet saris clinging to their bodies, their inky blue hair dripping in the nectar of Ma Ganga. The strange words mingled with the sounds from the loudspeakers, the splashing water and the general hubbub from the millions of people in the immediate vicinity.

Summer slipped off her sandals and rolled up her ethnic-style Indian trouser legs.

'Come on Jen, are you coming in with me?'

I thought about it for a split second. I needed a new life. Eyeing the dirty looking water with suspicious looking debris and garbage floating around in it, I changed my mind. My salvation would have to wait.

'No thanks, Summer. I'll hold your gear if you're going in, though.'

We watched as she waded in until the water reached up to her knees. Her long lilac hair looked almost silver and the stud in her lip glinted. She closed her eyes and her lips moved as she repeated her mantras over and over. Her prayer necklace dangled in between her hands as she passed each bead between her fingers. She looked beautiful, untroubled and devout.

* * *

THE SUN SLIPPED towards the horizon and the last golden light shimmered on the Ganges. The crowds had thinned out now and Har Ki Pauri ghat resembled a magical fairy wonderland. Each temple roof, strung with sparkling lights, shone against the darkening sky. Lilting Indian music floated from a cafe near the exit and before leaving we decided on a final cup of steaming masala chai.

The others sat around the outside tables drinking and chatting while I busied myself taking photos of the evening lighting, trying and failing to get the exposure right. An aura of serenity surrounded the whole area. Lost behind my camera lens, I didn't see Fraser approaching until he stood in front of me.

His voice was low. 'D'ye ever put that camera down, Jen? It's permanently stuck to yer hands.'

He lifted the strap from around my neck, passed the camera to Summer and pulled me towards him. Without saying a word, he held me by the waist, I lifted my arms around his neck and we swayed to the music. The gentle pressure of his torso moved against my breasts as we shifted in harmony from side to side. He pulled me closer. The natural scent of him filled my senses, and his breath caressed my cheek. I looked into his dark cobalt blue eyes.

They locked onto mine – smouldering, searching. His face flushed in the soft rose red lighting and my gaze fell to his glistening lips, full and inviting. Strains of fuzzy sitar and flute were carried along on a slow, lazy drumbeat accompanied by the dreamy voice of a female vocalist. I relaxed my tingling body and melted into him. In an instant, I was struck by lightning. What the hell was I doing?

* * *

LATER THAT NIGHT, I sat in my hotel room trying to convince myself I'd somehow captured the magic of the Kumbh in my photographs. But it was no good. As I scrolled through hundreds of shots, I knew I hadn't succeeded. It deflated me. I'd witnessed an out-of-this-world event. A bewitching, spectacular celebration of mankind. I was in awe of this country and its people. I wanted to share my experience with others. When they looked at my images, I wanted them to feel they were there, standing alongside me. In frustration, I slung the camera onto the bed. There was a soft knock at the door. My heart skipped a beat. What if that was him?

'It's just me, Jen.' Alexandra.

'I'm rather too stimulated to sleep and wondered if you wouldn't mind company,' she said, settling onto the bed.

'Would you like a nice cup of British tea?' I asked.

We reminisced about our visit to the Kumbh. It was difficult to find adequate words to describe our feelings about what we'd witnessed. When I remarked that I thought I'd have to drink a mug of pee to escape the Aghoris she laughed so hard she snorted. But somewhere amid the laughter there was a shift in Alexandra's demeanour and her eyes filled with tears.

'Eeeh Alexandra pet, what's wrong?' I hugged her to me.

'I'm sorry, Jen. I'm grieving,' she said through huge sobs. 'Today has brought so much pain to the surface.' I passed her a tissue. 'My best friend died two months ago. She had cancer.'

Her words struck my heart like a knife. The shock knocked the breath from my lungs and for a second I couldn't speak. The desperate need to keep my situation a secret strengthened me. I gathered myself.

'Oh Alexandra, I'm so sorry love.' I hugged her closer until her tears had stopped.

I listened for an hour as she told me how her friend of thirty years had discovered a lump in her breast. Alexandra had nursed her through her treatment. And finally lost her. Tamara had helped Alexandra through a nasty divorce when her husband had left her for his secretary. The betrayal had devastated her.

'Tamara was my rock, and now she's gone.'

'But you're so brave, Alexandra. Tamara would be proud of you.'

'It was Tamara who convinced me to come out to India. Before she died, she said she had a feeling it was important for me to sign up for the Ganges Voyager. She didn't know why. It was just instinct, she said.'

Later that evening as I lay in bed trying to sleep it struck me that the single most important thing to possess in life is your health. All the money in the world can't bring you happiness or save you from a deadly disease. Fear nibbled at the edges of my conscious thought, trying to gain entry and, determined to get some rest, I slammed the door shut before its tentacles could creep any further.

12

Ping.

A Geordie Up The Ganges sprung to life with a message from Martin.

Hi love. Did you show those guys in the Sikh Gurdwara kitchens how to make stotty cake and pease pudding? It's nice to read your travelogue of the places you've visited. You're not missing much on the Tyne, it's freezing here. By the way, Newcastle beat Sunderland two nil in the derby match. They're still celebrating on the Quayside three days later. Love and miss you. Martin x

Hello Jen. I'm following your blog from Scotland. Your Scottish travelling friend will agree with me when I say forget Geordie stotty cake, what India needs is haggis!

Hi, I'm from Ireland. What rubbish. Nothing holds a candle to Irish stew.

I'm Hank from Arkansas. Y'all don't know what you're talking about. Once ya'll taste possum pie nothing else will do.

We had two hours before meeting for lunch. Time to update my next blog.

These photos are no better than the ones before. I'm not improving. They're good. Yes, technically perfect even. But what's missing? Scrutinise them up close, Jen. What can you see? Aha, I know what it is. Yes, that's it. The problem isn't what I can see. The problem is what I can't see. I can't see emotion in these shots. They're all so two-dimensional. But how the hell do I capture feelings like I witnessed at the Kumbh yesterday? I haven't got a clue how to do that. You'll never be a good enough photographer to apply for that job on the cruise ships. You're rubbish at it.

Here's a few nice ones of people bathing you can upload. This one here of the sadhu with his willy wrapped around the sword blade should shock a few people. This is a nice one of you with that lovely family. Here's a good one of the whole group. Bloody hell, I wish Derek would smile for once. Summer and Charlie have become so close they're joined at the hip. Look at this shot of Fraser, you've taken loads of photos of him. For someone who's always joking around he looks miserable on a lot of these. He's smiling on this one, zoom in on his face. He's so good looking. No, stop zooming in on his crotch. That's naughty. You've got the hots for him and it's wrong. Don't be so disloyal to Martin. Eeeh but I couldn't stop tingling after that smooch with him last night. He's so exciting. Stop it. Stop it. You're a married woman. Get on with writing an overview of what happened yesterday. Don't mention Betty's attempt at mooning millions of people, though.

Wednesday, 3rd March

... So, thank you for reading my account of this spectacle, so immense it can be viewed from the moon. I've now recovered from the sight of millions of men's dangly bits. One such appendage had a bell and a piece of string attached. For a small fee devotees could give the string a tug and delight everyone with a chorus of "Jingle Bells".

It's so exciting to reach the magical number of one hundred followers. I'm delighted to have your company as we head off to our next stop, Rishikesh.

I'm discovering the essence of India. It's intoxicating.

And there, lurking within my private messages:

Don't you think you'd be better off at home in Newcastle. When the cat's away the mouse will play! Forever Yours, Marra.

My posture stiffened. It was that creep again. Don't let it get to you. You know Martin. He'll never cheat on you. I stabbed at the delete button and the disturbing words vanished.

* * *

It was an hour before we were to meet at the restaurant for lunch and I grabbed the opportunity to lose myself in the bustling streets. A tailor sitting on a stool in his kiosk smiled for me as I snapped a shot of him. His foot moved back and forth on the treadle of his sewing machine. The gnarled old lady selling tiny flower-filled leaf boats grinned at my camera, her teeth long gone. A boy sat on his hunkers at the side of the road. The air surrounding him wafted out to passers-by, tempting and pungent as his cooking pans bubbled on a stove. I was so engrossed in capturing the essence of the surrounding tableaux I didn't see Derek at first, but yes, that was him. He stood with his back to me, peering into the doorway of a shop selling musical instruments.

'Hi Derek,' I called out as I made my way across the street towards him. 'Thinking of buying some bongo drums, Derek?' He spun to stare at me, confusion carved into his face, his eyes darting from side to side.

Taken aback, I looked around for Betty. At that moment she appeared from out of the throng looking flustered.

'There you are, Derek.' Turning to me, she said, 'We got separated in the crowds.'

'I'm not surprised, it's really busy. I was taking a few shots of the boy selling chai when I spotted Derek.' I turned to face him. His bewilderment had vanished.

'It's almost time for lunch, ladies. Come on, let's make our way to meet up with the gang,' he said. Back to his normal self.

* * *

'I'LL NEVER MASTER CROSSING these roads,' I said. We'd bumped into Summer and Charlie on the way to the restaurant, and now the five of us teetered on the edge of the pavement. Hesitant and nervous after a few false starts, the traffic chaos befuddled my mind. Derek grabbed my hand shouting, 'There's safety in numbers, if we wait for a gap and all step out together they'll have to stop.'

'Here's a gap,' shouted Charlie as he stepped off the pavement. He hadn't noticed the tuk-tuk which had swerved to overtake a lumbering oxen and was now hurtling straight at him.

'Charlie, watch out,' screamed Summer as the vehicle rammed into him with such force his feet left the ground and he hit the floor with a thump.

The driver launched himself into the road shouting and waving his arms in anger while Charlie lay stunned and moaning on the floor. Summer got to him first and cradled him as he struggled to sitting.

'I'm n-not hurt S-summer. J-just a bit dazed. I'll be okay in a minute. Aw, don't cry I'm fine.'

'Oh God Charlie, I got such a fright,' said Summer. With tears running down her face she kissed him tenderly.

'They'd make such a lovely couple,' whispered Betty.

'Yes, they would indeed Betty pet,' I said, smiling.

Seeing Charlie wasn't injured the driver shouted a word which sounded like an insult, jumped into his tuk-tuk, cranked it into gear and sped off to disappear into the lawless throng.

* * *

'The chicken butter masala sounds cool,' said Charlie as he supped on his bottle of water, none the worse for his close encounter with the tuk-tuk.

'I'm having the lamb roghan josh this time, finished off with gulab jamun,' said Summer.

'What's gulab jamun, hen?' Fraser scraped his hand across his beard.

'They're sticky, sweet deep fried dough balls dripping in syrup,' Summer answered.

'Oooh, that sounds like heaven in a bowl, I'll try them as well,' I said

The restaurant was full with people who were visiting the Kumbh. Laughter and happy chit chat in an unfamiliar tongue filled the air, blending with harmonious, mystical Indian music. Dazzling posters of Hindu Gods and Goddesses adorned the walls. I sniffed the air relishing the heady fusion of scent from hanging marigold garlands, mingling with aromas of spices and curries competing for dominance. I'd decided to live dangerously and ordered the pork vindaloo and steamed basmati rice.

'You're brave, hen,' said Fraser, who'd slid along the bench seat to be next to me.

This was a traditional Indian restaurant and eating with hands was expected. I tore a long chunk from my naan, remembering to use my right hand. Vijay had advised in the strongest of terms against using our left hand, which in India is used in toilet activities. It was more challenging that it looked. I used my thumb and forefinger to tear off a strip while holding the rest of the bread with my other fingers. I scooped up a tender piece of pork dripping in fragrant, deep red masala sauce and, feeling pleased with myself, popped the whole morsel into my mouth. The explosion of chilli, vinegar and spices bombarded every taste bud with my first tangy bite. My tongue tingled with the first hit of pepper, cinnamon, cloves and cardamom. Then came the earthy nutty flavours I recognised of cumin, coriander and turmeric. The multi-dimensional heat detonated, blasting every part of my mouth. Beads of sweat formed on my top lip and forehead as I breathed in and out through rounded lips, struggling to stem the burning. Derek grabbed Betty's fan and flapped it inches from my nose.

'Take a drink of coconut milk,' suggested Ivan.

But I didn't want to dampen the heat. It was stimulating the release of pleasurable, sensual endorphins.

'Golly Jen, your face is as red as a chilli. How was the vindaloo?' asked Alexandra

'Delicious,' I said as I tucked into my dessert of gulab jamun. The intense floral flavour merged with cardamom coated the inside of my mouth in a juicy, sticky rose syrup which clung to my teeth and lips.

Fraser said something I didn't quite catch. As I turned to face him, his hand reached out, and he gently wiped the syrup from my bottom lip. My gaze rested on his mouth as he licked the syrup from his fingers. Butterfly wings quivered in my chest and this time the heat radiated from a place other than my mouth.

I jumped up like a jack-in-the-box. 'I think it's time to leave for Rishikesh.'

13

On arrival at the Rishikesh hotel, our base for the next three nights, the manager draped a pretty marigold garland around each of our necks. My room was huge with an enormous, comfortable bed. From my window I drank in the green and mountainous view. I snapped a few frames with the camera and rushed downstairs to meet everyone for our transportation into Rishikesh Town.

'Someone needs to speak up,' grumbled Charlie as Betty and Derek emerged from the hotel door twenty minutes late.

* * *

'I'll sit up front.' I jumped into the tuk-tuk next to the driver as Ivan and Charlie pulled themselves into the back seats. We were to take tuk-tuk rides from the hotel to the Laxman Jhula bridge where we could cross over the Ganges into the centre of town. A unique aroma reached my nostrils. In the driver's hand was a giveaway reefer. Marijuana was illegal in India but I'd read that in some places, including Rishikesh, its use was common. The driver, looking spaced out, grinned at me through decayed, brown and red-stained teeth. He was a middle-aged man but his nut brown, deeply wrinkled leathery skin gave the impression he was many years older. My first instinct was to dive out, back into the street. Too late. The driver cranked the gears into place and the tuk-tuk jerked forward. I hung onto the side handle for all my worth, my body jolted back and forward as the driver changed up the gears. The vehicle kangaroo'd into the midst of the traffic.

I'd watched the traffic chaos in Delhi and Haridwar with astonishment. Now, here I was, stuck in a tuk-tuk with a driver who was as high as a kite.

The streets were chock-a-block with traffic of every description. Instantly we were in the thick of it. If there were any road regulations, no-one was following them. Cars attacked from the right, tuk-tuks from the left. I grasped my mouth when out of the melee two cars appeared heading straight towards us. Just when I thought a head-on collision was inevitable, the two cars parted and passed along either side of us with only inches to spare. My hair stood on end. It wasn't only because of the breeze which whipped around me through the open sides of the vehicle.

We zig-zagged through the hectic streets at breakneck speed avoiding everything in front of us; people materialised out of nowhere; cows rambled by oblivious to the danger; bicycles; horses and traps; fruit-seller carts. You name it, it was on the road in front of our tuk-tuk. At one point I turned to the driver and unintentionally lapsing into my broadest Geordie accent shouted, 'Eeeh, howay man, slow doon.' But I think something was lost in translation. He looked at me with glazed eyes, shifted up a gear and rammed his foot further to the floor.

Part of me was loving it. The sensible part was terrified. Near miss after near miss ensued. We hurtled down the road towards the bridge. Twisting; turning; breaking abruptly; jolting forward; bumping over holes in the ground.

'I feel like I've fallen asleep and woken up in the middle of a Keystone Cops car chase,' shouted Charlie above the chaos.

* * *

RELIEF FLOODED over me as I stepped from the tuk-tuk. My heart pounded and sweat covered my skin.

'Well, I could certainly recommend that for the relief of constipation.' Ivan looked shaken as his feet faltered on the firm ground.

I gazed at the Holy River Ganges. This river was at the centre of India's beating heart. But for me, it had become a representation now of my battle against the dark unspoken terrors which threatened to destroy me.

'Lost in your thoughts again, Jen?' Alexandra's quiet voice brought me back to the present. 'Golly, are you okay? You look rather worried.' She linked her arm through mine. 'If you need to talk, I'm a jolly good listener.'

I looked at this kind-hearted woman and an overwhelming desire to unburden myself washed over me.

For a split second I imagined how good it would be to tell her everything. But how can you open your heart to someone you've only known for a few days?

'Oh, I'm fine Alexandra thanks, I was just mesmerised by this amazing place. I've imagined standing here in Rishikesh and now, here we are.'

It was true, I was awestruck by the scene before me. Grey

and white puffy clouds had developed with the occasional sighting of a tiny section of blue sky. The surrounding trees swayed in the stiff, cool breeze which carried the aromas of greenery and earthy soil. Green tree-covered mountains rose from each side of the Ganges like ever-watchful guardians.

Two large iron suspension bridges; the Laxman Jhula bridge, where we now stood and further away, the Ram Jhula bridge, spanned the river. On the other side was the main town consisting of buildings of all shapes and sizes. Some resembled fairyland castles, others reminded me of many layered wedding cakes painted in burning orange, sunny yellow, rustic green, cool blue and all hues in between. The largest of them all were the multi-storied temples, ashrams where seekers gravitated to practice yoga, meditation and gain enlightenment. At the centre of it all the wild river surged, rough water frothing and crashing on the side rocks. The current raged, giving credence to the reports of people drowning here in the rolling water.

My hair flew around, whipping my face. My coat and trousers flapped in the breeze and the Laxman Jhula swayed under my feet. I steadied myself on the hand rail and stopped dead one third of the way across. There to my left-hand side and, too close for comfort, was a rhesus macaque monkey, and it was looking at me. It sat on the rail but it looked about three foot tall. Soon it was joined by a second, and then a third.

'Don't look into the eyes, Alexandra. I've read somewhere that if you give them eye contact, they can get aggressive.' My voice rose to fever pitch.

Two men strolled past where we stood motionless, paying no heed to the monkeys. As we inched past, one of them made a move to climb down from where it sat on the handrail. That galvanised us into motion and we both set off at a run. Once we'd got far enough away, we stopped to glance back. It seemed we were the only panicky people on the bridge. Everyone else just walked on by, not giving the monkeys a second glance.

'Eeeh we're a daft pair Alexandra, we'll have to get used to those. I've read there are bloody loads of them over there,' I said, pointing towards the town.

* * *

'This place looks like it hasn't changed since The Beatles came here in the late sixties,' said Summer as she side-stepped a cowpat.

'It's got a peaceful hippie vibe about it, hasn't it? So many interesting characters,' I said.

As if to prove my point, a holy man wandered by. With a staff in his hand, his long grey hair and beard danced in tune with his saffron robes in the breeze. His face was finger-painted with bright red and yellow swirling and zig-zag patterns. I snapped a quick shot.

Sprinkled amongst the lovingly tended ashrams with lush gardens and pristine architecture, were neglected, dilapidated buildings. The once magnificent temples with collapsing rooftops, crumbling walls, faded paint and flimsy woodwork carvings were a sad reflection of a prestigious past. Now they were ravaged by years of monsoon rains, blistering heat and whipping winds.

'Ye'll photograph anything, ye will Jen,' said Fraser as I stopped to frame a shot of a half demolished building. 'Can't ye just stop for a minute to look around?'

'There's beauty in decrepitude, you know.' I pointed the camera at him and grabbed a shot.

'Sorry if I cracked yer lens, hen,' he joked.

A myriad of shops, restaurants, markets, ashrams, bazaars and guesthouses flanked the rough, pot-holed main street. Yoga-inspired clothing on hangers around shop doors danced seductively in the breeze. Shopkeepers competed with their neighbours offering their own particular brand of yoga equipment, Indian style bags, spiritual souvenirs and jewellery.

'Watch out, Derek. There's a stampede on its way,' Fraser shouted in warning as a huge shaggy-haired, sandy-coloured cow sauntered up the middle of the road. Derek was an obstacle in the holy cow's progress and he stepped aside to allow it to pass. Without a second glance it plodded on, the pretty pink necklace around its neck an indication of the animal's importance in Rishikesh society. These streets were just what I needed after the crazy tuk-tuk ride. Along with the evocative music and chanting floating in the background, the sweet smell of incense wafted on the breeze. It blended with the ringing of temple bells to reinforce the serene ambience of this sacred Indian town. Tranquility settled over me as I allowed the fresh mountain air, imbued with eons of mystical energy, to seep into my being.

'Did you get some good shots of the bridges over the river, Jen?' Derek asked, looking happy and relaxed. Perhaps the magic of the place had worked on him as well. 'You should get some great shots at The Ganga Evening Aarti Ceremony.'

'You're right. Now, which night are we going? Oh, yes we're there on our last evening in Rishikesh. We need to leave the hotel dead on time then, to make sure we get a good spot at the front of the crowds,' I said pointedly.

We wandered in our group investigating shops and markets. Soon, it seemed normal to see cows of all shapes, colours and sizes running the show. They commanded the right of way on the cowpat-strewn roads.

'People-watching is so absorbing here,' said Summer as holy men, yogis, western hippies, Hindu devotees and spiritual seekers mingled in a profusion of spirituality.

A woman approached, one calloused open hand outstretched towards us, the other clutching her baby to her breast. Her lifeless eyes were as dull as her torn, faded sari. I pulled twenty rupees from my knickers.

'Don't you think that's a little too much to be giving Jen? Vijay advised ten rupees was enough to give beggars on the str...' Alexandra's words tapered off as I swung round to glare at her.

Not taking my eyes off Alexandra's face I stuffed my hand down my trousers, retrieved another twenty rupees and handed both notes to the lady holding the now screaming baby.

Unsettled, as I roamed along the street window shopping, a poster grabbed my attention. It compelled me to negotiate my way around the cowpats to the other side of the road. I stood in front of a shop window with the huge white painted words "White Water Rafting". A shiver ran up my spine. The photos were of people in orange inflatable rafts. Unrestrained excitement shone from their faces as they powered their oars through walls of crashing, wild, raging torrents.

Ten minutes later, I re-joined the others, clutching my booking slip to take part in the Brahmpuri to Laxman Jhula "White Water Experience for the Adrenalin Junkie".

14

I drew my room curtains on our first morning in Rishikesh to bright blue skies and puffy white clouds. The leaves of trees outside my window shimmered in the early dew, quivering in the light breeze. They didn't call this town The Yoga Capital of the World for nothing and I was to spend the day with Summer. We were to attend a yoga class with a renowned yogi and then she would teach me to meditate. I was excited.

Before that, though, I had laundering to do. It was hot outside and my clothes would dry out on the balcony. I filled the shower tray with water; threw in a handful of washing powder; and dropped in the combat pants I'd been wearing at the time of the little mishap on the sleeper train. I stepped into the shower and trampled on my trousers, whipping up soapy suds. Where must my shewee be now, I wondered.

Later I gathered my gear together and rushed through the hotel door. I didn't want to be late for the minibus. We had to get to the Laxman Jhula on time. The ashram where our yoga class would be held was over the bridge in town. It was a drop-in session, which meant Summer and I couldn't pre-book our places. Once all mats were taken that was it. Any late-comers would miss out.

* * *

'I DON'T BELIEVE THIS.' Summer's normally unflustered demeanour showed signs of cracking.

The minibus engine ticked over as we waited once more for Derek and Betty to show up.

Each of us displayed various symptoms of impatience. Fraser whistled; Charlie rocked from side to side; Ivan's head tilted back as he gazed at the ceiling; Alexandra tapped her foot; Summer let out a loud sigh and Vijay patted his red clipboard against the palm of his hand. As for myself, my frustration turned to irritation as my breath grew heavier and louder. They were ten minutes late now and the throttling engine seemed to increase in volume along with the sound of my own breathing in my ear.

Five minutes later, they emerged from the door of the hotel. As usual Derek displayed an air of haughtiness and strolled nonchalantly towards the bus, and poor Betty trotted after him, trying to keep up, looking drained.

'At last.' Ivan clapped as they climbed the steps and took their seats at the back without a word to anyone.

That does it. Someone has to be frank and speak to them. I made my way to the back of the bus, took a deep breath and adopted a placatory tone.

'Sorry to mention this, guys, but please would you arrive on time in future when Vijay has asked us to meet? You're often late to turn up and it's really frustrating for the rest of us.'

Derek's eyes turned black and his face shifted to thunder. 'And are you our tour group leader now?' His tone was threatening, sarcastic and superior.

I channelled Emma's voice, telling me to control my breathing.

'No Derek, I'm not the tour leader. I'm just one of your travelling companions who would like it very much if you would respect the rest of us by turning up on time like everyone else. You're fifteen minutes late and that affects us all because some of us have plans for this morning and need to keep to a schedule.'

My calm manner took him aback. He glared at me but I could see he had no reply.

I knew that was all I needed to say and as I made my way back to my seat, Ivan shouted,

'Hear, hear.'

I took my seat next to Alexandra who squeezed my arm and nodded in support. As the bus pulled out of the car park, my insides did a merry dance.

* * *

THE DRIVER PUT his foot down, and we arrived at the Laxman Jhula in record time. As we rushed over the bridge, I paid no heed to the monkeys flying through the air, jumping and cavorting on the metalwork structure.

The yoga class was held at the Parmarth Niketan Ashram. Hindi script, Om symbols and a myriad of exotic paintings in eye-watering colours decorated the studio walls. Ganesh the elephant-headed God, the remover of obstacles, bestowed a benevolent smile to everyone who gazed upon his earthly depiction.

'That goddess with the many arms is Durga. She's the warrior goddess, she combats evil and demonic forces that threaten peace, prosperity and goodness,' whispered Summer.

There were another fourteen practitioners warming up or chatting. Summer and I claimed the last two mats at the back of the room. Swami Prajakash entered and the quiet chatter died down. Gentle Indian sitar music enhanced the calm aura. Without saying a word, Swami seated himself cross-legged on the small raised dais at the front of the room. He was dressed in the Indian-style long white shirt top and white pants. With his eyes closed and hands upturned, index finger and thumbs touching, he appeared a vision of serenity. His chest barely moved. He was deep in meditation. His long, sleek, straight black hair parted in the middle, reached down to his elbows, gleaming. His lips curved in a faint smile. A short black beard extended to about two inches below his chin. From his closed almond-shaped eyes I could see he had long thick black eyelashes. Everyone settled. A hush descended. The sweet buzzing reverberation of the sitar filled the room. Swami Prajakash opened his eyes raised his hands in prayer position and greeted us all with a bow of his head. 'Namaste.'

'Namaste,' replied everyone.

In a voice that flowed over me like silk caressing my skin, he instructed us to lie on our backs with eyes closed. It was time to begin the opening relaxation section of his instruction.

For once, I was able to silence the chatter in my mind. I gave full attention to my body and the effects of each posture. When I struggled to achieve the correct pose, Summer encouraged me in her gentle way to just do the best I could.

'There's no pressure to stretch or push yourself into any

of the poses. Listen to your body. Turn your thoughts inward,' she said.

Swami addressed the class, 'And finally before we close with relaxation we will perform headstand. The king of all poses. This is the most invigorating and energising of postures.'

With clear instructions from Swami, I prepared with very careful placement of my arms and hands supporting and stabilising my head. I slid my weight onto the top of my head now placed on the floor. Swami assisted as I inched my legs up, knees bent at first. I was performing the pose against the wall and straightened my legs with heels touching the cool plaster. Once I'd gained my balance, I felt courageous enough to move my heels away from the wall, Swami standing by to assist if needed. For a few seconds my legs wobbled. It was astonishing. Here I was in headstand. The king of poses.

The class ended with a relaxation session where I fell asleep to the sound of Swami's treacle tones and woke myself up with my own snoring.

We said 'Namaste,' to Swami and, in a post-yoga buzz, floated out of the room.

* * *

STEPPING foot into the gardens where Summer would teach me to meditate was like entering a different sphere. Away from the bustling streets the green, lush flower-covered space was a spiritual haven. Workers pottered around maintaining the pure, clean sanctuary; they polished the statues of deities; dead-headed flowers; cut the grass or swept the paths. Yogis, yoginis and holy men and women strolled around the walkways. Visitors stopped to admire the architecture and beauty on display.

We found a quiet corner and settled opposite each other, cross-legged on the grass.

I followed Summer's instruction and wriggled myself into a comfortable position. Then rested the backs of my hands on my knees, tips of thumbs and forefingers touching and closed my eyes. Blackness. The sun beat down on my face and arms and my sense of smell amplified in response to the deprivation of sight. I noticed the aroma of fragrant jasmine, my favourite essential oil and somewhere in the distance the Ganges roared, tumbling ever onwards. The sensation of my fingers pressing against my thumbs intensified along with the heavy touch of my bottom and legs in contact with the grass. My mouth watered copiously and I swallowed a few times, pushing my tongue up against the roof of my mouth to stem the flow.

I was comfortable and concentrated on my breath as Summer had advised. Visualising the flow in through my nostrils, down my windpipe, inflating my lungs, flattening my diaphragm and then its return journey up and out through my nostrils again. I watched inside my body as my organs responded to the life-giving breath and tried to clear my mind.

What was that? Urgh, something was crawling on my arm. I jerked my body, disturbing my peace. Whatever it was flew off, and I settled myself again. Oh God, what was that creeping on my scalp? My hand flew up to my head, fingers ruffling my hair. I forced my body to stillness and calmed myself once more. Something tickled my leg inside my trousers. I ignored it. I listened to my breath entering and leaving my nostrils, trying to clear my mind. An image surfaced of millions of people dancing with joy in the Ganges. Then a vision arose of a wizened old shepherd. Confusion contorted his face as he twirled a bright pink plastic contraption around and around in his hand, wondering what the hell it was.

I erupted into uncontrollable giggling and gave up.

'That's normal, Jen, your mind will bring up all kinds of strange thoughts and forgotten memories from the past. Just practice for ten minutes every day and you'll soon notice the benefits.'

I wasn't so sure.

* * *

Our group meal that night was a quiet affair. Even the curry sauce was subdued.

'How's your chicken korma, Jen?' asked Betty.

'It's delicious and mild. Would you like to try some?' I stretched my plate over the table for her to pick up a square of meat on her fork. She popped the tasty morsel dripping in pale straw coloured sauce into her mouth. 'Would you like some, Derek?' I asked, proffering my plate.

He smiled and shook his head.

'Well, thanks for meeting on time tonight, guys. It's really appreciated.'

'We're really sorry for being so inconsiderate, Jen. We just need to get a bit more organised Derek and I, instead of running late all the time. Don't we, darling?'

Derek nodded in agreement and his pleasant smile indicated there were no hard feelings.

Fraser tried a third time to dissuade me from my white water rafting trip planned for the following morning. 'It's a dangerous sport, hen. People have died on the rapids here.' He waved his hands, emphasising his words. 'Ye'll have no-one te look after ye.' Concern lined his face. 'Ye'll be on yer own oot there.'

But it was to no avail. 'I'm sorry, Fraser. Thanks for caring so much but I'm as stubborn as a mule. Once I've decided to do something, I do it.'

He couldn't begin to know why I needed to do this.

In exasperation, he stormed out of the restaurant door.

* * *

Back in my hotel room later, I decided I needed an early night. My taxi was picking me up at seven in the morning to take me to the meeting point at Brahmpuri for eight.

There was a knock at the door. Alexandra strolled in uninvited and plonked herself beside me on the bed.

With an inward sigh I prepared us some English tea, it was clear she wanted to talk. Alexandra relived childhood tales of ballet and violin lessons, evenings at the Covent Garden opera, her pony she'd named Galileo and school-days of innocence and fun. She went on to university where she'd gained a master's degree in English. Her father had been a hot-shot lawyer in London and her mother, a society lady. When it was my turn, I steered the conversation away from my childhood. My mam and dad had loved me and that alone had been my salvation, but the rest I kept locked away in a box. It had never been allowed to disturb the comfort I'd found in Martin.

She needed to talk, so I put aside my plans for an early night. As she spoke about her painful divorce and losing her best friend Tamara, I could sense a knot of pain within her begin to unravel itself. I warmed to her. She was vulnerable like me. I realised we weren't so different after all. Just two lost people trying to find their way.

'How does Martin feel about you having an adventure without him?' Alexandra asked.

'Oh he's fine about it,' I trilled. 'Can't believe I signed up for white water rafting!'

'You're jolly well braver than me, Jen. Why on earth do you want to do it?'

'Well I came to India for an adventure and rafting fits the bill,' I said.

'Where does your courage come from, Jen?'

'I wouldn't call it courage, Alexandra. I'd call it stupidity.'

We giggled like schoolgirls.

* * *

Afterwards I had time to check my blog and upload a few shots of Rishikesh along with a brief description of the scenery.

Ping.

One hundred and twenty-six followers.

Hi love, where are you now? The photos of the Kumbh Mela are great. Why is that guy torturing himself with a sword? Can't believe how many people were there. Thanks for the helpful information and statistics about the festival. I hope you didn't go in the water. You must look after yourself and not take any chances with your health and safety when you're there. There was a Street Spice Food Festival in Newcastle last week and about two hundred people got Salmonella. Just goes to show...you don't have to travel thousands of miles to get Delhi Belly. Love and miss you. Martin xx

Typical Martin, I grumbled. Still trying to control me from five thousand bloody miles away.

I hovered my mouse pointer over the link to my private messages. The fingers of my left hand drummed on the wooden table as I chewed the inside of my cheek. Thank goodness. Only one message, and that was from Priti.

> *Hey Jen, they advertised the cruise ship photographer job on Metro Radio this morning. That job was made for you but there's bound to be loads of people interested in it. I hope you're taking plenty of photos to include in your interview portfolio. By the way, you're in photographer's paradise. When are you going to upload images of the quality I know you're capable of, instead of snapshots? It's too quiet here at work without you. Miss you my friend xx*

I smiled at Priti's lack of diplomacy. She'd never been one for mincing her words and anyway, what she said was true.

A new message popped into the Inbox. Username "Marra". No. Don't open it. Click.

> *I saw him last night. He looked happy in the arms of that other woman. You're losing him.*

A sickening tingle pulsated across the bridge of my nose. There was only one person I could think of who would want to hurt me like this.

15

And so I gave in to the temptation to remember that fateful evening at the King's Head.

The resident band belted out the number they always performed at the same point in the set every Saturday night. It was party time again, only I didn't feel much like partying. Our regular alcohol-fuelled Saturday evenings were losing their shine and a peculiar sense of outer-body detachment clouded my vision. I was one of the Greek Gods from the film *Jason and the Argonauts* looking down from Mount Olympus, watching the earthlings going about their lives.

An inky blue crushed-velvet curtain encrusted with tiny diamond lights provided the backdrop to the small stage. At those times when an alcoholic haze clouded my reality, of which there were many, I could swear I was sat outdoors below the night sky. The ageing star of the show was crooning another Elvis tune, unaware that the ultra-violet lighting revealed suspicious yellow stains around the fly area of his white cat-suit. The two female backing singers flanking him were doo-wapping and shoop-shooping along. At the back, five musicians were playing trumpet, saxophone, guitar, keyboard and trombone with the skill that grows with performing the same songs week after week. The sounds were floating through the ether towards me, and the lyrics registering in my mind as an echo.

Myself, Martin and our friends of five years Pat and Brian were sat together on one of the circular tables arranged around the small dance floor. Two middle-aged couples with the shared goal of having as wild a night as possible.

The lights were dim and the smell of perfume, alcohol and sodden beer mats permeated the air. In front of me was my intoxicant of choice, a large brandy. I picked up the warm, smooth balloon glass and took a swig, allowing the familiar heat to linger on my tongue. I paused a moment to enjoy the rich golden-brown alcoholic aroma for a second before swallowing. The pleasing flame spread upwards and outwards from my abdomen. Pat was shouting above the noise. 'Here she is, Dancing Doreen.'

The bar we frequented in the shadows of the Tyne Bridge was a magnet for many of the extrovert characters in Newcastle. Dancing Doreen was one of the regular unofficial entertainers at the venue. She slunk onto the dance floor in a shiny red ball gown, gold dancing shoes and fishnet stockings. As she gyrated and performed her raunchy routine, she twirled a white feather boa in the air. As the band launched into 'Sex Bomb', Doreen threw herself into her few minutes of fame.

Every week at that part of the evening, I always looked for the out-of-towners in the room. It was fun to watch the expression on their faces when Doreen performed a particular move. At the mid-point of the song it was time. She spun to face the audience on the right-hand side. With an amazing level of fitness for a woman in her late sixties, she lifted the hem of her ball gown and kicked her height. The look on the unsuspecting faces was always the same, complete shock, followed by raucous laughter. Next she performed the move to her left-hand side and again, there was shock followed by laughter. She turned to face the centre of the room to execute her final move, right in front of our table. She flicked her fishnet stockinged leg to the height of her head and it was confirmed that yes once again, she wasn't wearing any knickers. From somewhere behind me a drunken out-of-towner shouted, 'bleeding hell that looked like a cat with its throat cut.'

Everyone on our table was guffawing. But I wasn't smiling. For me, the joke had worn thin.

'What's up with you tonight, you miserable sod?' said Pat.

'There's nothing wrong. It's been a long week at work, that's all.'

'Howay, get up.' Pat raised her voice above the opening bars of 'our' Shania song, swaying her hips to the beat as she stood up. The sparkles from the glitter ball rotating above the dance floor flickered like icicles on her face. I remained rooted to my chair, looked up at her and shook my head.

'Sorry Pat, I'm not in the mood for dancing tonight.'

As her sashaying dwindled, her face shifted to a glower. She was tall, slim and flame haired, with a temper to match. I'd witnessed that look many times over the last five years, but never directed at me. She looked vexed.

'What the hell is up with you, Jen? You're acting like you don't want to be here, you miserable cow. Think you're better than us, do you?'

Her sarcastic tone rang warning bells. Unscramble your thoughts, Jen. You need to diffuse this situation, and bloody quick.

'You know me better than that. The only thing that's wrong is I'm not so well tonight.'

She raised an eyebrow in disbelief. 'Come on, outside,' she gestured to the door. 'I want to talk to you.'

Once we got outside, she came straight to the point.

'Right, come on out with it Jen. I've known you long enough to figure out you're not being honest. What the hell's up? Is it Martin? Is everything okay between you two?'

A spark of annoyance rose within me at her line of questioning. 'For God's sake, Martin and I are just fine. There's nothing wrong with our relationship. Mind your own bloody business will you?' The space between us crackled as I snapped at her. I pressed my fingers against my temples, trying to push away the burgeoning headache.

'Why are you treating me like this?' She waved her arms, palms up. 'Why are you shutting me out? I thought our friendship meant more. I tell you everything.'

It broke my heart, but the last thing I could do was open up. So I went on the defensive.

'No Pat, why are you treating me like this? Questioning my relationship with my husband; accusing me of believing I'm a cut above everyone else. You're so damn judgemental.' My body shook and my voice quivered.

This was the first argument we'd ever had and our voices and tempers rose in equal measure.

It was dark outside in the street, but I detected a cold, hard, flinty look in her eyes. Two passers-by quickened their pace and kept their heads down as they hurried by. Shania had finished and the thump, thump, thump of the next track was reverberating out from the window under which we stood. The pulsating of the bass seemed to ratchet up the tension between us. I wasn't sure if the jumping sensation inside my chest was my heart beating harder, or the music seeping into my body.

She jabbed her finger towards me. 'D'ya know what, I've had enough of this shit. I know exactly how much you value our friendship now Jen, and ye can take yer emotional baggage and gan te hell.'

With false bravado, I fired back, 'Aye, wey ye can gan te hell as well, Pat.'

Alone on the street, I cupped my nose and mouth with my hands in astonishment. My stomach was heavy. My ribs too tight. In that instant we had torn our friendship in two, and a tremendous sense of loss washed over me.

16

The following morning, I stood on a small sandy cove on the edge of the mighty Ganges. I was surrounded on each side by the majestic Himalaya and wondered what the hell I was doing. I glanced around at my fellow rafters. There was to be seven of us paddling, plus a guide to sit at the back and help manoeuvre the raft through the rapids. The group comprised six young, vibrant, strong, fit, healthy Indian men and women. And me.

Bet they don't offer this activity on those holidays designed for the over-fifties, I thought. A little voice whispered to me that there was no shame in backing out. I was struggling to find the words to answer it when a taxi pulled up and screeched to a halt in a hail of gravel and sand. The door was wrenched open, and the passenger jumped out through the pall of dust.

'Did ye really think I was going to let ye do this with no one to look after ye, hen?' said Fraser, passing his receipt to the rafting guide.

'So that's where you went to in such a hurry last night?'

He nodded and I threw myself at him. He gave me a bear hug, lifting me off my feet.

* * *

'I AM YOUR GUIDE. My name is Maalik. In Hindi Maalik is meaning "Boss". I will be the boss on the raft. You must listen carefully for my instructions and follow them to the letter to avoid flipping the vessel. It is imperative that you work as a team.'

While Maalik continued to talk of the dangers which had in the past resulted in more than a few deaths, I glanced at Fraser. He made a motion with his hands that signified his desire to wring my neck as he flashed me a huge grin.

'The rapids are formed where the river bed has a steep slope, this causes such turbulence it aerates the water and causes an unstable current.'

Steep slope, turbulence, unstable. I didn't like the sound of that. My thoughts resembled rapids. My heartbeat quickened. My blood pulsed as Maalik continued.

'This is when whitewater occurs and it becomes more apparent when the flowing water splashes over and around rocks.' Everyone paid close attention as he continued. 'The stretch of the river you will negotiate is from here at Brahmpuri finishing at the Laxman Jhula Bridge in Rishikesh.'

I glanced at the shimmering turquoise water. Diamond sparkles glinted off the surface from the morning sun. It was a beautiful day in the foothills of the Himalaya. The chattering from the small tawny coloured birds wheeling in circles in the cloudless sky reminded me of spring mornings back home. Behind me something scampered around on the rocks. A quick glance confirmed it was a lizard darting for cover. The Ganges gurgled playfully.

I relaxed as Maalik continued in his broken English, 'The four rapids you'll encounter are graded from one, the easiest to navigate to level two plus, which can be exhilarating and challenging. Their names are: Initiation; Double Trouble; Hilton and Terminator.'

Terminator? Did he say Terminator?

Whoosh. My pulse went through the roof.

I was wondering if there was still time to back out as we were each kitted out with a scarlet safety helmet, life jacket and paddle. I'd bought a plastic waterproof case for my camera in town. I tightened the strap, so it was snug and secure to the left-hand side of my body. I didn't want it flapping around when I was paddling.

It was time to board the raft, but first Fraser gathered everyone into a circle. With arms around each other's shoulders and in unison we jumped up and down, whooping in a rhythmic, guttural, deep intonation from the abdomen like neanderthal cavemen.

The team was pumped. I was pumped. Full of bravado. I was the oldest, but I refused to be a weak link. It was time to smash those rapids.

'Are you ready?' Maalik shouted and punched the air with his fist.

'Yes boss,' we screamed back at him.

I clambered into the raft and seated myself on the right-hand side tube behind Fraser. 'Och, no hen, you're sitting in front of me. I'm here te keep an eye on ye remember.' He pulled me forwards and into the front space. I wriggled my bottom into a comfortable position on the bouncy rubber tube. Acceptance over whatever was to happen over the next few hours flooded into me. It was empowering.

I sat on the side of the raft with my left foot tucked into the foot hold. With the paddle in my hands, I watched my partner at the front on the opposite side. The young Indian woman and I dipped our paddles into the water at the same moment and everyone behind us followed suit. Our paddling was in sync and we glided into the centre of the gentle flowing river, facing downstream.

'Well done, now watch each other's movements, work together, keep that precise paddling synchronicity and paddle forward,' shouted Maalik.

The air smelled of warm rubber and fresh tree bark. Welcome splashes of water cooled my face where the sun was beginning to make its mark. I had time to shoot a couple of frames of the breathtaking scenery around us. Just as we were enjoying a leisurely paddle, taking in the enchanting views, Maalik shouted, 'There it is. Your first rapid. *Initiation*.'

17

I looked to where Maalik was pointing and my heart skipped a beat. The roar of the violent waves hadn't registered, but now I could see the frothing, turbulent water getting closer and closer each time I dipped my paddle in. The sound became deafening. A milky whiteness swirled around rocks that broke the surface on all sides, but a clear way through was visible.

'Paddle hard and fast straight forward,' Maalik shouted above the din. It was overwhelmingly counter-intuitive to propel myself towards the wall of crashing water. With every ounce of courage I possessed, I forced myself to paddle with all the strength I could muster.

The raft crashed into the tumultuous rapid and reared up at a terrifying angle before smashing down with a deafening thud. Hard, freezing walls of water pounded into my body, lashing every bit of bare skin I had. The shock of the cold water took my breath away, and I opened my mouth wide to take in large gasps of air. A slap of water hit my face, found my gaping mouth and stole away my breath again.

We were in the middle of the vortex. 'Paddle, paddle, paddle, paddle,' Maalik screamed. The raft leapt from side to side and bounced up and down. The water raged. Everyone smashed their oars into the foaming waves trying to stay in sync with the rest of the team. The waves reared even higher trying to engulf us. There was no way out. 'Paddle, paddle, paddle, paddle.' The roar was piercing my ears and I could hardly hear the screaming guide. The raft was out of control. In the next instant we powered our way through the final waves and into smooth water. We were out of the rapid, and out of breath.

My arms ached, a fire burned inside my body and I'd never felt so alive. I was swallowed up in euphoria. I turned to look at Fraser who was laughing uncontrollably, glistening water droplets running down his face.

Through his laughter he shouted, 'Yer eyes are sparkling, hen.'

Fraser was right. I was ultra-awake and rejuvenated. Every part of me down to my fingertips tingled with adrenaline.

Someone shouted 'aaawesome,' and at that everyone erupted into wild cheering while jabbing our paddles up to the sky in triumph.

* * *

We floated downstream in a smooth run of river, glad of the chance to recharge our batteries and marvel at the sight of mother nature in her pristine beauty. I took the opportunity to snap a few more shots for my blog. My left hand was sore where I'd gripped onto the T handle of the paddle and I thanked my stars for the yoga training where I'd learned to engage my core. This helped me to place as much of my body power as possible into the act of digging my paddle into the untameable waves.

The young lady on my left told me her name was Meera. When Maalik shouted that our second rapid, 'Double Trouble', was in view I said, 'Howay Meera, get ready for another rendevouz with the rapids.'

'Paddle forward,' came the command, and we all sprang into action.

We picked up speed, entered the rapid, and headed straight towards a rock the size of a smart car. Vicious white water swirled around the obstacle. In an attempt to avoid a collision, the guide yelled, 'Stop.' But it was too late. 'Hold tight,' yelled Maalik. And I did. I held on for dear life. The raft hit the rock side-on with a thunderous boom. Our bodies jolted with the violent impact but we all managed to stay inside the vessel. The gushing water engulfed the raft and flowed around it with such force that it pinned the raft against the rock. The raft was wrapped. We were stuck.

'How can we get free?' screamed Meera.

Maalik clambered between us to the side of the raft. 'Stay where you are everyone and get ready to paddle when I command.'

He jumped up and down while Fraser used his oar to apply leverage between the raft and the rock. The frothing water leapt into the air and rained upon our heads. Merciless, hard and icy. The guide jumped high and hard. The raft bounced. Fraser saw his chance, rammed his oar against the rock and we were free. The vessel swirled round twice in the aerated, boiling water and when the nose faced downstream we paddled for all our worth.

* * *

It wasn't long before Maalik shouted, 'Up ahead, look, it's Hilton.'

The whitewater raged at the point where the river bent round to the left. The raft was moving forwards at a rapid speed. Someone on the left-hand side of the boat stopped paddling when we bumped against a hidden rock. We lost our co-ordination, and the raft spun round into a sideways position. Seated on the upstream side of the raft I noticed the water pressure building. I sensed myself rising as my side of the vessel lifted. Up and up.

'Oh God, we're going to flip,' I shouted. My voice had an edge of hysteria.

The world stopped turning. Everything around me faded away. I looked skyward. The glaring sunlight blinded me. I squinted and between its rays I could just discern birds swooping in a graceful, gliding dance in an empty azure sky. From a distance I could hear the muted sound of a raging river. Echoes of someone shouting in another universe. The far-away voice drifted closer now. It had an urgent quality.

'High Side Right. Now. *Now.*' Maalik's deafening words pierced my eardrums and penetrated my consciousness. The noise of ferocious battering, as unforgiving water hammered against rubber, boomed around my head. The big bass drumming of my heart pounded against my chest wall. My body rose higher on the side of the raft. Instinct kicked in and I leaned backwards.

Everyone on the left-hand side of the boat reacted to Maalik's command. He'd taught us in the pre-rafting training to re-distribute the weight in this situation to prevent the raft from flipping over.

The manoeuvre worked. The raft levelled out and swung around to face downstream.

With everyone back at their stations we followed the commands. 'Paddle backwards. Now paddle forwards. Dig in. Paddle, paddle, paddle.'

We forced our way out of 'Hilton' rapid.

Too exhausted to speak, we floated down the next stretch of smooth water en route to 'Terminator'. The final rapid before our end point at the Laxman Jhula Bridge. My body ached, I had a blister on my left hand and I was drenched to the skin.

But there was to be no rest.

I could see as we neared 'Terminator' that the rapid was dotted with rocks.

On the count of three, we co-ordinated our arm movements and our paddles dipped into the agitated water at the same moment. Our team behind us followed our lead in complete synchronicity and the raft powered forward towards frothing, milky white water crashing over rocks.

In an instant our raft was being thrown around inside a maelstrom. The thunderous commotion pierced my ears, and I didn't hear the words until it was a second too late.

'Bump. Lean in. *Lean in*!'

Everyone followed the procedure we'd been taught on the beach. They leaned towards the inside of the raft and placed the T-handles of their oars on the floor. With their hands still gripping the paddle handle, the blade end of their oars stuck up into the air. But it was too late for me to follow suit. The raft rammed into the jutting rock with a deafening thud followed by a screech of rubber against stone. Hard, freezing water cascaded over the vessel and crashed over everyone.

Like a pea on a drum I bounced twice and felt the bottom half of my body somersault, fly into the air and flip over the side. My legs hit the icy water. In desperation I hung onto the side of the raft, half in and half out of the churning river. The raft heaved and rolled. I could hold on no longer. The vessel lurched, I lost my grip and was hurled like a rag doll into the raging rapid.

18

The shock of the impact when I hit the glacial water knocked the breath out of me. My heart was racing, an iron grip closed around my chest. I bobbed around in the boiling river like a cork. Through a wall of water performing a wild dance in front of my eyes, I could make out the orange outline of the raft. Its nose reared up in front of me, hovered for a second then began to fall. The icy fist of realisation punched me in the face. With every ounce of strength I could summon, through my wide open mouth, I gasped one momentous breath of air before the raft came crashing down on my head. Instantly I was submerged beneath the raft. It swirled around in circles, an ominous dark orange shadow above my head. The momentum created a whirlpool beneath, pinning me inside its rotating walls. The current held me in a vice-like grip as my body whipped round and round resembling clothing in a washing machine. Water filled my nostrils. My cheeks puffed, swollen with life-sustaining air.

I can't get out of here, the force of the current's got me trapped. God, please help me. Panic's rising. Fight it. You'll die if you don't. Come on. Move your arms and legs. Try to swim through this wall of water. Oh God, I'm not strong enough. My arms won't move. My legs are like blocks of wood. My clothes are too heavy. It's freezing. My legs are going numb. Cramp. It's agony. My chest's on fire. I need to breathe. The raft's bouncing about on top of me, keeping me under. Get ready. Take another breath when it lifts and you can get your face above the water for a second. Now. Now. Good, you did it. Jesus, I still can't swim out from under the raft. Please don't let me die. I don't want to die like this. Why didn't I listen? My bones are like lumps of ice. I'm sleepy. My eyelids are so heavy. Maybe you should just go to sleep, Jen. No, don't close your eyes. What's that tightening around my neck? It's crushing my windpipe. Cutting off my air. It's the camera strap. Quick, get it off. Good, now let go of the strap. You've got to let the camera go, Jen. Can't you see? You've been hiding behind that camera since the diagnosis. Using it as a shield to stop you facing up to reality. You've got to stop looking at life through a lens. Stop living in a dream. Face up to reality. Drop the fucking camera. NOW.

* * *

THERE, it's gone.

19

I felt my body jerk forward and rise upward. Fraser was underwater next to me gripping onto my lifebelt. Pulling me out from under the raft. Our faces broke the surface. We gulped huge breaths of air through wide-open mouths as the angry water raged around us. The veins on the sides of his forehead bulged as he put every ounce of his strength into pushing me up towards the grasping hands on board. I landed on the bottom of the raft with a squelching thump. Gasping for breath and fighting the urge to panic. A second later, Fraser joined me.

We couldn't rest. We had to escape the rapid. I grabbed my paddle from the floor and regained my sitting position along with the others.

Maalik shouted, 'Paddle forward hard and fast. Paddle, paddle, paddle.'

We propelled the raft forward and in the next moment we barrelled our way through 'Terminator'. Our final rapid. When the vessel had settled in smooth running water, I turned to Fraser and hugged him close.

'You saved my life, Fraser. I'll be forever grateful. Thank you.' Tears of gratitude rolled down my cheeks.

'Och, it was nothing, hen. The others would kill me if I didn't get ye back to the hotel in one piece.' He looked around my body. 'Where's yer camera?'

'I had to let it go. It was strangling me.'

'Aye. I'd noticed,' he said, just as the Laxman Jhula bridge came into view.

Spontaneously we broke into our caveman chanting again, jabbing our oars skyward in victory.

* * *

I WOKE before daybreak the following morning naked and shivering on top of the covers. Apart from an angry purple bruise spreading from hip to knee on the outside of my right leg, I'd escaped unhurt. My hand opened and the dark shadow of my camera body and lens dropped into a watery chasm. The canvas strap fluttered away from my open fingers like a flag in the wind as I pictured it falling away from my grip in slow motion. A long sigh of dejection escaped my lips at the thought of my two-thousand-pound camera lying somewhere at the bottom of the Ganges.

There was a knock and Alexandra poked her head round the door.

'Oh golly Jen, Fraser told us about your lucky escape.' She hugged me so tight she hurt my sore ribs.

'Did he tell you he saved my life?'

'Oh, he jolly well played it down, but we guessed he'd averted a tragedy. Oh bugger Jen that's a wicked looking bruise. How are you now?'

'Just a bit shaken, but I don't regret one moment of it, Alexandra.' I was sure my eyes must have been shining as we hugged. I chivvied her away in time to join the group's shopping expedition whilst I rested body and soul.

After she'd gone, I logged onto A Geordie Up The Ganges.

Ping.

One hundred and sixty-two followers.

Hahaha, I love the photo of the cow inside the jewellers shop. Was she shopping for a new necklace?

She was going to buy the gold necklace but decided she liked the udder one better.

Those monkeys on the bridge look deranged. I've heard you sing, Jen. Give them a few verses. That will frighten them off. P.S. Hope you're having a great time and haven't picked up Delhi Belly, fallen down one of those squat toilets or had your nose pierced. Love Priti xx

Hi Love, how did you enjoy the rafting? Photos please. It can't be long now until you attend the Rishikesh fire ceremony. I can't wait to see those images. I know you'll get cracking shots. Love Martin xx

Hi, I'm Madeleine from Paris. Love your blog, it's bringing so many memories back for me. I attended the fire ceremony there last year. You're in for a treat. Yes, Martin is correct and you'll treasure the photos you took there for years to come. Thank you for taking us along with you on your wonderful journey. I'm with you to the end.

It was too much, I was unable to stem the hot tears. I was numb and couldn't prevent another dejected sigh from escaping my lips. Right, you've got to pull yourself together now. Make the best of the situation and drink in every moment. Think yourself lucky it was only your camera you lost and not your life. The private message header from "Marra" leapt out at me. Anger burned. I clicked.

> *What? Are you still in India? If another woman was moving in on my husband like that, I'd be on the next flight home. Love always, Marra.*

'Bitch,' I screamed inwardly at the words. 'I know it's you, Pat.'

I had always been aware of Pat's nasty streak, but wouldn't give her the satisfaction of a reply. The words melted as I hit the delete key and leapt to my feet. I needed to get out of my room for a while.

* * *

IT WAS JUST after lunch and the ghats below the Ram Jhula bridge were quiet. I rested on the top step watching a child of around ten years old making the miniature leaf boats I'd seen bobbing on the dancing waters of the Ganges. She teased and moulded the yielding leaves into a mini vessel with dexterous fingers. The girl placed a marigold flower head in each boat before dropping a tiny candle at its centre. She worked fast and soon her sales basket was overflowing. I envisioned the images I could have captured and my stomach clenched. I hadn't produced one quality image for the portfolio I needed to apply for the cruise ship role, and I had no chance now. My dream of working as a professional photographer had turned to dust.

My head hung heavy as I stared at the ground. I felt a

tiny hand slip into mine where it rested on my knee. 'Hello Lady, why are you so sad?' I looked into liquid black eyes shining with a wisdom beyond their years. 'You could buy one of my boats, sail it on Ma Ganga and ask the Divine Mother to bring happiness to your life.'

She told me her name was Prafula. 'It means "in bloom",' she said with a hint of pride.

'It suits you. Shouldn't you be in school, Prafula?'

'I go to school on mornings and on afternoons I work to help my family. When I grow up, I want to be a doctor.'

'Well, I wish you the best of luck. How much are your boats?'

'Ten rupees.'

'Here's fifty, but you must help me launch it on the river.'

We hopped down the steps to the water's edge hand in hand.

She chanted a mystical verse while we launched my boat together. 'What did you say?' I asked.

'A powerful mantra to get rid of enemies and people who are jealous of you.'

20

I decided against blogging the tale of my near drowning. The last thing I needed was Martin getting on the next flight to India to drag me home. For the rest of the afternoon I slowly packed my bags. We were to take the sleeper train to Allahabad the following day where we'd begin three days of sailing and camping on our route along the Ganges, destination Varanasi. The city reputed to be over five thousand years old. But first we were to witness the sunset Ganga Evening Aarti Ceremony. Vijay had described the ritual as a divine light ceremony when thanks are given to Mother Ganga. I didn't want my 'incident' holding up the group – especially since my words with Derek!

Someone was knocking on my bedroom door. 'Hello madam.' It was the Hotel Porter. 'Parcel for you.'

Mystified, I turned the package over in my hands. It was neatly wrapped in lustrous candy pink paper with a crimson bow on top. I lifted it to my ear and shook. Teased the tape from one side to reveal a plain white box. I pulled open the flaps on one end, tipped up the box and shook it above my open hand. The contents slid from inside, landing in my palm. 'A camera,' I said out loud. There was a note.

> *It's the photographer who makes a great shot. Not the camera. This is all you need to create your magic. Get back out there and get shooting. Love from your friends.*

Each member of our group, including Vijay, had signed the card.

Why would they do this? There must be an ulterior motive. Shame at my thoughts burned in my chest and the taste of bile stung my throat. Tears sprang to my eyes then spilled over, trickling down my face. Could I ever learn to have faith? To trust? I was determined to put aside deep-rooted cynicism for once and see this act for what it was. A pure loving gesture. I pressed my fingers to my smiling lips as the pent-up tension melted away, leaving a tingling warmth in my limbs.

I switched on the camera. It had a fixed telephoto lens. There was no option to choose aperture, shutter speed or sensitivity. No button for white balance, depth of field preview or exposure compensation. An explosion of infinite space and freedom filled me. *You have permission to stop looking for that unforgettable, perfect image, Jen. Absorb what's going on around you from now on. Slow down, and when your body and mind tingle from experiencing the essence of India then, and only then, take your shots.* My gaze roamed to the view outside my window. A graceful, swooping single bird played on the thermals in the wide open sky. Streaks of pastel pink already tinged the forget-me-not blue. It promised to be a good sunset.

* * *

I BOUNCED up the steps of the minibus, my new camera jiggling around my neck. 'I don't know how to thank you all.' I hugged everyone in turn.

'Just jolly well enjoy India. You always seem so very distracted,' said Alexandra as I dropped into the seat next to her.

We arrived at the Parmarth Niketan, taking spaces amongst the devotees seated at the top of the steps leading down to the water's edge. Facing us, sat cross-legged on a bridge over the river was a magnificent marble fourteen-foot statue of Lord Shiva, a picture of serenity in meditation pose. The Ganges surged behind him. The sky had become darker as the sun slipped towards the horizon and the breeze had dropped, giving way to a clement evening. Joyous temple bells chimed, encouraging all to join together in ceremony irrespective of culture, language, religion or walk of life.

The trainee priests of the ashram, sitting cross-legged, led the devotional chanting and singing of mantras. Each displayed a red painted dot in between their eyes and was dressed in saffron and maroon robes. At the centre of the group one young priest played the harmonium as he sang with eyes closed into a microphone accompanied by drummers. Others played tiny little prayer bells, clashing them together in rhythmic harmony. We sat on carpets laid on the concrete floor to ward off the cold. Amongst the crowds of devotees the warmth from so many bodies in close proximity was soothing. After a while the music became hypnotic, and I found myself swaying back and forth. No matter that I didn't understand the strange words, the rhythmic sounds compelled my body to move in harmony. When there was a mantra I knew from my yoga studies I sang along. My voice boomed in happiness to the Hare

Krishna Mantra, any inhibitions about my dreadful singing voice now forgotten.

With each new song the audience became increasingly joyful, the singing and clapping getting louder and louder. It delighted me to watch the growing elation of the group of Hindu ladies sat in front of me as each new mantra began. They swayed in unison from side to side, holding each other's hands smiling with delight at each other, love shining from their faces. One lady heard me singing behind her. She turned and pulled me forward into the middle of their group. A new chant began. I didn't know the words. It mattered not one jot. The ladies on each side of me put their arms around my shoulders and we swayed in harmony. My body tingled. The lady on my right turned to look at me, her eyes gleaming with laughter. I raised my camera for permission and they all shouted 'Haan' and nodded with enthusiasm. I bubbled with excitement and happiness and took their photographs as I laughed along with them. Pure and simple. Click, click, click. No fussing over the technical aspects. For the first time I was comfortable zooming in on faces. It was natural. I was immersed in my surroundings, understanding and connecting with the moods of everyone around me.

The sun dipped below the horizon and the sky turned pastel shades of candyfloss pink and purple, enlivening the statue of Shiva so he seemed almost real. Music merged with the frothing and crashing sounds from the steady flowing current of the rolling river. The air smelled fresh and earthy, and positive energy vibrations surged amongst the crowd. The palpable sense that there is more to life than what we see before our eyes, something inscrutable, a connection with everyone and everything else, enveloped the gathering. Large oil lamps, four tiers high, were lit by the children and passed out amongst the crowd. Ten flames flickered from the largest bottom plate, the second smaller plate held eight flames, the third six flames and a single flame flared from the smallest top plate.

After each person, holding the large handle with both hands, waved the lamp in a circular motion chanting and praying, they passed it on to the next person. When my turn came, I struggled to hold the lamp horizontal to the floor. A hand grabbed the handle to help me and I turned to see Derek. Together we waved the lamp round and round while the priest who was mingling in the crowd, chanted prayers for us. 'Thank you, Derek,' I smiled. He smiled back and hugged me as we passed the lamp onto Charlie and Summer.

I was itching to make some images which would reflect the emotions lighting up the faces of the revellers, but told myself to be patient. I would just sit and observe. Look for those unguarded moments. After a while, when I'd stopped being wrapped up in thoughts about myself, I allowed my instinct to lead me. Happiness coursed around my body and I was fascinated by the scenes I was witnessing. Time to make some more images. I moved through the emotional crowd capturing the oil lamps, swirling in the dark. Round and round, their handles clutched by people with unfettered joy glowing from their faces.

I stepped gingerly down the steps to the water's edge, the toes of my bare feet curling against the chill of the wet marble. Behind me the swirling flames from the oil lamps danced against the now black sky. Devotees floated the tiny little leaf boats to honour their ancestors and worship the holy river. The current carried them away, and they bobbed, looking like fireflies playing on top of the flowing water. I rolled up my trouser legs and moved down the steps until the freezing cold water flowed just under my knees. The music, chanting and prayers filled the space behind me and as I gazed up into Shiva's white, calm face, peace drifted over me.

'Jen, please come here, the priest he is wanting to bless you.' Vijay beckoned and my relieved feet warmed through as I padded back up the steps.

The temple priest dipped the ring finger of his left hand into a pot of red paste. I moved my fringe aside, and he pressed a red dot in the space between my eyes.

A shiver fizzed up my spine when he said, 'Your journey will provide the answer.'

Before leaving I made a donation to the ashram and a holy man wrapped a red raksha sutra around my left wrist. He chanted as he wound the thread round and round, tying it in place with a tight knot.

'What did the priest say in his mantra, Vijay?' I asked.

He translated for me. 'I am tying on your hand this Raksha, with which the most powerful and generous King Bali himself was bound. Oh Raksha don't go away; don't go away.'

He explained further, 'The power of the mantra is protecting the wearer from all evil influences Jen. It will ward off dangers, diseases and enemies. The sutra is sacred protection thread symbolising long life. It must stay in place until it falls off naturally on its own. It will bring you luck.'

21

It was two hours before we were to leave the hotel. Enough time to choose a bunch of photographs from the Aarti Ceremony and write a few lines describing the experience. As I downloaded the images from my new camera onto my laptop, I knew not to raise my hopes. It would be same old, same old. Even the kind generosity of friends clubbing together to buy a new camera couldn't make me a better photographer.

My mouth fell open with a gasp when I looked at my first image on the laptop screen. I flicked through the next, then the next, feeling giddy. I sensed a tentative smile playing on my lips; it built as surprise sank in when I viewed each image. A flush of adrenaline tingled through my body.

My God, the images were fantastic. Not technically, perhaps, but something had changed. You could see it on the faces of the ladies I had been singing with. They were looking straight into the lens and it was almost as though the photos were showing my own feelings reflected back at me. Last night I'd been happy, relaxed and at peace with myself and it showed in the images.

And then I realised that I had been travelling in a bubble. The earlier images looked distant, and fearful, because the way I had been feeling had been transferred into my photographs. Last night, for the first time I had allowed myself to interact with and care about the people I was photographing. For the first time, I didn't just snap a shot with a wide-angle lens from a distance and run away.

I spent the following half hour agonising over which images to upload. Each one was special in its own way. Real and immersive.

Ping.

One hundred and eighty-five followers.

My reader numbers were increasing steadily. Maybe after this blog post my subscribers would nudge over the two hundred mark.

I was inspired to accompany the photos with a compelling narrative to match, and my fingers flew on the keypad. The words flooded out of me like a body of water breaking down the walls of its dam. I described in rich, colourful detail every emotion I'd experienced at the ceremony, opening my heart in a way I'd never been able to before. When I finished, I was exhausted.

Sunday, March 7th, Rishikesh

... So, wherever you are in the world I hope, whilst reading my words, you felt you were alongside me at the Ganga Evening Aarti last night. Nothing on earth will compel me to remove my raksha sutra myself. It will remain on my wrist until it falls off on its own accord. And now I have some happy news I'd like to share about two members of our group. Summer and Charlie are an item. I'm so happy for them. They're made for each other. India has a way of making people fall in love.

I smiled as I thought of the blossoming relationship between Summer and Charlie and hit the publish button with gusto. There was a message from Priti.

Have you filled in that application form yet? I'm not letting you off the hook. Here's the link. Click on it NOW!

I clicked on the job application link and the online form burst into life on my screen. When are you going to start believing in yourself? You are good enough. Can't you see that now? One hour later, I clicked the submit button and my completed application form disappeared into cyber space.

As if to test my positive mindset, the words flashed announcing a private message had just landed in my Inbox.

Wey howay man, your raksha sutra will not help you when Martin announces he's leaving you for another woman. They were at it again last night. I saw her leaving your house in the early hours.

Nausea engulfed me at the thought of another woman in my bed. With my husband. The sharp pain in the back of my throat instigated a coughing fit, and I struggled to catch my breath.

As I hit the delete button, I thought I could hear someone crying softly. Yes, there it was again. It was coming from outside my window. I peeped through the net curtain. There on the balcony next to mine was Betty with her face in her hands. Her shoulders shook as she strove to quell her tears. She turned and seeing me stepping out onto my own balcony, wiped at her face and sat bolt upright.

'Are you okay, Betty? Is there anything I can do to help?' I asked.

'Uh, oh I'm fine. Just a bit tired is all.' She looked at me and pain ached in her huge expressive light blue eyes.

'Is it Derek? He does seem a bit overbearing with you sometimes.' There, I'd said it.

'Oh, that's just Derek. He's not been feeling too well lately.' She looked at the floor.

I could see she didn't want to talk. 'If you ever need a natter, Betty, just give me a shout. We can have a girly chat and a good moan about our husbands together.'

She smiled.

As I turned to go back inside she said, 'Jen.'

'Yes Betty.'

'Thank you.'

I nodded and went back inside, leaving her alone.

* * *

Grabbing my bags, I rushed out of the door to meet the others for our minibus journey to Haridwar station.

The seat next to a glum looking Fraser was free. He snapped his absent-minded gaze away from outside the bus window, and in an instant his demeanour brightened when I dropped beside him. The vehicle jolted over the uneven roads towards Haridwar and all the while, where our bodies came into contact, I was aware of a tingling heat. I knew little about him and wanted to know more. I decided the direct route was best.

'Do you have a wife and kids at home?'

'Och no hen, no-one would have me. Besides, I'm married to my job. How long have you been married?'

'Thirty years.'

He whistled. 'Long time. Ye must be happy together.'

It was a statement rather than a question and I was relieved it didn't require an answer as my reply stuck in my throat.

'How long have you been a Personal Trainer?'

'I set up my own company in Glasgow ten years ago. I've got two others working for me. We've got thirty clients between us.'

'Eeeh, I'm so unfit, I could do with a Personal Trainer myself.'

'I'll teach ye a few good exercises if ye want.'

'Wey aye, that would be great Fraser, thanks.'

We spent the rest of the short journey in a comfortable silence. When I caught him regarding me he smiled, not hiding his intense, searching gaze. By the time the bus ground to a halt, I noticed our bodies leaning in towards each other.

* * *

We were to board the sleeper train that evening for the four hundred and fifty-three mile, twelve-hour journey to Allahabad. Before leaving we needed to stock up on supplies for our supper after first snacking on the famous Indian street food. We crowded around a stall where an assortment of delicious looking morsels were being prepared and sold. The vendor dropped unsavoury coloured strings of batter, dough balls or patties into bubbling hot oil. They sizzled until becoming a rich golden brown before being ladled out and piled high onto metal plates. My tastebuds danced a wild jig when I sampled the tangy yet spicy potato curry sauce of Aloo Puri for the first time. There was one ingredient with a subtle aftertaste flavouring the whole dish. It reminded me of a sharper, more pungent version of thyme.

'That's carom seeds you're tasting,' said Vijay, reading my mind as I dunked the puri, a crisp, golden soft puffed-up pillow of delicate fried bread into the sauce.

To finish, I couldn't resist a plate piled high with Jalebis, fresh from the pan of bubbling hot oil. The aroma of cardamom and saffron had my mouth watering. My jigging taste buds calmed to a sensuous smooch as the golden iridescent swirls of crisp batter soaked in spiced sugar syrup hit the sweet spot. I chewed slowly, savouring the gelatinous, silken juices sliding over my tongue.

Arrival at the train station followed the same routine with the porters hoisting two bags each on top of their heads, with a further two large bags strung over their shoulders. As usual, people thronged the bustling platform. We stood in a circle around our mountain of luggage, our concentration fixed on Vijay as he read out our bunk numbers for the train. As Vijay gave out the last number he smiled, 'Now, look behind you everyone. While you were all concentrating on me, everyone else has been concentrating on you.'

We turned as one and broke into laughter. Around us in a huge circle, a crowd of ten deep had gathered watching us with great curiosity. The heads tilted on one side and quizzical looks spoke volumes. People at the back jumped up and down, trying to get a better view. Why are you here? Where have you come from?

The crowd dispersed, and I wandered around with my camera strung round my neck and carrying my earlier purchases, six huge oranges and a vegetable wrap, in a white plastic bag. With my photographer's eye, I scoured the scene for potential subjects. Two children dressed in Goddess costumes and makeup performed acrobatics on the railings of the walkway which descended from the bridge over the platforms. I hadn't used my Hindi speaking skills very much. Here was an opportunity to use the one phrase I'd practiced over and over at home. Please may I take your photograph? 'Krypaya main apane sir kaat kar sakate hain?'

They erupted into howling laughter. The elder girl spoke English in her thick Indian accent. 'Lady, you've just asked if you can cut off our heads.'

My faux pas had broken the ice. I'd connected with them, and instinct told me the rapport it generated between us would translate into the final image. As I pressed the shutter we chatted about their village school, their families and their excitement at going to the Kumbh Mela. They forgot about the camera and became relaxed and natural, striking poses, smiling or pulling cheeky faces. This was so different to the way I'd approached photographing people before. I was gaining in confidence and becoming more open with people. Hell, I was even becoming a better photographer.

The children ran off and the loudspeaker burst into life. I guessed that a train must be due to arrive as passengers picked up their bags and moved closer to the edge of the platform. Sure enough, a train came into view and rumbled into the station. Our train wasn't due for another half hour and I rattled off a few shots from my camera. Travellers boarded, then disappeared into the midst of the long row of blue and white carriages.

The train crawled out of the station, thinning out the crowds. On the platform that ran parallel to ours I noticed a large black and white pig snuffling around in the dirt, her brood of five piglets scurried around her. I became absorbed in the photo opportunities on the other side of the track. It was at the edge of the station in front of a row of single-storey buildings which acted as a playground for a group of rhesus macaque monkeys. As I fired off a few frames, I spotted one particular monkey, the biggest one, sat on the opposite platform watching me. It followed me with its eyes as I wandered around taking photos. I paused between shots to smile across at the animal. Our eyes met and he held my gaze. He was so handsome with the sun shining behind him, producing a halo around his fur. The perfect animal portrait.

I took a step forward and looked down to raise my camera. Someone screamed, 'Don't get too close to it,' just as the animal sprang to life.

22

A microsecond later, I saw to my horror the macaque was thundering across the track towards me. The look in its eyes was murderous.

The animal came at me with such speed. *It's going to kill me, bite me, rip my face off!* The only instinctive, desperate reaction I could muster was to turn my back on it. I hunched forward and clasped my camera into my stomach with my right hand. My left arm swung out to my side, out of control with the weight of the bag full of oranges dangling from my wrist. I took a terrified breath, steeled myself and waited for the impact.

At that instant there was a rapid succession of judders vibrating my left arm. I heard the squeaking of plastic followed by the sound of six hefty bumps on the ground. Squinting through half-closed eyelids I caught sight of my oranges rolling around on the floor of the platform. A horde of lightning-fast macaques appeared out of nowhere, snatched the oranges and ran hell for leather. My gaze ran the length of my left arm to the white-knuckled hand which gripped the empty plastic bag. Its bottom now shredded, it flapped in the light breeze like washing on a line. There was a moment of speechless shock amongst everyone on the platform. I held the bag up higher for everyone to see and that prompted hysterical laughter.

As the monkeys sat eating my supper on the opposite platform, Fraser strolled up.

'Och hen, ye'd think it would be frightened of a Geordie wouldn't ye?' Seeing how shaken I was, he gave me a hug.

'Thanks Fraser, but you should be careful you know, you might show everyone what a caring guy you really are.'

'Well I would nae want that now, lassie would I?'

A voice boomed from the tannoy. The next train was the overnight sleeper to Allahabad. With no time to buy more food I had no choice but to climb on board. We found carriage B and busied ourselves preparing our bunks for the long evening ahead. As the train chugged out of the station, I watched from the window as one large monkey tucked into the vegetable wrap which was to be my supper. I glowered at it in resentment. It bared its teeth in my direction. I could swear it was laughing at me.

The journey got underway, and I sat on the top bunk tapping into my laptop, preparing my next blog. I planned to upload it in four days' time when we got to the hotel in Varanasi as there would be no wifi access during the sailing and camping days. Alexandra appeared and swung a carrier bag up onto my bunk.

'We've had a whip round. Couldn't jolly well leave you with no supper. The yoghurt came from Ivan; the grapes from Derek and Betty; Fraser gave up his chapati; this bean and rice concoction's from Summer; the apple's from me and Charlie donated the last of his breadsticks.'

As she drew each item from the bag, tears pricked the inside of my eyelids.

I hadn't made it known I was out of food for the train journey as I didn't want to be beholden to anyone. Alexandra had noticed. Now it struck me as incredibly stupid that I would rather not eat than ask for help. As I looked at the pile of food on my bunk, a strong sense of belonging washed over me. It felt safe. It was good. Really good.

We were the only westerners in our carriage and I spent the time before lights out chatting with the friendly Indian family sharing our section of the sleeping bays. I took the opportunity to try out a little more of the Hindi I'd learned and delighted the children with my strange Indian accent.

The view from the windows changed from cities and large towns to wide open spaces with trees and green paddy fields. It was close to dusk and the raking sun rays cast long deep shadows on small village scenes reminiscent of films I'd watched of medieval England. Children played on the hard, russet brown earthen floor amongst ramshackle buildings, some little more than mud huts. Cows, horses and pigs roamed around the buildings and mothers washed their children in ponds on the outskirts of the villages. The evening flew by, and it was soon time to settle for the night. I closed my curtain and snuggled into my sleeping bag.

Through the tiny gap in the swaying fabric I could see Fraser on the top bunk opposite me. I was caught off guard by a sharp intake of breath which was followed by a flutter in my abdomen.

I whipped the curtain shut with a sharp tug, closing the gap. My body rocked along in synchronisation with the carriage, carrying me off into a deep sleep as the train rumbled on its way to Allahabad.

* * *

TWELVE HOURS LATER, I stepped onto the platform at Allahabad station feeling refreshed. I was becoming an expert at hitting a moving target in the squat toilets, sleeping in my clothes and pretending I hadn't heard unmentionable nocturnal noises. We were to spend the next three days sailing down the Ganges in our country sailing boats towards Varanasi. We ate at the station. It seemed perfectly normal now to feast on spicy food for breakfast. The zinging heat from the coconut chutney accompanying my dosas did more to enliven me than if I'd drunk ten cups of strong coffee.

I sat by Summer on the minibus for the short journey to the riverbank jetty to join our boats and crew. Rural India flashed by. It was early; the sun was rising, illuminating people in a warm pale golden light as they squatted in fields, already going about their work. Rainbow colours punctured the green vegetation as women in glowing saris plucked at plants, dropping them into baskets held under their arms. Women glided through fields of swaying crops, carrying sparkling metal containers on their heads with an ease practised since childhood. We streaked past small shanti towns, busy with life. Stall owners swiped ineffective hand brushes in a constant battle with the ever-present dust. There were vegetable carts with fresh produce displayed; potatoes, red carrots, cabbage, tomatoes and onions. Stalls with an array of street food. Multi-purpose shops offering a diverse range from car supplies to clothing, food and toys all housed within one building. People sitting outside on dusty white plastic chairs smiled and waved when the bus slowed down at a junction or traffic lights.

Like everything else in India, there was a stark contrast between the buildings in the countryside towns and villages. Houses made of wood, with roofs of straw or polythene, stood next to once majestic arched brick buildings in various states of disrepair. The painted Hindi words advertising Airtel faded and ravaged with time. A lucky homeowner may have a roof of slates or corrugated plastic. Those not so fortunate protected themselves from the elements with pieces of sacking sewn together, or hewed branches of trees with leaves still attached. Dotted around in the midst of the crumbling decay stood resplendent, ornate temples. A feast for the eyes amongst the drab, grey surroundings.

Cows, horses, dogs, chickens and goats mingled with mothers as they washed their children in green septic looking ponds. We passed pig herders guiding their animals through green fields and crops of yellow mustard plant. Smoke swirled up towards the sky from fires tended by men who poked at the embers, encouraging the flames to dance higher. In and around the towns the main mode of transport was the bicycle. Some with whole families clinging onto the frame whilst the strongest of them peddled as if their life depended on it. Other bicycles piled high with sacks, baskets or boxes appeared to be powered by themselves, the rider obscured by his towering load. On the main roads garish lorries thundered by decorated in Om signs, emblazoned in Hindi or Roman script advertising soft drinks. Everywhere the constant sound of toot, toot.

* * *

THE TRIBESMEN ACCOMPANYING us on the next leg of our journey greeted us at the jetty and placed fresh marigold garlands round our necks. Two country riverboats bobbed on the water, eighteen feet long and eight feet wide, alongside a utility boat which would carry our luggage, camping gear and cooking facilities. The boats had mattresses, blankets and cushions spread on the deck and a green tarpaulin draped overhead as protection from the sun. Two oarsmen would row and steer each boat. We'd decided over breakfast that Alexandra, Fraser, Ivan and myself would share one boat, with Derek, Betty, Summer and Charlie in the second one. Vijay would sail on the utility boat.

I began side stepping down the riverbank when a commotion erupting behind me stopped me in my tracks. Derek was saying something and jabbing his finger at Charlie, who stood with his arms wide up in the air, shaking his head.

'You've been coming on to my wife. I've been watching you,' said Derek in a menacing tone, taking a step towards Charlie.

Everyone stopped mid-step. There was a stunned silence before everyone erupted into laughter. This must be a joke? But Derek's face turned an angry crimson red.

'Derek,' shrieked Betty. 'You stupid old fool. I'm more than thirty years older than Charlie.' Fraser sprang into action and stepped into the space between the two men.

'And besides,' continued Betty, 'we can all see that Charlie and Summer are always side by side. It's not me Charlie's interested in.'

Summer stepped up to Derek and laid a gentle hand on his arm. In her calm manner, she took the wind out of Derek's sails. 'Betty's right, Derek. Charlie's with me.'

Derek's bravado waned and his arms dropped to his sides.

'Well, I'm jolly glad we've got that little misunderstanding cleared up,' said Alexandra. 'Let's change our arrangements, shall we? Jen and I will sail with Derek and Betty. Summer and Charlie, you can sail with Fraser and Ivan.'

'Yes, I think that's a wonderful idea,' said Summer, linking arms with Fraser and Ivan. The threesome sauntered down the riverbank with Charlie following up the rear.

I opened my mouth to protest, then stopped myself as I caught sight of Betty's face. Her relief was plain to see as she smiled at me. All I could do was nod my acceptance, though inside I seethed at Alexandra's meddling.

Left alone with Alexandra at the top of the bank, the heat flushing through my body combusted. I couldn't contain my fury one more second.

My voice trembled with rage. 'What the hell do you think you're doing?'

'Calm down, Jen. Why are you so jolly angry? I thought it best to keep Derek and Charlie apart for now. We don't want World War Three erupting in a boat in the middle of the Ganges do we?'

'So you just take control without consulting anyone else. Didn't it enter your mind to ask the opinion of other people?'

'Someone had to act quickly, and that's what I did.'

'Yes and sod everyone else's feelings, eh? I'm sick and tired of you manipulating everyone, Alexandra.'

'You're being selfish, Jen. I can't understand why you're so furious.'

'Can't you see how your controlling ways affect other people? The last thing I wanted was to spend three whole days in a tiny boat with Derek and Betty.'

'Jolly well chill out, will you? It's only three days out of the whole of your life.'

'Don't you dare patronise me.'

'This isn't about not wanting to be in a boat with Derek and Betty, is it?'

'What the hell are you getting at?'

'I think you know, Jen.'

I spun on my heel and stormed off down the country lane, not wanting to hear one more word. As I pounded down the road trying to get as far away from Alexandra as possible, the rushing of blood in my ears drowned out my scrambled thoughts. My face tingled as burning indignation propelled me along. Outrage clouded my vision. I turned a corner and stopped dead, not expecting the sight that greeted me. There encircled in the protective branches of a copse of trees was a small temple. Exquisite detailed carvings of gods, goddesses, devotees and depictions of Indian mythology covered every inch of its dove-white marble facade.

I was drawn to the entrance by rhythmic chanting from a lone voice within. The mandir was deserted apart from a saffron-robed priest busy draping a marigold garland around one of the deities. I needed solace and pointed to the dim interior. 'Yes?' I asked.

The priest nodded. 'No inner temple,' he said, and I understood. As a non-Hindu I would only be allowed into the outer rooms. My research had paid off as I knew to slip off my trainers and socks and leave them outside the temple door. As I stepped over the threshold, the priest signalled that I should ring the bell at the entrance. The reverberation, haunted and ethereal, reached down to my bones and made them tingle.

Surrounded by mystical statues, I squirmed into a comfortable kneeling position on the floor cushion. My surroundings melted into the background as the subdued light, cloying incense and spiritual chanting induced a clarity to the thoughts racing in my mind. Yes, Alexandra is bossy and yes it's annoying. But the reason you got so angry isn't because you have to share a boat with Derek and Betty, is it? I had to admit the truth. I was gutted because she'd snatched away my chance to spend three whole days up close and personal with Fraser. Anger flared again, but this time I directed it at myself. *You've behaved like a stupid schoolgirl. You need to apologise to Alexandra and put Fraser out of your mind.* With a clear head, I dropped twenty rupees into the donation box and stepped from the dusky interior into blinding sunlight.

I squeezed my eyes together. It took a few seconds for them to focus. Where were my shoes? I was sure I'd left them at the side of the door. Yes, there was the imprint of the soles in the dusty earth. I rubbed my chin and glanced around looking for answers. It took a few more seconds for dawning realisation to settle. After a wander around the building I had to accept that my footwear had walked. I shrugged my shoulders and tutted. *Oh well, I hope their new owner gets plenty of wear out of them.* I set off on the barefoot walk back along the earthen road to the riverbank.

23

As I limped round the corner, and the jetty came into view, Alexandra sprinted up the bank. 'Someone nicked my shoes,' I said as she hugged me to her. 'Alexandra I'm so sorry. I was out of order.'

'Me too Jen. I know I need to reign in my overbearing tendencies. Let's say no more about it.' She pulled off her trainers as she spoke. 'Here put these on.'

'I can't take your shoes, pet.'

'I accepted your hat. Now you will accept my shoes.'

'Bossy mare,' I said.

* * *

'Balance the boat. Balance the boat,' Anil our oarsman shouted in his thick Indian accent.

Derek, who had stood up for no reason, causing the boat to rock, looked around mystified.

'Come on, Derek. Sit back down now or you'll have us all in the water, love.' Betty grabbed his hand and guided him back into sitting. The boat steadied.

On paper we were the perfect foursome to share this type of boat. One tall and one smaller person sitting on each side, legs extended between each other for balance. We had two oarsmen, Anil and Mukunda, who sat at the prow to share the rowing, and we drifted off for three days of escape from sensory overload. As we floated down the river, the tranquillity settled into my whole being. On the river banks we observed day-to-day life in India. People came down to the water's edge from the villages to bathe, praise the sun, swim and wash clothes, pots and pans. Children ran and jumped headlong into the water and the sound of their laughter was uplifting. Men were all soaped up from head to toe, scrubbing as hard as they could to remove the dust and grime. People seeing our boats waved and shouted in greeting.

One little girl hollered, 'How are you?'

We shouted back, 'Very well, thank you,' and everyone laughed.

Fishermen in coracles flung their nets, allowed them to spread on the surface of the water then sink, before hauling them back onto their boats, writhing with small fish. A herd of buffalo enjoyed their daily bath, their attentive herder splashing them with water, the sun glinting off their brown leather hides. Cloth in vivid hues lay stretched out to dry on the buff-coloured earth; and on the water gold circles of marigold flower necklaces floated undisturbed on the glassy, glinting surface. The vivid sunny orange stood out against the steely blue and as we approached, they bobbed up and down, disturbed by the action of the oars. Every so often I could hear chanting from the many temples along the banks, the mystical sound seeming to float towards me over the airwaves. Most of the time the only sound was from the oars hitting the water and the creaking of timber. The air smelled fresh, the sun illuminated all around, and the warm breeze tickled my face and arms as the boat glided onward.

My body moved in rhythmical motion in tune with the pull of the boat. I had the time and space to reflect and it filled me with a yearning for home.

Vijay's voice interrupted my thoughts as he shouted it was time to raft our two boats together for lunch. Our boat crew had prepared dishes of delicious local food which we passed amongst us between each boat. The whiff of aromatic spices followed each dish on its journey. There were no potatoes left by the time the platter reached me. Derek reached over with his dish and nudged his potatoes onto my plate. After his outburst earlier, it seemed his mood had lifted.

As we sat floating on the river, the boats tied together, perfect harmony pervading everything, there was a sudden splash.

'A Gangetic dolphin. Over there.' Ivan pointed to his right.

'Another one,' I shouted. The long thin snout broke the surface, followed by a glistening, greyish brown stocky body with large flippers, then splashed back into the water.

Eyes peeled, we hoped for just one more sighting of this wonderful endangered species. We were lucky as around us dolphins leapt out of the water now and then. Probably to take a look at the strange foreigners floating along in a state of complete relaxation on their Holy River. 'Here in India the government has abolished the use of dolphins in aquatic theme parks,' said Vijay. As we ate and watched the dolphins, birds swooped down skimming the mirror-like surface of the water and rose to the cloudless, bright blue sky again. The air was full of trilling birdsong. In the distance, as if in a dream, floated the familiar sound of the Hare Krishna Mantra. Repetitive, hypnotic, evocative.

As we continued our journey with the sails unfurled, swollen with the wind, the Hare Krishna Mantra became louder. It was as if we were being pulled down the river by an invisible rope towards the source of the chanting. We reached a temple at the edge of the riverbank where a cremation was taking place. The chanting became more excitable, accompanied by a drum beat as smoke spiralled up into the sky. We sailed on until without warning, the two boats changed direction and headed for the riverbank, grinding to a stop on the sandy, gravelly shoreline. Anil pointed to the deserted, undulating ground in front of us and said in his limited English, 'Toilet'.

We looked at each other, uncomprehending.

'I think this is our toilet break girls,' said Betty.

'But there's nothing here,' replied Alexandra.

'Howay lasses.' I pulled the blanket from under me. 'We need to be innovative.'

Summer joined us on the sandbank from the other boat and we each took turns holding the blanket as a screen to allow privacy. We giggled when Summer, trying to balance on her hunkers, fell backwards coating her butt in sand.

'Well, I'm jolly well not wiping it off for you,' snorted Alexandra.

* * *

WE SPENT the next part of the journey in comfortable silence, each lost in their own thoughts. The hot breeze was enough to power our boats. With the sails full of wind, we made good progress to a small jetty jutting out from the river bank. Above us towered the surrounding walls of an

Indian country village. We climbed the rough-hewn steps carved into the light orange earth, emerging through the trees fringing the village. A crowd of children greeted us with exuberant Hindi chatter. As we walked to the village centre, the crowds following us grew larger and now included adults. Delighted villagers welcomed us into their homes. The adults smiled, greeted us with 'Namaste', and stared, heads tilting to one side in typical Indian fashion, not hiding their curiosity. Children, pulling on our hands, were proud to introduce us to their schoolroom with cheerful, radiant painted walls depicting maths and other lessons in Hindi script.

Little stacks of cow dung patties, built up into neat pyramid shapes, were everywhere. They dried in the sun to be used later for fuel, or for protection on the outside walls of buildings. Cows, bulls, buffalo and goats shared backyards equipped with water pumps and metal machines for grinding corn. Clothes were spread on roofs of straw to dry and lines of washing danced in the breeze; bright hued saris; working clothes; children's uniforms or men's trousers and shirts. The air was natural with no artificial aromas to contaminate it; straw, soil, fresh cut wood and a slight undertone of cow dung.

The noise increased as we headed towards the edge of the village and the small buzzing marketplace. Lines of black, yellow and green three-wheeled tuk tuks sat idle, awaiting customers. Children shouted and laughed as they played cricket on the hard, dry earth, and cows roamed wherever the fancy took them. We sat at a table drinking masala chai and parents brought their children to us to say hello in English and have their photos taken.

Although we were reluctant to leave, it was time to be on our way. As we strolled back to the riverbank a group of children in the schoolyard, one hundred yards away, caught my attention. It was the shouting I'd noticed first. A childish rhyme in a strange language. Repeated over and over. They ranged from around ten to twelve years old, girls and boys, holding hands as they skipped around in a circle. The hairs on the back of my neck stood up. One boy had a bamboo switch in his hand, and he was raining blows on something in the group's midst. I shielded my eyes from the sun, straining for a clear view. My God, there's a child in the middle of all that.

I screamed 'stop it,' and propelled myself forwards. 'Stop that. Stop that now.'

I flung dust into the air as my feet pounded the earth, my arms pumped back and forth and my hair streamed behind me in a wild frenzy. The children glanced up to see me bearing down on them like a screaming banshee. They scattered in all directions, leaving a small girl swamped in a filthy t-shirt cowering on her hunkers on the floor. I flung myself onto my knees and gathered the crying child in my arms, cradling her and swaying from side to side, saying 'Shh, shh, shh' to comfort her. Her crying subsided. I checked her over for any injuries. She seemed unhurt. She looked up at me, her dark molten eyes shining in gratitude. Then she pulled away from me and ran off into the rabbit warren of village streets. Shaken, drained and tearful, I tramped back to where everyone waited.

'My God, Jen. Are you okay?' asked Alexandra.

My assertion that I was had a chilly edge which I hadn't intended, but at least it prevented anyone from questioning me about what they'd just witnessed.

We continued on our way to our evening rendezvouz point. These large empty spaces were a world away from Delhi, Rishikesh, Haridwar and the Kumbh Mela. This was pure relaxation. As the huge orange ball of sun suspended in the sky dropped towards the horizon, we arrived at our campsite. A large, flat, empty expanse of sandbank.

Our boat crew erected the toilet tent first, complete with a deep, neat hole dug into the ground. They assembled our one-man tents next in a semi-circle around the campfire, followed by the larger mess tent. Then they laid blankets on the floor in the middle to serve as a communal seating area. As the sun fell it changed to red, and raking shadows painted the ground, spreading out from the trees on the riverbank. A rich, warm golden glow bathed the surrounding land. The lower the sun dropped, the deeper became the hue of the iridescent pink sky graduating into shades of deep purple. Trees transformed into ghostly silhouettes as the luminous quality of the sky rippled, like flowing silk on the mirror-like surface of the river. I closed my eyes, soaking up the last rays of sun as it slipped out of sight. Soft chanting from a temple away in the distance floated on the airwaves. Mystical, spiritual and melodious.

In our home-from-home, our crew gave us a thin mattress, pillow and blankets. In the dark as I fiddled with a dodgy door zipper on my tent, thousands of moths and flies attacked me. They flew at and around me from all directions attracted by my torchlight. They flew in my face, in my hair. All over me and my tent. They were inside it, too.

Just as I was wondering how I would cope all night with the mass of flying creatures, the onslaught died down. Vijay explained that the insects only have a short life to fly between five thirty and nine o'clock in the evening, then they die.

Now all I had to deal with was the marauding man-eating tigers and king cobras sliding silently across the sand. Destination? My tent.

I suddenly felt nervous as we sat on our communal blanket sipping steaming chai. I'd never slept on my own in a tent, let alone a tent on a sandbank in the middle of nowhere in India.

We gathered in the mess tent for our evening meal cooked on the open fire, prepared for us by our boat crew. The spiced potato and vegetable curry with rice and chapaties left a lingering gentle heat. I reached into my bag for the bottle I'd brought with me from England. At the start of the trip I'd wanted to keep it for myself, but this was the perfect time, and these were the perfect people to share it with.

'Who'd like a shot of the best cognac you can get?' I held the bottle of premium tipple up for all to see.

An hour later, the bottle was empty.

'Would ye all like a wee sing song?' said Fraser. He waved a harmonica in the air and launched into a rendition of Beatles tunes to which we all sang along with gusto. Alexandra asked me to sing a Geordie song. I jumped into the middle of the mess tent and burst into 'The Blaydon Races'. Not caring that I had a singing voice that sounded like a howling dog.

When it was time to say goodnight, we all hugged one another. I knew this was risky. Fraser folded me to his body and gave me a lingering kiss on the cheek. The touch of him. The smell of him. It was getting to me. A little voice whispered, *If you wanted to, you could invite him into your tent tonight...*

24

Of course, I did nothing of the sort, though I did feel a stab of envy as Summer and Charlie headed off to her tent, arms draped around one another. I heeded Summer's reminder about the revealing nature of torchlight inside a tent. Plunged into all-encompassing inkiness, I pulled Martin's Newcastle United shirt over my head and slid into my sleeping bag. Buoyed by cognac-induced Dutch courage I dismissed my creep-crawly phobia with a giggle and was asleep in seconds.

The next day, I woke very early; the sun hadn't yet risen, but I was wide awake. I peeked outside the door of my tent. Not another soul was around and I thought this would be a perfect opportunity to practise meditating. I'd followed Summer's advice and had sat for ten minutes each morning. I'd enjoyed the brief periods of inactivity, although my monkey mind persisted in performing cartwheels in my head. Now here was my chance to meditate on the banks of the Ganges at sunrise.

I undid the zipper, crept through the door into the silent dawn, and found the ideal spot away from the tented semi-circle. The sky was a pale apricot as the sun, not yet in view, made its slow ascension. The tree shadows had receded. A flock of brown birds in a V formation flew overhead to an unknown destination. The setting was perfect. I settled onto my knees, positioned my hands and closed my eyes.

I concentrated on my breath and watched the flow. In and out. In and out. I began to perceive the peace I craved. The heat from the sun seeped into my skin as it peeped over the horizon. So focused was I on my body, I could sense the pores opening in my arms to welcome the warmth. My mind started to empty, the thoughts coming less and less, until there was no chatter in my brain to disturb my stillness. Time had ceased to exist when a vision flashed vivid in front of my eyes.

A group of children standing in a circle were shouting. Their words dripped with venom. 'Dirty Gerty. Dirty Gerty.' Over and over again. In the circle's middle stood a girl of eleven years old. Her hazel eyes didn't reflect their usual sparkling warmth. Today they smouldered with rage as she turned round, glaring at each of her tormentors. One of the older screaming children yanked on a handful of the girl's chestnut brown hair, pulling her head to one side. Her scalp burned. Tears pricked the insides of her eyelids but she refused to cry in front of them.

'Susan says her house bloody stinks,' shouted the biggest boy.

'Wey aye man. She lives in a pigsty,' shouted his friend

'Oink, oink, oink.' Their cruel laughter was peppered with pretend snorting and grunting.

'Dirty pig, dirty pig, dirty pig.' They clapped along as they chanted.

The trapped girl saw a break between the packed bodies and tried to make a run for it. But it was futile. The freckle-faced girl with the bright ginger hair pushed her back so hard, she fell over her feet landing on her backside in the middle of the screaming pack. The girl called Susan, who she thought was her friend, picked up a handful of mud from the side of the riverbank where they stood. She hurled it with devastating aim. 'Pigs love to eat shit. Here's yer dinner.' The ball of foul, reeking sludge splattered into the face of the girl who now struggled to stand. It found its way between her eyelids and into her mouth. She spat out the fetid slime. Her eyes stung.

'Howay everybody. Feed the pig,' shouted the biggest boy.

The only thing the cornered girl could do now was curl into a ball on the floor while clumps of putrid, oozing malodorous filth rained down upon her.

At last the bombardment stopped.

'Divvent come to play on our estate, Jenny Watson. We divvent want dirty pigs like ye near wor houses. Stay in yer pigsty,' shouted the girl with the bright ginger hair as the gang ran off down the banks of the Tyne.

Left on her own and covered in sludge, the girl could hold back her pain no longer. Her body heaved with huge gasping sobs. They'd lied. She wasn't dirty. Her house didn't smell. Her Mam had always kept their cramped rooms, in the poorest part of Newcastle, spotless. The faded clothes she wore had come from the second-hand shop on Scotswood Road. Aye her Mam had mended the rips and tears again and again, but she hand-washed her dresses every week. Yes, it was true her family had nowt. But it wasn't her Dad's fault his accident at the pit had crippled him, forcing him into a wheelchair for the rest of his life. Her Mam had saved money so she could invite her best friend Susan for tea on her eleventh birthday. Why had

Susan told those rich kids about her family's poverty? Now they all despised her. The little girl's sobs increased. She hated Susan. She hated them all.

Hot tears cascaded down my face, I shook my head to bring my senses back to the present day. Nausea engulfed me as misery slashed at my heart like a scythe. Those memories of rejection and suffering, meted on the riverbank so long ago, came flooding back and I remembered every single agonising second in heart-rending clarity.

I was shocked and shaken and pressed a fist to my mouth looking around, trying to quell the trembling inside. The sun had risen over the horizon now, and a new day had begun as the Ganges came to life. The sound of birdsong and splashing water reached my ears. It was warm and promised to be a beautiful hot day. I heard my name and looked up to see Alexandra halfway between the tents and where I sat. She was holding up a mug, beckoning to me.

'Come on Jen, I've made you a jolly wonderful cup of chai.'

I wiped the tears away. How would it feel to tell Alexandra about my past? The high-school years marked as an outcast, the poor kid nobody wanted as a friend. The taunting, the shame, the ridicule. I saw now how that painful rejection had become deeply ingrained in my attitudes to others. No wonder I found it hard to trust; and yet I knew I had to move forwards, to let the past go just as I had my expensive camera kit.

As I walked back to the tents, I made a promise. I'd begin to trust myself and others a little more. In the right circumstances, of course.

A new day had begun indeed.

I joined everyone sitting on the blankets enjoying breakfast alfresco.

* * *

'WHERE DID you learn to play the harmonica, Fraser?' I asked, in between mouthfuls of toast washed down with hot chai. 'Your repertoire is very impressive.'

'Och, I picked up a few ditties in the army, hen. I was the unofficial music man of the Royal Scots Dragoon Guards. None 'o the other squaddies could rattle off a Lennon and McCartney classic like yours truly.'

'Did you go on any tours of duty?' Ivan asked.

'Aye, in nineteen ninety one me and the boys saw active service in the Gulf War.'

His blue eyes resembled the depths of the ocean as they darkened and glazed over. Intuition told me to change the subject. 'Are you enjoying India?'

'Aye, I'm lovin' it, hen. It's a place I've wanted te visit for years.'

'Are you a spiritual person then, Fraser?' Ivan looked surprised.

'Och nay lad, just like Jen here, I'm in it for the adventure.'

But I didn't believe him. I certainly wasn't here just for the adventure anymore and I suspected hidden depths in Fraser's reasons for signing up for the trip, too.

* * *

THE WARNING CAME as we jumped from our boats onto the vast sandbar which was to be our home for the second night's camping.

'Dust storm,' shouted Anil, pointing towards the horizon where an ominous wall of brown air stretched skyward. The afternoon's sailing had been idyllic with empty cornflower skies and a warm breeze filling the green, patched canvas sails pulling our vessels onward. But now our boat crew sprang into frantic action and Vijay's grim expression was enough to alert me to the fact that we could be in danger. Things were happening fast. I struggled to process my thoughts as the sinking feeling opened up a hollow ball in my stomach.

'How long do we have?' said Vijay as the eerie dusk, tinged with a burnt orange light descended, and muddied the sky.

'Maybe fifteen minutes,' answered Mukunda through gasping breaths, as he and the boat crew dragged tarpaulins over the boats, lashing them down with rope, covering the bags and equipment. The muscles in their arms bulging with the effort.

'What can I do te help?' shouted Fraser.

Vijay guided him away from the shoreline to where the rest of us stood. 'Fraser, you must all be coming with me. Your crew will be securing the boats. We'll find shelter in the village on top of the hill. Come on everyone. Follow me. Be quick, please.' The urgency in his tone galvanised each of us into sprinting towards the steps carved into the hill, leading up to the walled village.

We forged our way across the sandbank and every minute seemed to last a lifetime as our feet sank into the shifting sand, slowing our progress. As I neared the top of the steps, I glanced behind me. My heart leapt. Our elevated position revealed that the proximity of the flat, muddy wall was nearer that it had first appeared. I grabbed Alexandra's outstretched hand and pulled her, panting, over the final step. 'This way,' Vijay bellowed over the swishing tree branches, whipping back and forth in the whistling wind.

The village was in an uproar. People scattered in every

direction seeking shelter. Some gathered the animals tethered in their yards and dragged them mooing and bleating inside their homes. Others ripped washing from the line as clothing flapped about in a frenzied dance. The stale stench of dust permeated the air and instinct told me we only had minutes to get to safety.

25

I heard Vijay shout, 'There's the door to the schoolroom.' He pointed to a huge "Om" sign just visible behind a wall of dirty air. Bent over double we pushed on until, one after the other we stumbled through the door coughing and wheezing. Grit, sand and dust filled my ears, nose and mouth, and my face stung where sand had pelted my skin. The door was flung open again and our boat crew fell inside, banging the door closed as the dust storm reached its peak.

The violent flapping of sackcloth hanging at the window opening allowed clouds of dust to belch into the room. It covered the furniture, coated our hair and stuck to our clothing. The roar of the wind bombarded the mud-caked schoolroom walls, and I held my hands over my ears trying to drown out the sound of the slapping palm fronds. The bedlam outside rendered everyone silent as we waited in the dim classroom for the onslaught to end. I glanced at Derek and Betty holding onto each other and longed for Martin's protective arms. Pelting sand grains pounded the corrugated iron roof, and I pressed my hands to my ears harder, trying to silence the ear-splitting drumming.

'Gosh, that sounds like bullets peppering a wall,' shouted Alexandra. The wind screamed in anger. There was a crack of tree limbs splitting, followed by the almighty smash of a tree crashing to the floor. I hunched forward in shock as if ducking from a flying object. As I straightened up, I noticed Fraser pacing from wall to wall in the small room. The faraway look in his eyes troubled me. He was having difficulty breathing.

'Are you okay Fraser?' I shouted, but he didn't hear me. His pacing only stopped when he shoved chairs and tables aside to shrink into the dark corner of the room. It looks like he needs to shut everyone else out and deal with this situation on his own. Leave him be, Jen.

* * *

'It's passing over now,' shouted Vijay as the buffeting wind eased. But as he finished his sentence, the room lit up with flashing light, illuminating the times tables drawn in a neat hand on the sunny yellow walls. Within seconds a deep, rolling thunder clap vibrated the sackcloth curtains.

'We will be stuck here for the night now,' said Anil as the first drops of rain plopped onto the corrugated roof.

'Well, I've slept in places a lot worse than this,' I joked, relieved to see Fraser emerge from the corner of the room.

'After tonight our sleeping bags will feel like a duck down duvet,' said Summer as she and Charlie settled next to each other on the floor.

'Well, I've spent many hours in classrooms but never at the mercy of a high velocity dust storm,' said Ivan.

'We have visitors,' remarked Alexandra as the door

inched open and a villager struggled into the room lugging an enormous cauldron. His dripping wet clothing clung to him and his hair stuck to his scalp. Another followed him with arms full of bowls, cups and a metal teapot. The unmistakable spicy aroma of masala chai carried on the steam drifting from the spout overpowered the odour of grimy dust.

'Danyevad. Thank you. Danyevad,' we said as the dripping wet men handed out chapaties.

'The people of the village are offering this food to their very welcome visitors. They hope you will be returning to their village one day when the weather is more clement,' said Vijay as he ladled generous helpings of hot goat curry into our bowls.

Warmed by the mouth-watering delicate heat of curry and chai, we claimed our own space on the earthen floor. The only sound now came from the hammering on the roof, while the lightning cracked and the thunder boomed. Lost in our own thoughts we waited for morning.

* * *

'OH MY, OH MY.' Betty struggled to hold back her tears. 'The storm has decimated the village.' The clean, fresh smell the morning after the storm was a stark contradiction to the chaos now playing out before us. Trees with their branches split asunder lay where the raging wind had dragged them from the earth, snapping their roots. Villagers scurried back and forth, clearing debris from their homes. A group of men hoisted the remnants of a wooden shed from the roof of a green and yellow tuk-tuk; its once shining metal surface scuffed by the grinding force of sand grains. Spring flowers floated in pools of muddy water, their once pretty petals faded and crushed.

My voice cracked. 'The roof has been blown clean off that house.'

Alexandra held out a mangled sheet of metal. 'It's the school sign.'

'I don't know about anyone else, but I can't leave without helping. How about we delay our sailing until later today?' I asked, and everyone nodded their agreement.

* * *

WE SPLIT ourselves into teams to work around the village, Fraser and I opting to get the schoolroom and surrounding gardens back in order. 'Let's clear the playground at the front first,' I said and he nodded.

'Ye'll get plenty of exercise today sure enough hen. Come on grab the other end,' said Fraser as he hoisted one end of a mangled tree branch onto his shoulder. Conversation between us was stilted as we worked, the heavy lifting stealing away our breath. There was something I wanted to ask him. Sensitivity was needed and instinct told me to bide my time.

'One, two, three,' we shouted in unison, co-ordinating our movements to perfection, heaving the crushed metal remnants of the school's only swing onto the growing pile of rubble.

Two hours later we stood at the centre of an orderly playground. 'High five,' I said, my arm raised in triumph. Fraser smacked his palm against mine, his face creasing into the first smile I'd seen from him since before the dust storm began. We spent another hour washing the grime from the furniture in the classroom. 'You'd make someone a lovely wife Fraser.' His answer was to turn his spluttering hosepipe in my direction, threatening to soak me, and missing his target by a few inches as I leapt aside.

Our final task was to repair the bamboo fencing around the back of the building. 'C'mon Jen, let's see how handy ye are with a hammer,' said Fraser. He helped himself to a bundle of bamboo canes and a hacksaw from the pile of materials the villagers had provided.

We knelt side by side working along the fence, with me holding the bamboo canes in place while Fraser hammered in the nails. We were alone. It was quiet and Fraser was relaxed. I took a breath. 'Tell me to bugger off if you want Fraser, but what happened to you last night during the storm? You had me worried pet.'

He stopped working and the hand holding the hammer dropped to his knees where his gaze rested. His body slumped. 'I'm sorry if I scared ye, hen. What ye saw was the baggage I carry around from Operation Desert Storm.'

'That was the Gulf War, wasn't it?' I asked.

He looked up, and in the deep, dark pools of his eyes I saw again the turbulence which had took my breath away when we'd first met. 'Aye hen. When I came home, I brought the battlefield with me. It's every soldier's nightmare. Post-traumatic stress disorder.'

'Oh, Fraser, I'm so sorry.' He tore his gaze from mine as we inched along on our knees to the final fence panel where he hammered another nail through the bamboo. The vibration pulsed through my hands with each thump.

'It only developed six months ago. Hit me out of the blue at a firework display. One minute I was oohing and aahing at the rockets shooting into the sky; the next I was reliving the horror of seeing trucks and enemy soldiers being blasted off the face of the earth.'

Silence descended, the only sound the thwack, thwack, thwack of the hammer

He began again. 'The last few months I've been plagued with nightmares and flashbacks and now I've developed insomnia. The feelings of guilt are eating at me. I get very jumpy sometimes, hen. The only way I knew how te deal with it was distraction, so I kept busy. I didn't allow myself any downtime. My logic was, if I'm busy I'm not thinking about it. But I burnt myself out working too hard. I needed time away and saw this trip advertised. A country steeped in spirituality might provide some respite, I thought.' He gave a hollow laugh. 'I didn't think for one moment a dust storm would grab me by the throat and punch me in the face.'

'Haven't you asked for help? Promise me you'll get help when we get home.'

'Aye, this latest episode has convinced me I need te get in touch with my regiment. They have a programme to help soldiers with PTSD.'

An uncomfortable lump developed in my throat but I choked back my emotions; my tears would be no use to Fraser. He fell silent and rested against me when I put my arm round his shoulder.

'There you are. I wondered where you were.' Summer's smiling face appeared around the corner of the building. 'Come on you two, Vijay's said we need to set sail now to make sure we get to our next stop before dark. The villagers have packed some food for us, and they want to wave us off from the sandbank.'

* * *

THERE WAS STILL WORK for the villagers to finish before the hamlet would return to normality, but our contribution to the clean-up was in evidence as we wound our way towards the sandbank. Volunteering to clear garden areas, Derek and Betty had gathered the scattered remains of haystacks and organised them into neat piles; they'd re-planted shrubs which the gales had torn from soil and mended wooden barrels. They piled the barrels high with fruit that had been ripped prematurely from trees during the storm. The shimmering orange and lemon contents serving as a reminder that bright days had returned.

Charlie and Summer had joined forces to reclaim undamaged bricks to help rebuild the walls of homes, now barely recognisable in piles of rubble. 'This family nearly lost their father. He just made it out of the house before the walls collapsed.' Said Charlie as the homeowner shook his hand, chattering in Hindi, a huge grin expressing his gratitude.

The task of helping to reconstruct the roofs of houses had been allocated to Alexandra and Ivan. They had assisted with weaving straw, nailing down sheets of plastic and setting corrugated sheeting back in place.

'Is this our new group member?' laughed Ivan. Vijay led a plodding charcoal coloured cow on the end of a rope from one of the houses that had survived intact, and tethered it in the yard.

'Well she can sleep in your tent tonight Ivan, there's no room in mine,' laughed Fraser. An involuntary breath of relief escaped me. Thank goodness he's back to his old wise-cracking self.

* * *

'NAMASTE. Bye bye. Danyevad. Thank you again.'

The villagers waved and shouted their chorus of goodbyes from the shore as we set sail. The Herculean task of tidying up the village had been hot but satisfying work. As Mukunda got into his rhythm, my body swayed in time with the thrust of the boat. I'd been witness to the inescapable force of nature once more. Like the raging current on the Rishikesh rapids, the storm had been a powerful, uncontrollable reminder of human fragility.

That night as we sat in our circle in the mess tent, the flickering candlelight illuminated our faces as we enjoyed another tasty meal, prepared over the camp fire by our multi-talented oarsmen. Vijay sat outside the tent talking with the boat crew. We chatted amongst ourselves and soon the discussion turned to the next stop on our trip. Varanasi.

'Sounds like an awesome place, but I don't know much about it. Can you give us the lowdown on it, Ivan?' asked Charlie.

'I've got to admit I know little about Varanasi and I've left my guidebook on the boat.' Ivan sounded disappointed.

'Well, I'm afraid I can't help,' said Alexandra. 'I've been jolly lazy with my research.'

Now, I'd spent hours researching everything about Varanasi, but still I hesitated. My monkey mind had gone into overdrive. Thirty-nine years of conditioning was a hard habit to break, but I remembered my promise to myself. In the dark I glanced around at the faces lit by candlelight and took a breath.

'I did a bit of research at home.' Everyone turned at once to look in my direction. It was disconcerting. 'Sorry in advance if I bore you all.'

'Stop apologising for yourself,' Alexandra whispered in my ear, and instantly I recognised a habit I'd had for years.

Much louder now, Alexandra said, 'We'd all be jolly grateful if you'd share your knowledge with us, Jen.'

So I imparted the knowledge stored in my head about Varanasi and soon forgot my self-consciousness. I told them that the city, also known as Benares, stretches for seven kilometres. It has a population of just over three million, is reputed to be six thousand years old and is regarded as exceptional holy land. I knew I'd fascinate them with one legend of how the God Shiva had founded Varanasi. In a fight between the two mightiest Gods, Brahma and Shiva, one of the five heads of Brahma was torn off by Shiva. The victor carried Brahma's head dangling down by his side wherever he went as a sign of his bravery. When Shiva came to the area which is now Varanasi, the head dropped from his grasp and disappeared into the ground. I became increasingly animated as I explained that the city has around eighty-four ghats leading to the water's edge, all with different functions.

'There are the bathing ghats; also the main ghat where Vijay has planned for us to witness the Agni Pooja celebration, known as "Worship of Fire"; not forgetting the burning ghats where mourners carry out open-air cremations.'

I finished by saying I'd read the Ganges was very polluted there, contaminated by raw sewage and dead bodies. There were restrictions to the burning of bodies; pregnant women; children; priests or anyone who had died from the bite of the cobra. In these instances, families wrapped up the bodies, weighed them down, and gave them a watery grave in the holy river.

Just talking about Varanasi had increased my excitement levels and later, all snug in my sleeping bag, my mind whirred. In the dark I thought of home and wondered if Martin was worrying about me. My scalp prickled with a niggling discomfort when Marra's words flashed before my eyes. I wonder what Martin's doing right now. I switched on my laptop and tapped onto the keyboard. It wasn't possible to log on here on the sandbank, but at least I could prepare my next blog. It would be ready for upload when I got to the hotel in Varanasi. When I'd finished, switching off the laptop plunged me into darkness. Tiredness took over, and I fell asleep in seconds.

I woke in the pitch dark with a gripping pain in my stomach. It was so severe I pulled myself up to sitting and bent forward, trying to ease the agony of the knife now piercing my abdomen. I knew that sensation. Everyone knew it. It was universal. I was about to be struck down with the Rangoon Runs. In a tent. In India. In the middle of the night. On a sandbank with no facilities. Beads of sweat stood out on my forehead as I scrambled around in the dark for my clothes. The knife stabbed me again. Now dressed and with toilet roll and hand torch at the ready I unzipped the tent door with excruciating care. Slowly, slowly so as not to alert anyone. At last the opening was large enough for me to ease myself through. The knife took another stab, and I bent myself double, jamming my fist into my stomach. Outside the sky was as black as the proverbial cat, only this time it wasn't lucky. I waited for a second until my eyes became accustomed to the darkness. Yes, there it was. I sprinted towards the outline of the toilet tent.

Squeezing myself through the half-open door flap, I switched on the torch. I reeled back in bewilderment. Where was the hole? I jerked the small beam of light in desperation around the floor of the four by four space. I couldn't see the hole. Surrounded in silent blackness I was disoriented and confused. I swirled the light beam in desperate circles. As cognisance dawned, horror set in, sparking the heat of adrenalin coursing through my veins. Oh my God, they must fill the hole in at night time for sanitary reasons. What the hell was I going to do now? I couldn't just leave a nasty surprise for my fellow camp mates to stumble upon in the morning. The knife stabbed two more times in quick succession and caused me to groan quietly. I didn't have much time and had to find a solution damn quick. I remembered a tale Fraser had joked about. In his time in the army, he'd been caught short and had dug a hole in the sand with his flip-flop.

Yes, that's what I had to do. I had to make it back to my tent. My flip-flops were just outside my door flap. I switched off the torch and dashed back, skirting the semi-circle of snoring travellers until I reached my tent. I grabbed one of the flip-flops and stood for a second looking round. Through the dark, in the direction of the river bank, I could just make out a faint outline. Yes, that was a bush. It was the only one in the area. It was closer than the toilet tent but far enough away for privacy. I sprinted towards the shadow with the flip-flop in one hand and my ass in the other. Sweat covered my skin, I felt faint and still the knife stabbed. The bush was further away than I thought. At last I was there. Grateful to be hidden behind its cover. In the pitch black I dug manically at the ground with the flip-flop, flinging sand up into the air in all directions.

I was just in time for salvation.

Afterwards, I filled the hole back in with my trusty flip-flop; wiped the sweat from my face; and crept back to my tent in the dark to search for the Imodium tablets. I prayed they were fast acting. The pain had now eased, and I dropped off to sleep again waking to the sounds of breakfast being prepared and arranged on the communal blankets. The Imodium had worked, and I knew the worst was over. I emerged from my tent to see I was the last to rise.

'Good morning sleepy head,' Fraser greeted me with a cheery smile.

I grabbed a slice of dry toast, glancing around furtively. No one seemed aware of my drama in the wee small hours. I decided to keep that little tale well and truly to myself. Not being in the mood for partaking in breakfast, I grabbed my camera and wandered further up the shoreline to explore.

The huge orange ball of sun was still low. The sky was a delicate shade of pink then lilac, progressing to pale blue. On the opposite bank stood a large white temple with two turrets stretching up to the heavens and through the morning haze it looked ethereal. Birds chirped as they swooped between trees and the cool crisp evening smell gave way to the aromas of sun-warmed earth. A delicate gossamer mist clung to the tranquil flowing river, swirling like ghostly apparitions from a hidden world beyond.

Into the all encompassing pastel shades of the morning, a group of six village ladies strolled towards the river. They were here to perform their Morning Puja worship of the sun. The striking vivid hues of their clothing elevated them from their mellow surroundings. The gold and silver threaded designs on their saris fizzed like sparklers on bonfire night. They waved hello and nodded in agreement when I raised my camera for permission. But gone were the days of indiscriminate pointing and shooting for me now. My approach to my photography had evolved. I didn't just want to capture these special moments, I wanted to live them. I wanted my images to be my expression of what I saw and felt through the viewfinder. So I quelled the excitement and provocation to spring into action and begin shooting, and I simply observed.

They entered the water fully clothed and sprinkled flower heads around themselves. As the mist swirled, with hands in prayer position they faced the rising sun, chanting quiet mantras. They submerged themselves in the glistening water, then filled silver pots and poured out the holy water as an offering to the sun. All the while the fuzzy, luminous temple on the opposite bank seemed to float on air as it watched over them. As I allowed my senses to drink in the scene before me, I stood in wonder; overjoyed that I was there, a spectator in what was an awe-inspiring spectacle to me, but a part of everyday life for these ladies worshipping in the river.

The mood of the ladies crept into my consciousness and the distinction between the observer and the subject melted away. I was immersed in the moment and felt at one with the devotees. My body tingled, and I knew now was the time to take my photographs. As I moved among them they forgot I was there. Their masks had dropped and their eyes and faces shone with devotion. I watched for those glorious unguarded moments and, when the essential soul peeked out, that was when I released the shutter. And all the while the essence of India bubbled with joy in my heart, bringing with it a sense of connection. At that moment I had no desire to be anywhere else on earth.

26

They emerged from the water looking chilled. I had an idea. I walked to our campsite, grabbed the pot full of steaming chai and a stack of plastic cups, and made my way back to the devotees. They smiled and shook my hand and through my limited Hindi we learned each other's names as we sipped chai together in comfortable harmony. I felt so privileged to have been allowed into the private moments for a short time of these gracious, kind women. The thought which dropped into my awareness was, these ladies have just taught you a valuable lesson, Jen...A lesson in trust.

* * *

MUKUNDA PULLED on the oars with rhythmic strokes, propelling us towards the majestic crescent riverfront of ancient Varanasi.

'Oh golly, I've been transported back in time thousands of years,' said Alexandra, shielding her eyes from the raging sun.

I was awestruck and, for once, couldn't find the words to

describe my feelings. I gazed ahead of me at the sight of the vast array of diverse architecture soaring above the steep ghats. High red-walled fortresses rubbed shoulders with majestic palaces; monasteries stood cheek by jowl with mosques and ornate temples with sky puncturing spires. Marble arched pavilions, many tiered houses and shrines devoted to Gods and Goddesses stood shoulder to shoulder. The buildings appeared to float, rising through the haze, and stretched as far as the eye could see.

'The architecture is so varied, but the buildings blend seamlessly together. What an amazing sight,' said Derek.

Betty's eyes glistened with emotion as she rubbed Derek's arm. 'Enjoy every moment, love,' she whispered.

We had a grandstand view of the sights and sounds laid out before us. Witnesses to the unique spectacle of daily life on the ghats. The cacophony from the periodic chiming of bells blended with shouting and laughter. Evocative chanting, whistling and announcements from loudspeakers pierced my ears. It sounded foreign and was in shocking contrast to the peace and quiet I'd become accustomed to over the previous days.

People bathed, submerging themselves then rose. Water glinting in the sun cascaded from their heads and faces. Cows strolled everywhere and the sound of their mooing and dogs barking mingled with the smack of our oars, pulling us on, deeper into the midst of Varanasi. There were many other boats on the river filled with sightseers. As they sailed past our boat, we waved to each other and shouted greetings. The slap, slap, slap of the dobi wallahs at their work filled the air. They swung their washing over their shoulders and bashed it with all their might against the slabs of stone.

Smoke rose in spirals, spreading a light haze over the city from the burning ghats.

'Oh my, it looks like we're approaching the area where the cremations take place,' said Betty, gripping her nose.

I remembered more details from my research. 'In the main traditional burning ghat, there's an eternal fire and the Master of the Crematorium keeps the flame burning. The flames are believed to be as old as the city and the fire they use to burn a body must be lit from that flame.'

We drew up alongside the main burning ghat where a live cremation was taking place.

'All I can smell is burning wood,' said Derek.

Betty looked relieved and stopped pinching her nostrils.

'Before they burn a body, they cover it in sandalwood, herbs, camphor, ghee...' I counted off the items on my fingers but paused, tutting to myself. 'Erm, and something else I can't remember. Oh aye, that's it, they also add a basic form of sugar and wood to aid the burning process.'

Everyone grimaced when I added, 'all of that disguises the aroma of burning flesh.'

Betty looked queasy as we sailed past and onto the next ghat. The music, chanting and prayers continued as we moved further along the riverfront. Crumpled washing hung in neat rows on railings; the bright hues shouted out against the white, cream and dark sand toned buildings, many of which were emblazoned with painted signs in both Hindi and Roman script. Men scrubbed their bodies and women soaped their children from head to toe. The soapy streaks dazzled, a vivid creamy white against brown skin.

We arrived at the boat jetty and it was time to say goodbye to Anil and Mukunda who had looked after our every need so well. Vijay said there was no requirement for tips as he'd provide for that out of our group kitty. But they'd worked so hard so we each donated a goodly sum of rupees. Their faces lit up when we slipped the notes into their hands before climbing up the steep steps of the ghat. A minibus was waiting to take us to our hotel for the next two nights.

We were to meet in the late afternoon at the hotel reception. From there we'd take bicycle rickshaw rides through the town centre to the Dashashwamedh Ghat to witness the Varanasi Ganga Aarti Ceremony held each evening at sunset. Vijay had arranged the group into couples for the rickshaw rides and had teamed me up with Charlie. But Alexandra intervened. My head shook and my jaw clenched as I watched, not speaking, as she re-organised everyone. She coupled her and I together, which I wasn't averse to, but I felt manipulated again by her controlling behaviour. I knew I needed to have a frank discussion to make my feelings known. Our budding relationship was too important for me to seethe inside for the rest of the trip and return home, never to see her again. I would fight for this friendship.

'Fancy meeting for a quick drink in the hotel bar before the rickshaw rides?' I asked.

'Rather.'

'See you at three.'

'I can't jolly well wait for a hot shower.' She pulled at her unkempt bright red hair.

'Aye, me as well Alexandra, I'm hakky.'

'Hakky? What's hakky?'

'It's Geordie for absolutely filthy.'

'Oh, I see. Well, I'm jolly well rather hakky too.'

It made me chuckle to hear such a broad Geordie word spoken in the same sentence by someone with perfect upper-crust enunciation.

* * *

I LINGERED in the shower for what seemed like hours and after scrubbing away three days of grime, my skin tingled and my chestnut brown hair shone again. There was time to update my blog and check for any messages. I clicked on the link and tapped my top lip with impatience, waiting for A Geordie Up The Ganges to flicker into life on my laptop.

Ping. Hooray. At last. I could see from the header it was a message from Martin. Ping, ping, ping, ping, ping. The message alerts kept on popping up on the screen. Ping, ping, ping. Alert after alert flashed in front of my eyes in quick succession. The electronic alarm persisted. Eventually mashing into one long, never-ending piiing. I slumped into the chair with a heaving sigh, covering my face in my hands. Oh bloody hell, that's all I need. Either my laptop's developed a fault or my website's crashed. Just when I need to connect with home. How bloody disappointing is that? Thank God, that annoying pinging's stopped now.

Eeh, what the hell's all this, like? The screen's flashing saying there's one hundred and fifty-two messages. That can't be right. My website's gone haywire. Two hundred followers. Yes, that's the target I had in mind when we left Rishikesh. No, wait a minute that number's not two hundred, it's two bloody thousand. Impossible. Hang on though, those messages are definitely for me. And look, there's a massive list of followers' names.

I knew some of those names; most of my colleagues from the hospital; teachers from Martin's school where he taught science; Emma, my yoga teacher and others from my yoga class. John Bell, our Postman's name was on the list; people I knew from Gosforth; and loads of people I'd never heard of. From all over the world.

Hi Jen, Wow love. Your latest blog about the Ganga Aarti ceremony in Rishikesh is out of this world. I don't know what's changed, but something's elevated your photography to another level. When I view your images, I feel I'm there. Stood next to you. Your written account of what you saw, and the description of your emotions has brought the scenes and the people to life for me. Your blog is so much more than just a few anecdotes from a travel guide now. The photo gallery's not just littered with record shots of places and people. It's not just a travelogue now, Jen. It's a deep, warm, honest portrayal of you, and I love it. I'm so proud of you. I passed the link on to my colleagues at school and they were all so impressed, they've shared the link with their families and friends too. Missing you, pet. Can't wait for you to come home. Stay strong. All my love. Martin xx

'I can't believe this,' I said out loud as I scrolled through the messages on the screen. With my spare hand pressed against my chest, fingers splayed, I could feel my blood rushing and heart pounding. Up popped message after message praising my photography and narrative skill.

Jack from London wrote: *Your photos shine and convey emotion; they show moods, character and feelings which transmit to the viewer.*

Honesty and truth ooze out of your portraits was the message from Annabel in Canada

And from Amanda; *Hi Jen, remember me? I'm the lady who's embarking on a "menopausal find myself trip" too. My bravery deserted me and, I was on the verge of backing out until I read your latest blog. Something has shifted within you. I can sense it in your words. You seem transformed, and your writing is inspired. I leave for India in two days' time. Thank you for encouraging me to follow my heart. I'd love to meet you one day.*

The comments box of A Geordie Up The Ganges was overflowing.

You've captured the real person; I'm able to connect with this shot; You have a real talent for writing; I feel a sense of belonging which makes me want to see more of your images. This photo speaks to my mind, heart and soul, I love it; The best blog about India on the net; This shot is unforgettable.

Warmed by tingling adrenaline, I basked in gratification. Eeeh Jen, this is what you've tried to achieve for years with your love of photography. To make unforgettable images which evoke strong emotions and stay with the viewer forever. And writing. Who'd have guessed you'd develop a passion for writing? Not me. Never in a million years.

A door somewhere within creaked open and the desire to share my experiences and tell others about the precious moments I'd been privileged to witness was all consuming. Experiencing the essence of India had lit a touch-paper within. A creative streak I never knew I possessed exploded into being. I tapped into the keyboard and the words flooded out. I held nothing back. Time stood still as I wrote like a demon, elaborating on every detail of the profound scenes I'd witnessed. Words unknown to me materialised from nowhere to paint a vivid picture. Words a child growing up in grinding poverty on the banks of the Tyne had never been taught in the bottom-grade class at school. My mind was fertile like never before. I ended on a light note.

Thursday, 11th March, Varanasi

... It gives me so much pleasure to share with you, dear readers, the enchanting sights, seductive sounds and profound encounters I've been privileged to witness over the last few days, while floating down the Holy River Ganges. Anil and Mukunda surprised everyone by serenading us on the final stretch to Varanasi with an impressive rendition of 'The Blaydon Races' as they pulled their oars in time to the beat. It seems they'd picked up the words listening outside our mess tent when everyone had sang along with me.

Our group are becoming so close now. Summer and Charlie are crazy about each other; Ivan watches over us and adds so much to our experience of India with his in-depth knowledge of the history; Fraser keeps us laughing with his humour; Derek and Betty are loving their retirement; I have found a wonderful friend in Alexandra.

One hour later, I hit the publish button and sank back into my chair. Elated.

My guard was down and without thinking I clicked on my private message button.

While you're "finding yourself" in India Martin is finding a new life here in Newcastle. He looks so happy with you out of his hair, and a beautiful woman on his arm. They went dancing last night. She stayed all night with him again. Isn't it time you came home? Forever yours, Marra x

The words burned into my eyes. I saw red. Before I could stop myself I fired off a reply.

Fuck You.

* * *

ALEXANDRA HAD GOT to the bar before me and sipped a glass of sparkling white wine. A cognac was awaiting my arrival, and I took a swallow enjoying the familiar heat on my tongue. It was quiet with only two more customers who chatted with the bartender. How could I instigate this awkward conversation? I gulped a nervous intake of breath. 'The ceremony tonight's going to be a real treat. I can't wait,' I said.

'Me too Jen. Did you do any research on it?'

'A bit. In Hindu mythology Lord Brahma created Dash..., Dashash...Dashashwamedh Ghat, I think that's how you say it, to welcome Lord Shiva to Varanasi. Brahma sacrificed ten horses in an offering performed in front of a sacred fire.

'Golly, it's amazing that the ritual has lasted for thousands of years. Hopefully we'll get to experience it if we survive the rickshaw ride through the town.'

'Talking of the rickshaw ride, I wish you hadn't interfered there Alexandra.' Her brow puckered, her eyes flashed in annoyance. She opened her mouth to speak but paused when I raised my hand. 'Please hear me out.' We sipped our drinks in unison. 'I'm so glad fate has brought us together on this trip. I feel I've found a soulmate and I dearly hope you feel the same way Alexandra. You're so supportive and I love your friendship, God knows I even love your crazy laugh.' A smile played at the corners of her mouth, her eyes softened. 'I want us to be friends for ever and so I think we need to be honest with each other. It really upsets me when I feel you're being too bossy. I've got a thing about being manipulated by other people. It drives me mad and I just hope you'll understand my feelings.' Her smile waned, concern etched on her face. A lump in my throat compounded my remorse, but I knew if our friendship was to last we had to come to an understanding.

'I do feel the same way about our friendship Jen, I'm glad you spoke up, and I know we're going to be friends for life. I'm sorry I've made you feel that way. People are always telling me I'm too bossy. I'll watch that in future. She held up her glass.

'Cheers to that,' I said and we chinked our glasses together. I relaxed with an inward *phew*, that went easier that I'd imagined it would.

'Now we're being jolly well honest with each other, I need to ask you something.'

Oh no. What was coming next?

'I detect a sadness in you, Jen. I sense that you hold back. There's a troubled look in your eyes when you think no one's looking. If you believe our friendship is worth anything, why can't you open up to me?'

This was my chance, and I wished I could unburden myself. But I couldn't bear to hurt her more today. She'd already lost one friend to cancer, after all.

'I'm fine, honestly. Haven't you worked out by now, sometimes I have a first class resting bitch face.

'Well, I agree it does jolly well look like a slapped backside sometimes.'

Had I put her off the scent? I wasn't sure. But the banter had provoked giggles, which caused snorting and eventual convulsive laughter. The bartender and two customers at the other end of counter looked on perplexed. I knew a strong friendship had blossomed between us. When the time came for me to open up about my illness, I hoped she'd understand why I needed to keep it buried deep inside for now. First, I had to learn to trust myself. Believe in my own strength. Process my thoughts and search my soul. My real soul. Not the soul of that false Jen. I'd faced the truth and accepted I needed to change. That was my first tentative step of transformation but I had a long way to go.

I jumped off the barstool. 'Drink up, it's time to catch our bicycle rickshaw down to the ghats.'

* * *

As usual, the streets and roads were over-crowded with people and traffic of every description. Vijay said he'd never experienced such crowds, and it was due to the Kumbh Mela. It seemed like the whole of India was following us as we progressed on our journey from place to place along the route of the Ganges. Alexandra and I linked arms and held on to each other as we careered through the town on our bicycle rickshaw. The top half of our driver's body bobbed up and down, his bald head shining in the low evening sun as he peddled furiously. I hadn't heard Alexandra use profanity before and couldn't help laughing as she screamed, 'oh fuuuuuck,' as we flew round a roundabout at breakneck speed. We swerved left and right, squashing against each other as we dodged people, traffic and animals. The warm breeze made our hair dance, and it was so noisy we had to shout to each other to make ourselves heard. We had an unfettered view of life on the streets of Varanasi.

We passed row upon row of shops, workplaces, ramshackle houses and eateries, all a hive of activity. It seemed as if time had stood still here. All of life available for us to view, nothing hidden, even toilet activities. We passed a shop with severed goat's heads displayed on a table and another with chickens hanging by their legs, their heads dangling on elastic necks. Men set up shop on the ground, some shaving their customers with cut-throat razors, others offering a shoe-shine service.

Along the whole length of the streets we traversed was an endless queue of worshippers which seemed to be miles long. People lined up patiently for their turn to enter the Kashi Vishwanath temple at this very special, auspicious time in the Hindu calendar. The happiness was clear on their faces. They waved to us as we zoomed past. 'Namaste,' they shouted. Many of the devotees were barefoot, the women wearing toe rings and anklets with tiny jingling bells. The sound of happy devotional singing, often accompanied by clapping, reached our ears as we whizzed by.

'Pheeew, I need another brandy after that.' I scrambled, swaying from side to side, from my seat and was glad to feel hard ground beneath my feet.

We'd arrived at the top of the steps of the Dashashwamedh Ghat in one piece. Vijay led us up a further flight of steps to a block of reserved seats. We had a fantastic view, facing the setting sun, and the raised platforms where the priests would perform their rituals.

The light faded as the sun dipped below the horizon. Boats full of sightseers jostled for position on the river. Long red cloths were spread on the ground as thousands of people took their places sitting in orderly rows. Excited expectation fizzed in the air as seven gold and burgundy robed priests climbed onto their raised platforms to perform their worship to the Holy River Ganges. Each priest rang a handbell, and melodic and mystical chanting filled the air from the loudspeaker; 'Govinda Jaia, Jaia, Govinda Hari, Hari.'

The strong smell of urine in the air was periodically smothered by the welcome, sweet aromas of incense. The priests blew the evocative sounding conch shells and everyone in the audience clapped along to the music. Next came the waving of the oil lamps filled with burning camphor and the smoke swirled around the men and up into the dark sky. Other offerings made to Ma Ganga were cow dung, incense, flowers and milk and honey mixed with Ganges water. The priests twirled smoking incense sticks in a floating motion with graceful hand movements, drawing swirling shapes in the air with the smoke. I glanced at my fellow travellers and their eyes shone at the unforgettable scenes they were witnessing.

I knew mine did, too.

27

It was four o'clock in the morning. The sights and sounds of the Aarti Ceremony from the previous evening running through my mind ensured I'd sleep no more. We were to meet at six o'clock to visit the bathing ghats to experience the Varanasi sunrise celebrations. I'd spotted a tranquil space tucked away in the corner of the hotel gardens when we arrived. This would be a perfect opportunity to practice yoga and perform a short meditation. Goosebumps formed on my arms as I stepped into the cool air of the morning twilight. I shivered as the delicate breeze slid through my hair and fluttered through my blouse. I'd popped on the cream chiffon floaty one, with the low-cut ruffled neckline. As I neared the tiny oasis, among the silhouetted shrubs encircling the patch of grass, a shadowy shaped moved. My gait slowed as I strained my eyes, trying to make out the shape. It was a person, sat on one of the logs, head in hands. They hadn't seen me. As I drew closer, I recognised the frame.

'Hello Fraser,' I whispered.

Something in his demeanour worried me. 'Are you okay?

You look like you've got the weight of the world on your shoulders.'

'Och aye, hen. I couldn't sleep. You too?' he asked.

'Me as well, Fraser. I thought I'd start the day with some yoga.'

'C'mon hen, this is a good time to teach ye some of my exercise routine. Let's start with sit-ups. Lie on yer back, hands behind yer head, knees bent. Take yer flip-flops off. I'll hold yer feet.'

I shuffled myself into position. The grass beneath me cooled my spine, but my feet tingled with increasing heat where his hands touched me.

'One,' he counted. I tensed my arms, engaged my core and hauled the top half of my body to sitting. He was on his knees holding my feet and as my torso stretched into an upright position, I found myself staring into his intense blue eyes.

'Two.' His gravelly voice was low. I pulled my torso upright.

'Three.'

I wished I'd worn something other than a flimsy blouse this cool morning. My nipples were sticking out like a couple of Newcastle Brown Ale bottle tops.

'Four.'

We were both trembling. For God's sake, I chided myself, don't let your knees loosen and open like that.

'Five. That's great Jen,' he rasped. 'Come on, I want another five. These exercises can help to increase flexibility and strengthen the core.'

'Six.'

Oh, God, we're close enough to kiss, I can feel his breath on my face.

'Seven.'

He moved closer, breathing hard although he wasn't the one exerting himself. I had to stop this.

I tugged my feet from his burning hands and sprang to standing. He rested back on his hunkers and looked up at me. A gentle smile played on his lips, his head tilted to one side as his eyes took a walk all over my body.

'Hi guys. I see I'm not the only one who couldn't sleep.' We hadn't heard Summer's approach, she hopped over the bushes into the bower with a grin.

'Uh, oh, hi Summer, erm, I woke early and thought it would be a good idea to start the day with a few exercises. Fraser got here before me. I can see you had the same idea,' I said, pointing to the yoga mat rolled under her arm. 'Great minds think alike, eh? Right, I'm off. See you both at six. Enjoy your workout.'

I left them chatting about the benefits of early morning exercise and headed back to my room for a shower. (Yes, it would be a cold one.) Thank goodness Summer turned up when she did.

* * *

WE ARRIVED at the bathing ghats at around six thirty. Even at such an early time the area was teeming with thousands of people, and there was a buzz of activity. After picking our way down the steps we boarded a rowing boat. The oarsman stopped pulling on the oars one hundred meters out where we drifted parallel to the water's edge. Far enough away not to interfere with the crowds of worshippers, but close enough for a stellar view of the activities.

The luminescent dawn light hung over the whole length of the Varanasi shoreline. The hard edges of the architecture melted into shadowy outlines as the haze from the rising mist clung to the masonry. Orange balls of fuzzy street lights along the ghats radiated outward from the receding layers of textures, hues, tones and contrasts; they projected onto the inky water, dancing like fire on the surface ripples.

The sun eased above the horizon bouncing golden yellow light off buildings and people. The clamour increased, fusing together into a wall of noise. The chiming of bells blended with chanting, singing and the splashing of water. Worshippers submerged themselves or scooped handfuls of water up into the air, cupped their hands together and chanted as the tiny stream trickled through their fingers back to its source.

The scene was a riot of colour as ladies bathed fully clothed. Many floated the miniature leaf boats I'd become so accustomed to now, as an offering to the river. Men entered the water bare chested in bathing suits. A vendor in a rowing boat filled with his wares drew up alongside us.

'Flower boats?' he shouted above the hubbub, holding a pretty example out towards us as our two vessels bobbed up and down. 'Beautiful boats to be honouring your ancestors. Be lighting the candle, sailing the boat and remembering your loved ones who are no longer here.'

'I'll have one for my Mam and Dad,' I told Alexandra as I handed over my rupees.

'It's a jolly nice way to remember our loved ones.' Alexandra searched her bag for her money. 'I'll sail a boat for Tamara.'

Everyone busied themselves handing over their rupees and lighting their candles with the vendor's cigarette lighter. Everyone except Fraser. The others were so wrapped up in their own private moments no one else noticed that he sat staring out to space, not moving. I leaned over the side and dropped my boat into the water.

'Miss you and love you Mam and Dad,' I whispered. The tiny leaf vessel swirled around three times then dipped up and down. It caught the current and sailed off to join the other tributes, on a mysterious journey to an unknown destination along the Ganges.

For a moment everyone sat in silence, lost in their own thoughts. Remembering. I thought of my childhood. Mam and Dad had loved me with a passion. I asked myself, *What would you rather have had when you were growing up, Jen? One of those fashionable Afghan coats everyone wore; a pair of platform shoes; the latest jeans or a maxi skirt?* The answer was easy. I wouldn't change a thing. My Mam and Dad blessed me with their love every day as a child. Now I knew. That had been enough.

* * *

WE HAD a free afternoon and evening. Derek decided he wanted to investigate the architecture and Betty, as usual had acquiesced, and plodded off alongside him.

'Well lassies, how would ye both like te spend the afternoon with a gorgeous hunk of a Glaswegian?' Fraser stood in between us and looked from Alexandra to myself, his arms hooked around our shoulders.

'Urgh, do we have to?' I grimaced.

'Well, we've got nothing better to do.' Alexandra playfully punched his stomach.

'Howay then, let's explore the streets of Varanasi together.' I smiled with delight.

'Is it okay if we tag along?' asked Summer as she, Charlie and Ivan fell into step alongside us. We banded together to get lost in the labyrinths of numerous lanes, passages and walkways.

A medieval tableau played out throughout the narrow winding streets of the Old City.

'What tales these lanes could tell,' said Ivan as he thumbed through his guidebook pointing out places of interest.

With mounting excitement, I watched Varanasi daily life happening around me. When the now familiar tingling heralded the time was ripe to take my photos, I sought out the most remarkable people to engage with and photograph. I was stumbling along in Hindi, talking about the weather with the local chai wallah, when I caught a flash of movement out of the corner of my eye. I turned to see two hulking cows, spooked by something, stampeding down the arms-width lane towards us.

'Watch out, guys,' I shouted. At my warning, everyone flattened themselves against the wall just in time. As the holy animals bulldozed past, I could feel the power of their bulk. The sound of their hooves on the hard earth was thunderous. The smouldering air that whipped across my face in their wake smelled of fresh cow dung.

'Shit, that was a close shave' I shouted. 'Shit' I roared a second time, because I'd just stood in a pile of it as I'd jumped aside, not watching where I was putting my feet.

With my red raksha sutra tied around my wrist and my shoes covered in dung, I hoped luck would be on my side over the next couple of months.

Surrounding us in the narrow streets, pungent smelling garbage lay rotting everywhere alongside animal and human dung. The overpowering whiff of urine hung heavy in the sweltering air. Vendors selling a variety of wares from open-fronted shops smiled, enjoying the attention as I spoke with them in my limited Hindi and photographed them at their work. Street food peddlers sat in holes cut into the ancient, dilapidated walls dropping morsels into huge pans of hot oil. The sizzling, fragrant spiced heat infused the atmosphere in the claustrophobic lanes and wafted across our faces as we passed by.

'There must be a parade heading our way,' said Charlie. The sound of banging drums, singing and chanting rose above the general day-to-day hubbub, becoming louder with each passing minute.

'It's probably a funeral procession,' said Ivan.

'It can't be, it sounds like a celebration,' said Charlie.

'They treat death differently here to the way we deal with it in the west. Here they celebrate the passing of loved ones. It's a happy celebration because the departed is going on to a better place.' As if to endorse Ivan's words a procession rounded the corner, winding its way through the warren of streets. The deceased, wrapped in shimmering orange cloth covered with marigold wreaths, was borne on a bamboo stretcher. The loud singing and chanting reverberated off the walls of the passageways. Out of respect I put my camera away as we followed the crowds towards the burning ghats.

'This is my auntie.' The man stopped singing as I fell into step beside him.

'I'm sorry for your loss,' I said

'No need for sorry. She had a happy life and now will achieve moksha, the release from constant rebirth.'

It struck me there weren't any women in the procession. 'Didn't she have any female relatives?' I asked.

'Women aren't allowed at the burning ghats. They get too emotional and will cry. If that happens it will prevent the deceased from reaching Nirvana. So, the women stay at home to cry.' He smiled and broke into an exuberant chant.

We watched the proceedings from a distance at the top of the ghat. They lined the deceased on their stretchers on the floor from the top to the bottom of the steps, awaiting their final ceremony in this world. The orange shrouds a contradiction to the grim subdued tones of the surrounding burning grounds. Smoke from the crackling flames of cremations already taking place filled the air. Sooty fumes cloaked the scorched buildings, the earth and huge piles of dark brown wood prepared in readiness for the funeral pyres. Cows, dogs and goats roamed at will and groups of men threw logs onto a pyre as they chanted, ash settling in their hair like snowflakes. On the water, tourists in canoes looked on.

The scene had me transfixed, unable to tear my gaze away from a body engulfed in leaping, hissing flames, burning in the open air. Clanging bells vibrated in my chest as another procession passed by. The family of the deceased singing with vigour to assist their loved one to achieve liberty. It was strange. Here I was staring at death and all at once, it didn't seem so scary after all.

* * *

As we watched in silence, there was a gentle choking sound. It was hardly noticeable, and it came from Fraser's direction. We all heard it and turned at once. My breath caught in surprise. Fraser was on the verge of crying. Fraser, the joker of the group, the tough looking alpha male, tattooed and scarred, for a split second resembled a tiny vulnerable little boy. Then the tears came. He could not control the flow as they spilled down his face. He turned his back. Embarrassed. We glanced at each other and an unspoken understanding passed between us. When he regained his composure, he turned back to us. We each hugged him, not asking questions.

'This place is such a melting pot of civilization, it's the constant reminder we're all mortal and life's short. It plays with your emotions doesn't it?' I said softly.

'You're so right there, Jen. Since I arrived in India I've been constantly reminded of Tamara,' said Alexandra.

We perched on the top of the steps and Fraser talked. It all bubbled up and spilled out.

'When I was a wee bairn, five years old, my parents were coming back from a night out. Their car skidded on a patch of ice and ended up wrapped around a tree. Both were killed outright.'

'Oh Fraser, I'm so sorry,' said Summer.

'I was an only child with no other relatives ye see. I was fostered into family after family. It wasn't the families fault, they were decent people, but I'm ashamed to say I was a horror. A bitter and twisted kid. Nobody could cope with my behaviour. To this day I don't know why I was so destructive.'

'Losing your parents at such a young age, Fraser. That's why,' said Alexandra.

'When no other families would have me the local authorities put me in the care system.' His voice quivered. 'And that's when I turned into an angry young guy. I got involved in a gang in Glasgow. Nobody else on the streets could beat me at stealing cars. My luck ran out and I was locked away in a young offenders' institute. The army saved me.' He looked around at our faces. 'Aye, the day I signed up was my salvation. The army gave me a sense of belonging. It showed me a different outlook on life. My comrades became my kin. I served my time and loved it. The army turned me from a wee shit into a decent person.'

'Well, at least I *think* I'm a decent person.'

'You're a lovely guy, Fraser, and I'm lucky to be spending this momentous trip with you,' I said.

'Och, I love my job as a personal trainer in Glasgow now. I still see mates from my army days hen, and I'm happy, but ever since I've arrived in India, those memories keep flooding back.'

'I know how you feel. I promise you that letting your feelings out will lighten your load, Fraser.' I said.

So this was the real Fraser who'd been hiding away. The broken child who had to mend himself. If he could break the shackles of his bad start in life, then so could I. I just had to trust myself to succeed.

* * *

We headed away from the cremation grounds back into the maze of streets for lunch. 'See you in an hour,' Alexandra said as she and I waved to the others. Neither of us wanted a meal, and we meandered off to find the lassi shop we'd seen earlier. We'd both developed a liking for those delicious Indian yoghurt drinks since our arrival in India.

'Here it is,' I said as we stopped at what was a huge square hole in the crumbling wall of one of the narrowest passages in the city. We stepped from bright sunlight through the hole and found ourselves in a tiny room with dim lighting. The walls were painted in swirling psychedelic patterns and covered with photos of customers, which added to the confined atmosphere of the small space. There were already four men inside and we filed in, nodding and saying hello, sitting next to them on the wooden benches around the edges of the walls. They were of European appearance but spoke in a Slavic sounding accent and we couldn't engage in conversation.

After the acrid aroma of the streets the blissful bouquet of sweet fruit and milky yoghurt seemed like heaven. A cross-legged local sat on the floor against the innermost wall of the room surrounded by metal pots and pans. Each contained a fruity yoghurt concoction which he pulped with a pestle and mortar and mixed with a long-handled spoon. He handed out menus, and we studied the flavours of the traditional Indian yoghurt drink on offer; apple, cashew, pomegranate, saffron, strawberry, pistachio, chocolate – the list went on and on.

We can prepare any combination of fruit for every palate. The only limit will be your own imagination, read the note on the menu.

'I don't know whether to go for a straightforward apple lassi or live dangerously and mix it with guava fruit. No, I'm going to live life in the fast lane and mix my fruits,' I said.

'Ooh golly Jen look, there's one called a Special Lassi on the menu. It's more rupees than the others. It must contain a large mixture of fruits. I'm having that one.'

'Two Special Lassis,' I said to the man, who busied himself pulping, mashing and mixing our drinks.

'Cheers,' we said in unison as we chinked our glasses together containing what looked like a green banana milk-shake with tiny little leaves.

'Mmmm, that's rather tasty and refreshing.' Alexandra raised her glass, turned it around in the air, studied the contents for a second and took another long sip.

As we sipped on our drinks, the voices of the Slavic sounding men increased in volume. They roared with laughter at something the smallest one said. Becoming more animated they rose to leave, looking unsteady on their feet. As they said their goodbyes the small guy recited a rhyme in stilted English. 'Goodbye, fly high.' The four men exploded into hysterical laughter, and disappeared through the hole to the outside, guffawing as they left.

'It wasn't that funny,' I said, and Alexandra nodded in agreement.

* * *

'WHERE DID you just say you went?' asked Summer, looking worried.

'The lassi shop round the corner,' I said.

'Was it the one with "Official Government Bhang Shop" painted above the hole in the wall?' asked Charlie, while everyone stared at us as we both nodded.

'What drink did you order?' Ivan asked.

'We both had the Special Lassi. It was jolly tasty,' answered Alexandra.

Summer's hand flew to her mouth. 'Oh God, you've been drinking Bhang Lassi. Do you both feel okay?'

I did feel a little strange. 'What the hell's Bhang Lassi?' I asked.

Ivan opened his guidebook and read out loud, 'Bhang Lassi is a drink made from yoghurt, spices, rose water and,' he paused, 'cannabis.'

'Cannabis,' I screeched, my voice seeming to burst from the top of my head.

28

Ivan continued reading.

'The holy city of Varanasi has several Government-approved shops where one can legally consume Bhang Lassi. Hindus drink bhang for spiritual reasons. They drink it to honour Lord Shiva, to improve their meditation, to get closer to God and to wash away their sins.'

I giggled, Alexandra snorted, and our laughter boiled over.

'C'mon everyone. Let's get these two druggies along to Assi Ghat at the southern end of the city. I've read it's a lovely place to watch the sunset,' said Fraser. To Alexandra and myself he said, 'Don't worry lassies, trust us, we'll look after ye and make sure ye come to nae harm.'

* * *

IT WAS a slow stroll of an hour to get there and we were approaching Assi Ghat when the bhang took effect. I felt light on my feet, like my body was a shadow with no substance. My grin spread from ear to ear and I giggled along with Alexandra at nothing. It seemed like I was dreaming, but it was so vivid that I still had a connection to reality. As I walked, I watched my feet. My trainers turned into streaks of black and white from the floating forward motion as I placed one foot in front of the other. The steps, the temple overlooking the ghat, the trees and the flowing water popped out in glorious technicolour and it appeared like I was in a 3D animated movie.

Fraser said, 'Let's sit at the top of the steps and wait for sunset.'

It sounded as if he'd spoken from within a tunnel far away and his words echoed over and over.

Alexandra wobbled and plonked herself down and it seemed the funniest thing I'd ever seen. I guffawed uncontrollably and couldn't stop. The ghat was busy and cartoon people strolled around everywhere. The students of a yoga class taking place on a raised platform, floated in the air above their mats as they moved from posture to posture. When I spoke, my words drifted out of the back of my head. The ground below was like a huge duvet, soft and springy. Fraser played his harmonica, and I was convinced the Royal Philharmonic Orchestra was right there in front of us. The symphony that filled the air was the most staggeringly beautiful piece of music I'd ever heard. It enchanted me, and all I wanted to do was dance. I danced for what seemed like hours, everyone taking turns to partner me as I invented a new genre of dance. A fusion of ballet, rock-and-roll, ballroom and head-banging from the mosh pit.

The sun slipped towards the horizon and my mouth was agape at the colossal size of the luminous orange globe. Ringed with flames that shot outward, the incandescent ball disappeared from view and the sky turned red. With the fading of the light came subtle feelings of paranoia. I thought I saw a shadowy spectre out of the corner of my eye and shivered. This was a sensation I didn't like, and I knew I wasn't in control of myself. As the time passed, I experienced lapses of short-term memory. I had a banging headache. I wanted to be back at the hotel, tucked up safe in bed.

We all linked arms and started on the walk back to the hotel. The journey was a mystery, but I was relieved to close my room door behind me and fall exhausted onto my bed. My headache had gotten worse, and I was nauseous. As I lay in the dark, I thought I saw the ghostly shadow again. The words of Marra flashed before my eyes followed by a vision of Martin making love to another woman. I jumped out of bed and switched the light back on. My skin was clammy and my heartbeat thrashed in my ears. I had an increased sensitivity to every sound. It terrified me and didn't want to be on my own. There was only one thing for it. I needed to be with someone I could trust.

I knocked on the bedroom door. Alexandra's pasty face framed by her shock of bright red hair peeped from the opening. When she saw me, without saying a word she pulled the door wide. I stepped inside and fell onto the bed. She flung herself down beside me and within seconds we were both in a deep sleep.

* * *

I LADLED the unappetising looking brown beans onto my plate. The consequence of being late for breakfast meant that my food choices were limited.

A thumping headache, tired muscles, raging thirst and intense hunger had replaced the high of the previous evening. I'd experienced a little of the wilder side of life but that was one escapade I knew I'd never repeat. I put my thumbs up to a dishevelled looking Alexandra who sat at the other end of the table and mouthed, 'You ok?' She replied with a weary nod of her head. I attacked the bland tasting beans with gusto, feeling like I could eat a mountain of food. It was our last day in Varanasi. We were to visit a silk factory after breakfast; return to the hotel and pack our gear in the afternoon; and make our way to the train station to embark on our third and final sleeper train journey.

* * *

WE PULLED up outside the silk factory and gathered in a group as Vijay made arrangements with the driver to pick us up in two hours. The bus pulled away, and we followed Vijay towards the door of the building.

'Derek, Derek, it's this way,' Ivan shouted.

Derek had headed in the opposite direction to the rest of us and was just about to disappear round a corner. We waited as Betty rushed to retrieve him. He hadn't been concentrating. From bitter experience I knew how easy it was to lose sight of the group. I smiled ruefully as a picture of me at the Kumbh Mela turning round and round in a circle, searching for familiar faces surfaced in my mind. The memory upset me so much it made me nauseous. I banished the vision from my head.

The silk factory was remarkable. We followed Vijay to the small workshop where we watched skilled craftsmen at their hand looms. They flicked tiny little bobbins of exquisite delicate threads back and forth in between two sets of threads stretched over the loom. The wooden frame click-clacked as the weaver moved the treadle with his feet, creating Indian inspired works of art.

'Here at the factory they are using traditional handmade techniques only. Some items they are making are silk saris, runners, cushion covers and pashminas. It will be taking eight hours to be completing one and a half centimetres of work. A wedding sari, typically, it will be taking seven and a half months for completion,' said Vijay

'The skill of the artisans at their work is captivating,' said Betty, and we all nodded in agreement.

In an upstairs sales room we could view the finished articles. There was no pressure to buy, but the pieces were so extraordinary I decided I wanted one to take home with me. I was contemplating a gorgeous wall hanging depicting Hindu gods and goddesses when an intense wave of nausea engulfed me. I beat a hasty retreat outside, it was hot and breezy but as I leaned against the wall the queasiness subsided. Not daring to return inside, I stayed propped up against the building feeling weak until everyone emerged clutching their purchases.

'Come on Jen, let's get you back to the hotel. You can grab some rest before we leave for the sleeper train.' Summer linked her arm in mine as I trudged towards the minibus.

I realised my fatal mistake had been eating the strange brown beans at breakfast. Nothing would prevent me from updating A Geordie Up The Ganges, though. I now had over three thousand followers and felt a responsibility to keep them updated.

Saturday March 13th, Varanasi

Dear Readers, how can I do justice to Varanasi and bring her to life for you with mere words? I can but try. It's a place where life moves incessantly yet it remains in a time warp. Ugly decay lives next to striking beauty and all of life is acted

out in that city where ancient practices play out against contemporary culture. The reek of stale urine and rotting garbage mingles with the aromas of sweet incense and fragrant flowers. The constant noise of chanting, temple bells ringing and spiritual music occupies the same space as deep meditation, profound silence and contemplation. So full of death yet abundant with life. Varanasi is one huge contradiction. It is a spectacular "City of Life".

There was a message from Martin which ended with...*I'm so lonely without you, Jen. Love Martin xx*

I sensed my eyes narrowing as I bit the inside of my lip. Hold that thought right there, Jen. If you begin to doubt Martin you're letting Pat win. I exhaled with a whoosh. No messages from Marra. Maybe my outburst at her last message had made her think twice about trolling me.

My punishment for being lax with what I ate in India was to spend the rest of the day fighting waves of nausea. I dreaded the upcoming fourteen-hour, five hundred and forty-seven mile sleeper train journey. Before leaving the hotel for the station, I spent an eternity indulging in the sport of projectile vomiting, and cursing myself.

* * *

PANDEMONIUM. Bedlam. Chaos.

These were the scenes as we arrived at Varanasi train station. My heart sank at the news our train was delayed by up to three hours. When I could stand up no longer, I joined the throngs of people sat on the ground. Sitting amongst the local people, propped up against our cases, feeling like death warmed up, I observed the surrounding activity with incredulity. Thousands of travellers jammed the platform.

Many sat on blankets in huddles as they waited for their delayed train. Others stood or wandered around often in bare feet, some carrying their luggage on top of their heads. My head was pounding, and I cursed the regularity of the announcements from the tannoy system, each one preceded by a loud, jarring, screeching very irritating harmonium type sound.

When a train pulled into the station, people hauled themselves up the train steps and pushed through the already crowded door entrances, to disappear into the midst of the carriages. Just as I thought not one more person could squeeze through those doors, more and more people forced their way through into the sardine-tin packed train. From the outside looking at the rusty blue carriages there were arms, hands and elbows sticking out through the barred carriage windows. Food sellers ran back and forth selling boxed meals to the anonymous hands stretching out. Once or twice there was shouting and animated discussions on the platform as it appeared one food seller had encroached on another's patch. As the trains pulled away from the station, people were still jumping on to the carriage steps. They heaved their bodies up and bulldozed through the throngs spilling out through the doors.

As I sat there thinking personal space must be a concept unheard of in India the huddle of people squatting next to me, so close that our bodies touched, unpacked their evening meal. My stomach lurched as the whiff of the unusual Indian food reached my nostrils and I had to fight the urge to vomit again. One lady gestured, asking if I'd like some of their meal. I declined as politely as I could, my hands in prayer position.

At last, exhausted, I dropped off to sleep. I woke up at one point, bleary-eyed, and thought I must be hallucinating.

From amid the fuzzy crowds of people on the platform there appeared, like a vision, a massive lumbering white cow strolling majestically through the rabble. Everyone made space for Her Majesty as she sauntered by. I really was on another planet.

'Thank goodness my suffering's nearly over,' I told Alexandra wryly. 'I can't wait to get onto my bunk and stretch out my body in my sleeping bag.'

Another disappointment was on its way.

I was on the top bunk and the space below the bottom bunk used for storing baggage was full. The porter looked at me, hoisted my baggage up onto the top bunk, shrugged his shoulders and disappeared, leaving me in the carriage, the only westerner there. Vijay appeared from the hubbub of people in the narrow aisle.

'I'm sorry, Jen, I couldn't get everyone's bunks located together.'

'Don't worry about me, Vijay. All I want to do is get off to sleep,' I said, unable to stifle a yawn and rubbing at my scratchy eyes.

'Here, you must be drinking this, you need to be staying hydrated.' He handed me a large bottle of water and a sachet of hydration powder. 'I'm in carriage B, bunk 3 if you'll be needing me Jen.'

He disappeared down the corridor.

I squirmed around in the tight space on the top bunk and managed to extract my sleeping bag and pillow from my case. Although my luggage occupied one-third of the space, I had just enough room to stretch out my body. I mused that the view of my bunk from outside must look funny. A pair of feet, clad in pink flowery socks, sticking off the corner of the bunk poking out from behind the curtain. I drank my re-hydration drink and my stomach spasms eased.

As I snuggled down into my sleeping bag and closed my eyes, the refrain of, 'chai, chai, chai,' reached my ears. The chai wallahs made their way through the carriages selling their brew. Any other time I would have enjoyed listening to that melody, but as they drew closer the sweet aroma reached my nostrils and I heaved again. Next came the vendors selling snacks, and I grabbed my nostrils to ward off the pong of spicy rice and beans.

The long whistle sounded and the train chugged out of the station. I was enjoying the gentle rocking motion of the carriage, and drifting off to sleep, when my curtain was wrenched open. I propelled the top half of my body upwards to sitting. An elderly Indian man stood staring at me. In an instant I recognised his abrasive demeanour as he waved his arms, indicating I should get out of my bunk, and spouting at me in his own language.

I took a huge intake of breath. 'Go away,' I bellowed in Hindi, pointing my finger at him and hoped my face displayed the anger coursing in my veins. The words I'd memorised for just this type of situation had the desired effect. He chuntered something I didn't understand before jerking the fabric closed again. I peeped out from behind my curtain to see him disappearing down the corridor, looking for someone else to annoy.

Just before I dropped off to sleep I thought of the next stop on our itinerary and wondered what on earth was going to happen next. The train thundered on through the night to its destination.

Calcutta. The City of Joy.

29

We arrived in Calcutta the following morning and I felt like a new woman, with thoughts of Varanasi station and Delhi Belly in the dim and distant past. I'd slept well with no more disturbances. The whole carriage had heard me roaring at my unwelcome visitor and that warning was enough to keep any other troublemakers at bay.

'He was a jolly lucky chap. You should never mess with a Geordie in any circumstances. But messing with a Geordie suffering with Delhi Belly is tantamount to taking your life in your hands,' said Alexandra when I told her of my altercation.

As we headed for the heart of Calcutta on the minibus, I was pleasantly surprised; wide roads carrying free-flowing traffic; large open green spaces and parks where men in whites played cricket; modern buildings and high-rise flats; white uniformed policemen; a huge horse-racing track. At one major junction where our bus came to a halt in the traffic, I could have sworn we were in London.

We checked into our hotel and had two hours to freshen up before sightseeing. I headed straight for a much needed shower, discarding the clothes I'd been wearing during my close contact with the filthy floor of the train station. I laundered my gear whilst I was in the shower, stamping on the soapy clothing while the hot water cascaded over me.

Our first stop was to be The Victoria Memorial, a building dedicated to Queen Victoria and inaugurated in 1921. For the first time since Rishikesh, Derek and Betty were late to board the minibus at the pre-arranged time. The engine ticked over. Five minutes passed. Ten minutes passed. When we'd been waiting for twenty minutes, Betty appeared running from the hotel door. She was screaming something, her red face blotched and contorted.

'What the hell's happened?' Ivan shouted, and we all jumped from our seats at the sight of her and pounded down the bus steps to the road.

'Derek's gone missing,' she shrieked. 'I don't know where he is. He was in the room one minute. I went to the bathroom and when I came out, he'd gone.'

The hysteria in her voice rose with each word, the veins stood out on her neck as she clenched and unclenched her fists. Ivan took hold of her shoulders and spoke in his quiet, reassuring tone.

'Calm down now Betty, he's probably checking out the gym facilities in the hotel.'

'No, no.' She shook her head wildly and gasped in between large intakes of breath. 'The reception staff said they saw him leaving the hotel about half an hour ago.'

'It's possible he's just looking around the back of the building,' said Alexandra.

Betty's eyes widened, and the white showed around the whole of the iris. She grabbed onto Ivan in a frenzy.

'You don't understand,' she yelled. 'Derek's in the early stages of Alzheimer's. This trip to India is our last chance to see a country he's wanted to visit for years. But I should never have agreed to us coming here.'

For a moment I was in shock, then everything fell into place. The mood swings, the confusion, the lack of a sense of direction, the staring into space and the constant turning up late at group meeting times. The astonishment was replaced with a sense of guilt when I recollected our altercation in Rishikesh when everyone felt Derek and Betty had been late once too often. Why on earth had they not told everyone?

Then I remembered the secret I was keeping and understood how skilled a person can become at pretence.

Vijay took control of the situation. 'We'll split up into groups of two and be checking the streets in the immediate area. Make sure you're all having the hotel address. Swap mobile numbers.' He spoke quickly. 'Betty, please be waiting here, he may be returning at any minute.'

I looked into her terrified eyes. 'We've got this, Betty. He can't have gone far. We'll find him.'

Alexandra and I, Fraser and Ivan and Summer and Charlie headed off in different directions while Vijay spoke into his mobile to the local police.

The streets, as we'd become accustomed to, were jammed solid with people, traffic and animals. As Alexandra and I jogged through the passages and alleyways, our eyes scoured the crowds for the familiar blue baseball cap. We turned corner after corner. The faces blurred into one as we asked again and again, desperate for a sighting of Derek.

'Look, there's the sign for the bazaar, let's head in that direction,' shouted Alexandra. I skipped after her and we sprinted across the road between the honking, hooting traffic.

'Let's ask this guy.' I raced up to the man sitting on his rickshaw waiting for customers and repeated my question.

I'd gotten so used to the quick replies of 'no' that he took me aback when he spoke a long sentence, nodding his head. I didn't understand a word of it. It was just one prolonged babble of unfamiliar sounds.

'I not understand.' I spoke the Hindi words slowly. 'Please slow.'

He spoke again, gesticulating to his right. An understanding of directions was one chapter in my language course, and straining my ears to listen to every syllable I could understand some words.

Thankful, we nodded, 'Namaste.'

'Howay Alexandra, he said he saw him walking up that long street on the right.'

We sprinted over the road and entered the street the rickshaw owner had pointed out. Jumping around people we forged ahead, approaching a busy roundabout when Alexandra shouted, 'There he is, Jen. I've just spotted his cap.'

As we got closer, I could see he was in a daze. He stood on the pavement staring at the chaos of the roundabout, looking this way and that, not knowing which way to turn.

'Derek, Derek,' Alexandra shouted. He turned and recognised us and the confusion in his eyes cleared.

We ran up to him and the three of us stood hugging for a moment.

Alexandra rang Betty first. I could hear her excited words of relief from the phone even though it was jammed to Alexandra's ear, as she explained Derek was fine. Then we rang the others to call off the search.

'Howay Derek, let's get you back to Betty,' I said.

Now the three of us were lost, but I said a private thank

you to Martin who had bought the language course for me. How valuable that present had turned out to be. I knew with a few Hindi direction words under my belt we'd find our way back to the hotel.

* * *

'HOW CAN we ever thank you all?' Betty stood, arms akimbo, in the aisle of the bus.

'There's no need for thanks, Betty. We've got to look out for each other. If you need help from any of us, please let us know.' Summer spoke for all of us and we each nodded in agreement. We'd made a pact to keep an eye on Derek for the rest of the trip. Calm had been restored, and we set off towards The Victoria Memorial, each lost in our own thoughts.

I mused that Betty wasn't the downtrodden little woman I'd imagined her to be. She was neither needy nor weak, but a very strong woman indeed. It was also clear she loved Derek very much. I'd been so wrong about both of them.

I'd chosen a seat next to Ivan and together we flicked through his guidebook. He told how the marble memorial, now a museum and tourist attraction, was dedicated to the memory of Queen Victoria. It had been financed by the Princes and ordinary people of India along with the British government.

'There's twenty-five galleries.' He counted a few of them off on his fingers, his eyes shining with the anticipation of our visit. 'There's the portrait gallery, the armoury gallery, the sculpture gallery and the book gallery.'

'Eeeh, that sounds great, Ivan. I'm a book lover myself.'

'Well, you'll love seeing some of the rare illustrated works of William Shakespeare, or the Rubaiyat by Omar

Khayyam.' Ivan's love of history shone through as he talked, and it rubbed off on me. I'd been apathetic about visiting the memorial but maybe I'd learn something interesting if I tagged alongside him.

After the tension of the events that morning it was a welcome relief to wander through the cool, spacious halls of the museum. This time, instead of splitting into smaller groups, we all meandered from room to room in unison. It was as if there was a collective unspoken need for us to band together and protect one another. Ivan led us through the halls and his impressive knowledge of the times of British rule in India and the period of the British Raj held everyone's interest. He had a real talent for teaching, becoming animated with eyes that shone with pleasure as he spoke.

After lunch an easy, calm mood hung over the group and we boarded the minibus for our next destination, the Kalighat Temple. The light was becoming dim as we approached the vicinity of the mandir. The whole area was one huge orgy of rainbow-coloured resplendence. The complex was busy and Vijay warned us more than once to take care with our belongings. Once inside the building, the colours took on even more saturation in the dim light. The scene was like something from an Indiana Jones film.

'Eeeh, Fraser man.' He lowered his camera to look at me. 'You can't take photos here.'

'Och aye, we can.' He took a shot of a statue of the monkey god, Hanuman. 'We're allowed to photograph in this area.'

'Fantastic,' I said. 'I must have misunderstood.' I took a quick shot of two men surrounded by garlands of crimson and saffron flowers.

Just as I raised my camera to my eye to frame another shot I heard a shout. As I dropped my hands, I saw the biggest policeman I've ever seen, striding towards me, wielding a huge wooden stick. For a split second I wondered what the conditions would be like in an Indian jail. He towered over me with an angry look in his eyes.

'No Photos,' he warned with a menacing tone.

I was mortified. Everyone was staring at me, the idiot Westerner taking photos in a prohibited area. All I could force from my lips was, 'sorry.'

My face must have shown my horror as the policeman gave me one final threatening glare, turned on his heel and strode away.

'Bloody hell, Fraser,' I said. 'You nearly got me incarcerated.'

He looked at me, shamefaced. I shook my head in exasperation. But I couldn't be mad at him for long.

* * *

VIJAY LED us to the inner temple where the statue of Kali resided, and I was agog at the scene. There was shouting, chanting, praying and a great deal of excitement in the air. A chaotic spectacle in a small crowded space. The atmosphere was electric and the hairs on the back of my neck stood up. There were bells ringing and a very strong, but pleasant, smell of incense. On the wall behind where I stood was a large bank of bells of diverse shapes and sizes in rows, rusted and ancient. The light was dim with a slight haze from the fire and burning incense.

The crowd pushed, shoved and jostled for position. There were two men raised on steps suspended above everyone hanging out over the top of the throng. They held onto ropes fixed to the wall with one hand, whilst they shouted and took donations of money from the melee. I stood at the back on tiptoes, craning my neck to catch sight of what everyone was so desperate to touch. I felt myself being pulled forward into the scrum. As I was being pushed, from behind someone took their opportunity to have a quick grope, and an anonymous hand squeezed my left breast. It was too busy to catch the perpetrator and then I stood in front of the object of everyone's devotion. The idol of the Goddess Kali. She had four arms, deep ocean blue skin and raging red eyes. Her mouth was formed into a vicious roar from which protruded a long, lolling, blood-red tongue. Around her neck hung a necklace of skulls and she wore a skirt made of severed human arms.

'Kali is being known sometimes as a Goddess of chaos; she embodies elements which cannot be controlled. Yet she is also an expression of a mother's protective love for her children; the feminine power will be rising up to attack anything or anyone who attacks her babies,' said Vijay.

On the floor in front of the goddess was a large bowl filled with dark red flowers and oil with a flame burning in the middle. The cloying aroma of the incense was intense, and the flame glowed in the subdued lighting. Animated people crowded around worshipping Kali in heightened emotional states; they prayed and chanted; hands in prayer position; the voices and strange words mingling together and adding to the dim, glowing, eerie atmosphere. The next instant a stranger's hands pulled me back out of the crowd. I was sweating, mesmerised by what I'd experienced.

On our way out of the inner temple we passed by a section of the room enclosed by a cage. The white tiled walls were splattered with blood.

'Every day at the temple live animal sacrifices are taking place. Goats and bullocks are being beheaded, skinned and disembowelled,' said Vijay.

The hairs on the back of my neck stood up again, and I felt queasy.

Once outside the temple it took a while for me to still my beating heart. I couldn't believe what I'd just been a part of. I could still see the scenes of fervour, hear the passionate sounds and remember the potent smell of that eerie place. So much intensity, hysteria and otherworldliness concentrated into a tiny space. I'd never experienced such a complete sensory overload.

Before dropping off to sleep that night I reflected on the events of the day. A morning of high tension; followed by an afternoon at the very cultured and genteel memorial; then to finish with, a visit to the most bizarre, crazy, mad, scary place I'd ever been to in my life.

Such a day could only transpire in India.

30

We were to visit Mother Teresa's Home in Calcutta before leaving in the afternoon by minibus to take the three-hour drive to Sundarbans. The biggest tiger reserve in the world.

We stepped from the coach in front of the white building, which at one time had been a Hindu temple. I gazed up at the blue painted sign above the door which read, "Mother Teresa's Home For the Dying Destitute". Vijay had given us the history of the home on the minibus. Mother Teresa had founded the free hospice on her forty-second birthday. Homeless people were brought to the home and instead of dying on the streets were cared for by the Missionaries of Charity. People were given the opportunity to pass on with dignity, according to their faith.

A sister dressed in a white sari with a blue border greeted us at the door and showed us into the vestibule. The peace and quiet of the interior was a welcome relief after the racket of the Calcutta streets. From the moment I walked through the entrance and saw the large picture of a smiling Mother Teresa, I sensed the spiritual atmosphere. The sister took us to the room housing the Mother's tomb where a visitor was kneeling in prayer. My breath caught at the simplistic beauty as we stepped through the door. On the top of the white marble tomb, spelled out in deep orange marigold petals, were the words, *Love until it hurts*.

I glanced at Alexandra, noticing the tears glistening in her eyes. We lingered a while in silence.

We followed the sister to the spartan room where Mother Teresa had lived and died. Then she took us to the small museum housing personal articles including her sandals, sweater and the Nobel Peace Prize awarded to her in 1979.

We'd gathered by the entrance door, each engaged in a private moment of introspection before leaving, when a door from the inner part of the building creaked open. We turned. Inch by inch, painfully emerging from within shuffled a man dressed in dark blue pyjamas. His skin hung loosely from his face in folds, his bones visible through the paper-thin skin on his arms and hands. His tortured staring eyes appeared too big for his bony face. He garbled something at the sister as he scuffed in half steps, bent over from the waist, further into the room. The sister reacted and, gently taking his arm, guided him through the door where a volunteer waited to steer him back inside. We all froze at the heart-wrenching sight of the poor man who seemed to be close to the end of his life.

'Oh that poor dear soul,' murmured Summer.

The sister whispered, 'He'll be comforted and well looked after at the end.' She paused. 'He has only a little time left. He has terminal kidney cancer.'

The shock of her last few words exploded in my head. I stepped back, trying to create space, hoping to process my thoughts. A blast of icy coldness radiated out from my core. I shivered. Everyone turned to stare.

'Jen, are you okay?' Alexandra sounded scared.

My mouth opened and closed searching for unformed words. I didn't know where to look, my eyes darted back and forth. I blinked over and over as I tried to make sense of what I'd heard.

'Jen, please speak to me.' Alexandra's voice was a distant echo.

I couldn't talk and swallowed, gulping in gasps of air, trying to dispel the hard aching rising up in my throat.

I ran.

Propelling myself through the door, I sprang into the glaring white light of the street. Alexandra followed close behind. As I pounded down the steps Alexandra, taking two at a time, caught up and grabbed my arm stopping me in my tracks. Without saying a word, she pulled me down on the bottom step. We sat in silence. Eventually she spoke.

'Something's very wrong, Jen. I want to help you. Please tell me. Trust me.'

I turned to her and spoke the words I never believed I could bring myself to utter to anyone on this trip. My voice was a whisper.

'I have kidney cancer.'

Her head jerked backwards. The shock in her eyes flickered. She wrapped her arms around me. Neither of us could speak. The others had followed and now stood behind. They watched helplessly as we hugged, our bodies swaying from side to side.

As we sat on the steps outside Mother Teresa's home, I was transported back to that fateful moment when the Consultant told me I had a life-threatening illness. Alexandra listened in silence as I related the events leading up to my arrival in India. As I spoke, hopelessness latched onto me. It pressed persistent on my skull before creeping over my shoulders and inching its way down to my feet. It made my skin crawl. On its journey it gnawed at the hope and determination I'd fought so hard to cultivate. I shrugged, shaking my head as I looked at the floor, feeling hollowed out. I was powerless. Defeated. My bravado melted away with each twist of my hands.

What am I doing here? My thoughts flitted around like black bats in a murky cave. *What if the cancer's spread to my lungs?* Mania was surfacing. *There's nothing I can do, it's futile. Maybe my time is over. Maybe I have to accept it. Maybe I'm going to die.* That final thought obliterated everything. Circumstances had dictated that I came face to face with the enemy. Fear had found a chink in my armour and it had won. I wasn't strong enough. I couldn't trust myself to fight on and win. It was time to surrender.

'I can't carry on with this trip.' My voice cracked. 'It's time for me to go home.'

Alexandra took me by the shoulders and looked into my eyes.

'But you've been doing jolly marvellous. You can't give in to it now. And we can help you.' She pointed to the rest of the group who had retreated to the top of the steps.

But I'd made up my mind. All I wanted now was to get away from the crowds and the noise surrounding us. I needed to get to my hotel room and arrange my flight home to Heathrow.

* * *

THE ATMOSPHERE on the minibus during the journey back to the hotel was subdued. I'd given Alexandra permission to fill the group in on the reason for my meltdown. There was a two-hour break to allow everyone to pack their belongings before the bus left for Sundarbans. I'd be able to pick up a flight home that evening. We hugged in the hotel car park and said forlorn goodbyes, promising to keep in touch. Everyone looked devastated and, not being able to cope with the mixture of pity and disappointment in their eyes, I beat a hasty retreat up to my room where I crumbled, unable to stem the tide of tears as a picture of the guy in the blue pyjamas flashed in front of my eyes. Exhausted, I flopped onto the bed and drifted into a merciful slumber.

* * *

A LIGHT TAPPING on the door woke me and a glance at the bedside clock confirmed I'd only been asleep for around half an hour. It was Derek and Betty.

'We want you to have this.' Derek handed over something wrapped in delicate tissue wrapping paper. I opened it with care. It was one of the elegant wall hangings I'd been admiring at the silk factory but had missed out on the opportunity to buy. With my hands forming a steeple and pressed to my lips, I said, 'Oh Derek, I can't accept this.'

'Please take it with our blessing,' smiled Betty. 'If it wasn't for you, Derek would have been halfway back to Delhi by now.' Each of us chuckled. We wished each other good luck, and I waved them off down the corridor.

Halfway through packing, there was another knock, this time louder. It could only be Fraser.

'Och aye, it's room service, madam. I've brought the bhang lassi you ordered.' He wanted to say a final goodbye and hugged me so hard it took my breath away. 'When ye've recovered from the surgery ye've got te come up te Glasgow and I'll finish teaching ye those exercises, hen.'

I looked deep into the fathomless, intense eyes of the man who, without knowing, had caused me to question my marriage. Those eyes had the power to spark thoughts so unsettling it made my heart ache.

Summer and Charlie came to say goodbye together. I could sense the bond which had grown between them.

'Your name is first on the list for my workshop at the Yoga Show in October,' said Summer.

I grinned as they left my room holding hands. I took pleasure in their happiness.

'Can I come in?' I opened the door wider for Ivan.

'There's something I want to tell you. Now, five years ago I was diagnosed with prostate cancer.' The surprise must have shown on my face. 'What I've come to say is that they gave me the all-clear after surgery.' He sat on the chair. 'Tell me.' He paused. 'Do I look infirm?'

A vision of a grey haired, bespectacled, deadly Ninja flashed before my eyes. 'No Ivan, you're a picture of health.'

'Yes, I am,' he said. 'And so are you going to be when you've had your treatment. One of the most important things is to stay positive.'

We talked for fifteen minutes and he told me of his terror when he was first diagnosed. It startled me that his feelings mirrored my own. When we said our goodbyes, I was more optimistic as I thought how well he had won his battle. Then it was time to say goodbye to Alexandra.

'I'm jolly well going to miss your Geordie accent.' Tears welled in her eyes.

Embracing, we arranged to meet up as soon as possible at home. A strong friendship had grown between us which we both knew would prevail. Vijay came to say goodbye with the Calcutta to Heathrow flight times. There were two flights leaving that evening, and I'd be able to get a seat. He thanked me for being a great group member, and he smiled when I congratulated him on his professional leadership and inspired presentation of his wonderful country.

Feeling numb and resigned to ending my trip early, I switched on my laptop. I was powerless over the present. Unable to guess at the future. I'd failed.

Ping, ping, ping, piiiiing.

Hi Love, your blog's getting so popular. You had over three and a half thousand followers from all over the world the last time I looked. There's even someone in Bolivia following you. Can't believe my wife is becoming a worldwide internet star! Looks like India is agreeing with you. The Head at school loves your photos of the ladies performing their Morning Puja. She thinks you have a talent for evoking stories with your photos and delving beneath the veneer of the subject and revealing their emotions. I'm missing you so much, Jen. The house is empty without you. All my love. Martin xx

Message after message popped up on the screen. Priti said my portrayal of India delighted her and her parents; and strangers praised my writing prowess, saying they were looking forward to my next blog. There were two private message notifications. Without looking I knew the identity of one of the senders. Don't click the link, Jen. Poisoned messages are the last thing you need right now. But I had no choice. Maybe the second message was important. Click.

Dear Jennifer, I'm pleased to invite you to attend an interview for the post of Cruise Ship Photographer.

I felt an unrestrained smile spread across my face as I took in the rest of the message. The interview date was one week after my return home from India. A swelling rose in my chest. I tingled with pleasure. What was that feeling? I felt valued, cherished. I took a deep breath to centre myself in the sensation. Ready for anything that Marra could throw at me. Click.

> *Martin is such a good liar. Anyone reading his comments would believe he was in love with you. Well, we both know the truth about that. Don't we?*

No Pat, I won't reply. I've wasted enough time on your vile game. Time to read one last comment before finishing my packing for my flight to Heathrow.

> *Hello Jen, my name is Henrietta and I just wanted you to know how much your blog has changed my life. I admire your spirit, passion and drive and it makes my day when I can lose myself in your words and images. I'm bedridden you see, and when I read your blog I can escape the confines of these four walls. I especially love wildlife and can't wait to read about your adventure in Sundarbans.*

My hand flew to my mouth at the same time as the sharp intake of breath. I swung round, wide-eyed in the direction of the clock. Ten minutes to three. I jumped off the bed like a scalded cat and began tearing around the room, shoving my belongings into my bag. Pulling open the door I darted down the corridor towards the lift and jabbed at the buttons.

The descent from the third floor was agonisingly slow and when I reached the bottom floor, the door inched and creaked open. Not waiting for it to open wide I squeezed through, pulling my case after me and galloped towards the hotel exit then into the car park. I was panting hard, swivelling my body round on the spot. The minibus had gone. I was on the verge of tears when I heard a horn and the bus appeared from around the corner by the side of the hotel. Frantic, I waved and jumped; the driver saw me and headed in my direction. The doors opened with a hydraulic swish and I bounced up the steps to be greeted by eight grinning faces. As I made my way to the empty seat next to Alexandra, Fraser shouted, 'Hey lassie, can ye make sure yer on time for the minibus in future.'

31

It was a three-hour journey to Sundarbans in West Bengal where we'd spend two days hunting for the elusive Royal Bengal Tiger. It would be our final destination before we returned to Calcutta for the flight back to Heathrow. As we drew near, Vijay updated us on the environment of the area.

'We're about to be visiting the world's largest delta which is enclosed by thick mangrove forest and huge saline mud flats. Sundarbans, it is being considered one of the natural wonders of the world. It is forming where the three rivers Ganga, Brahmaputra and Meghna are joining together and flowing out into the Bay of Bengal. This area is home to a wide variety of wildlife, including about two hundred and seventy Royal Bengal tigers. The tigers are known to be man-eaters, mainly because of the lack of other suitable prey in the area. This is a place where villagers, whose livelihood often depends on fishing, must be alert at all times.'

There were exclamations of shock when he announced, 'There are an average of forty maulings a year here.'

And I'd been paranoid about being bitten by mosquitoes!

I was certainly dressed for the occasion; mosquito-repellent impregnated shirt buttoned up at the neck, with the collar turned up; sleeves buttoned at wrists; mosquito-repellent impregnated cargo pants tucked into socks; wide brimmed mosquito-repellent hat, and any exposed parts of my person covered in high strength mosquito-repellent spray. It was the hottest place we'd been and, as I was hot and sticky, I rolled up my shirt sleeves. I rolled them down again when I entered my accommodation and saw the mosquito net around my bed.

We were housed in individual cosy, rustic bungalow style huts, with walls of baked mud and roofs of straw. The bungalows were scattered around small ponds containing moss coloured water and lotus blossoms. Walkways between the rooms wound their way through lush, leafy trees and a variety of vibrant tangerine, rosy red, lemon and violet flowers and plants. There was a lingering brackish, salty smell which fused with the heady sweet bouquet of jasmine. The aromas merged with a woody background scent which I could taste as I licked my dry lips. A dog bark echoed somewhere in the distance. A harmless insect buzzed by my face. This was pure relaxation, an oasis of calm – and just what I needed after my catastrophe at Mother Teresa's.

I thought about how I needed to be kind with myself – to the real me that was awakening day by day in India.

It came in a flash. I was my own worst enemy. I'd punched myself in the face day after day for as long as I could remember. I'd landed killer blows that had laid me flat out on the canvas for much of my adult life. It had been a mistake to bury my secret. I'd had opportunities to share my heartache and receive support, but had rebutted the intimacy of Alexandra's friendship. The walls I'd built didn't protect me. They segregated me. Turned me into an island. A vision swam before my eyes of me, squirming in pain, writhing on the floor. Now, sitting alone, I could swear I heard my Mam and Dad's voices, loud and clear, telling me, 'Get back up again wor Jen.'

* * *

ANY WORRIES I'd nurtured that my travelling friends would somehow behave differently towards me were unfounded. During evening meal, it was business as usual. Betty attended to Derek's needs, pouring his chai for him; Charlie cosied up to Summer, his arm around her shoulder, gazing into her eyes as they chatted; Ivan flicked through the Sundarbans chapter of his guidebook; Alexandra busied herself helping Vijay to order everyone's food and Fraser and I sat close enough that our bodies touched

'What did you order, Derek?' I asked.

'The tangra fish,' he said. His eyes were bright, and he was alert. Derek was having a good day, and I was happy for him and Betty.

'Me too, I've never had freshwater catfish fish before,' I said.

'Do you think we'll spot a Royal Bengal Tiger on our explorations tomorrow?' I asked everyone. Excitement animated the faces, and eyes sparkled in the subdued lighting at the mention of the endangered species.

'They're very elusive they are, but fingers crossed, we may be lucky. Keep your camera at the ready, Jen,' answered Ivan in his lilting Welsh accent.

I rolled the delicate flakes of fish around on my tongue,

savouring the hint of mustard, tomato, ginger and freshly ground spices infused into the traditional Bengali fish curry. We had a full day of wildlife spotting from a boat on the river the following day. A fish dish which caressed my taste buds with a mild heat, and which would also be light on my stomach was the perfect choice.

'I can be recommending the rasgulla for your dessert, Jen. It's being spongy, and juicy and made from Indian cottage cheese. Don't be having too many though or you'll be sinking our boat tomorrow,' said Vijay with a wink at the others.

My teeth sank into the white, squishy, sponge dumpling. Rose water, sugar and cardamom syrup squirted around my mouth, coating my tongue as a delicate aroma of cheese reached my nostrils. The sponge squeaked as I chewed languidly, a sense of tranquillity settling over me. The atmosphere was as light as the curried fish on the menu.

* * *

COUGHING and choking from emptying a full canister of insect repellent into my room, I lay counting the dead mosquitos on top of the net surrounding my bed. The lights went out, and I was enveloped in an oppressive barrier of darkness. I remembered that the electricity switched off at a certain time each night. The wall of black heightened my senses and amplified the ambient sounds. I pulled the bedclothes up tight against my chin and resolved not to get out of bed under any circumstances until daylight.

* * *

I SETTLED into my seat on the boat which would carry us around the waterways of the largest tiger reserve in the world as Vijay introduced us to our guide for the day; a nice young man who was lacking in one important job-related skill. His pronunciation of the English language was indecipherable.

Still, as we sailed on the river, our guide attempted to educate us about the flora and fauna of the area; the many and varied species of wildlife there; along with detailed explanations surrounding the ecosystems and plant life.

'What's that man doing?' Betty pointed out someone standing with his back to us on the prow of his tiny little boat. His hands held at waist level in front.

'Pissing,' the guide said, and I looked around at everyone who grimaced at his use of such a vulgar word.

An hour later our guide became animated and shouted, 'Piss, piss.'

I turned my gaze in the direction of his outstretched arm and saw fish, leaping out of the water, and dropping back in with a splash.

We sailed around the mangrove forests seeking out the wildlife: red fiddler crabs waved their enlarged claws trying to attract a mate; bright iridescent blue and orange kingfishers perched on overhanging branches, their unflinching gaze searching the moving water for an unwary and unlucky fish to swim by; water monitor lizards broke the surface of the river leaving a wake behind them, and macaque monkeys leapt, flying from tree to tree. We stopped for a lunch of dosas and chutneys at a wildlife sanctuary where deer and monkeys roamed free.

'Look after yer backpack, Charlie.' Fraser's warning came just in time. A monkey had crept up behind Charlie as he stood reading the information board about the ecosystem of Sundarbans and was undoing his backpack fastenings, its agile fingers as accomplished as any pick-pocket in Delhi or Calcutta.

We continued the boat ride in the afternoon viewing crocodiles squirm onto the mud-banks to rest in the sun. I floated through a wonderful reverie, reminiscing about all the amazing people I'd met; a new way of life I'd witnessed; events I'd watched and taken part in, and emotions I'd experienced. But most of all I felt grateful for sharing the experiences with the group of people who had become my friends. The boat trip ended in the most spectacular fashion when Vijay shouted, 'Tiger.' He gesticulated. 'In the water, there.'

Just that one word had everyone scrambling to the prow of the boat, cameras at the ready. In front of us with head bobbing up and down and leaving a tiny wake behind in the water was a huge Royal Bengal tiger. I held my breath, not believing our luck as I stared through my camera, the lens extended to its limit. I resisted the temptation to fire off frames at random. My finger hovered on the shutter button as the magnificent animal swam across the prow of our boat towards the opposite shore. It reached land and took one huge leap. I heard the satisfying click of my camera as I released the shutter at the decisive moment. I thought of Henrietta, in her bedroom somewhere in the world. *That one's for you, Henrietta. You'll never know how you've helped me.* The tiger landed on all fours on the mud flat and darted to the cover of the mangrove trees, the bright orange and brown markings just visible. Before disappearing out of sight in the dense forest, the tiger stopped, turned and looked back at us. It licked its lips, and I was grateful for the protection of the boat. Then it was gone. Spontaneous cheering, laughing and whooping filled the air. The rare sighting we'd witnessed had pumped everyone up with excitement. We'd been very fortunate indeed.

* * *

As nightfall arrived and our boat docked to a deep gold sunset backdrop, the local people invited us to a Cultural Evening they had arranged for us. A pang of guilt struck me. One of the village elders showed us to the best seats to watch the show as villagers were relegated to seated areas behind the performers.

'No, no,' I resisted. 'You should have a front-row seat to watch your children.'

'Please,' she said, 'the children have prepared this performance for our visitors. They're so excited to be singing and dancing for you. Please take these seats.'

The children, in ethnic costumes, danced and acted out scenes depicting life in Sundarbans. At the end of the show, tears pricked the back of my eyelids. I sang along when they led the whole audience in a rousing rendition of the song, 'We Shall Overcome'.

I'd picked up a bottle of Indian dark rum in Calcutta and now was the perfect time to share it, as we gathered around the communal seating area.

'This is jolly moreish,' said Alexandra as she drained her glass of the smooth tasting alcohol, topping it up again from the bottle.

Talk turned to regional accents and Charlie, slurring his words said, 'C'mon Jen, educate Vijay in some of your Geordie vernacular.'

'Hoya Hama Awa Hea,' I enunciated, and then followed up with 'Pitta patta went the watta doon the moontin side' before finishing with, 'Wey aye man pet, howay bonny lad.'

Vijay looked at me, his expression blank, and so did everyone else in the group. I knew in an instant how our guide must have felt on the boat earlier in the day.

* * *

I STROLLED BACK to my room arm in arm between Alexandra and Fraser, the heat from the rum adding to the inner glow dancing inside me after enjoying such a relaxing day.

We reached Alexandra's room first. 'Good night,' she said, slurring her words and hugging us both with a strength which belied her slim frame.

Then there was only Fraser and I. The chill in the night air made me shiver. Fraser put his arm around my shoulder, pulling me close as we sauntered on. I relaxed against the side of his body, grateful for warmth. The bushes and plants hugging the walkways pulsated with spots of light from fireflies which flew in front of us as we ambled. Fraser reached down to his side and swept his hand through the lotus blossom plant edging the path. He held his hand, now covered with blinking fireflies, in front of my face. I watched, enthralled, until the lights faded. We stopped and turned to face one another at his room door. I didn't want to look into his eyes. I knew there was danger there. He placed his hand under my chin and guided my face upwards until I had no choice. The question burning in the ocean blue depths was unmistakable. Holding me prisoner with his gaze, he turned the handle, and the door edged open.

'Would ye like to come in, Jen?' he whispered.

I wrenched my eyes from his to stare at the ground, unlocking the chains. A picture of Martin swam in front of me, and I knew I had to go home to the man I loved without any regrets.

I looked up again and in the illumination of the wall light, I recognised resignation in Fraser's eyes.

'No thanks Fraser, I'm so tired.'

I kissed him gently on the cheek and strolled away to the soft click of his room door closing.

32

Our final day in India.

It was an early bleary-eyed start for the drive from Sundarbans back to Calcutta, where we had free time to embark on our final exploration of the city. That night we were to meet for our last group evening meal before our flight to Heathrow on the following morning. Betty had accepted the offer for Ivan to sit with Derek on the bus journey. It was a simple gesture from Ivan, but the significance for Betty was huge. It bestowed a few hours' respite from the intensity of her constant caring role. Her ponytail jiggled and her body swayed on the seat next to me with the movement of the vehicle, as we bumped and jolted over uneven dirt tracks. Everyday life in rural India flashed by the bus window as we chatted.

'He was diagnosed three months ago with Alzheimer's. Kept forgetting what he was saying halfway through sentences. Then at times he couldn't understand how to use the television remote. But it was the mood swings and changes in his behaviour which convinced us to get him tested. It's breaking my heart, Jen. Derek's such a lovely man; kind, loving and intelligent. His organisation voted him top Hotel General Manager in the company five years running. And now this wicked disease is taking him from me. Sometimes I can't bear it. Sometimes I feel so helpless. But I love him so much and that's where I find my strength.'

Tears pooled in her eyes and spilled over, dripping from her cheekbones. I put my arm around her shoulder and she rested against me, our bodies rocking back and forth in motion with the bus.

'You're an inspiration to me, Betty,' I said.

Betty would never give up on Derek, and I knew I would never give up on my marriage, either. But both Martin and I needed to change. India had shown me that we weren't the same people anymore.

'Derek and I were so sorry to hear about your illness.'

'Thanks Betty. Now it's out in the open I can be myself. It's such a relief not having to hide myself away.'

'Yes Jen, I know how you feel.'

* * *

ONCE SETTLED into our Calcutta hotel, we met in reception for a short meeting.

'I'm going to find an Ayurvedic massage parlour. Do any of you other ladies fancy it?' said Summer.

'What's that? It sounds rather exotic,' replied Alexandra.

'We're all made up of five elements; earth, space, air, fire and water. These combine into three forces called doshas within each of our bodies. They call the doshas vata, pitta and kapha. When they're out of balance it affects our physical and emotional health. An ayurvedic masseuse uses different massage techniques to bring our doshas back into harmony,' explained Summer.

'Count me in,' I said.

'And me,' said Alexandra.

'Derek's coming with us lads to watch the cricket, Betty. Why don't ye go with the lassies?' said Fraser.

* * *

'WHAT DID SHE SAY, JEN?' asked Alexandra.

'I think she's asking if we want to be massaged all in the same room,' I answered, struggling to recognise the Hindi words.

'Well that's okay with me,' said Summer.

'And me,' said Alexandra.

'Me too,' said Betty.

'Don't know why she's asking that but aye, let's go for it lasses,' I said.

We were in the small dingy ante room, of a building in a narrow grungy side street, somewhere in Calcutta city centre. Dim yellow tinged lighting emanated from a bulb, hanging from the ceiling on a wire. It cast a subdued glow over the room. The rough plastered wall was covered in faded paintings of ancient sages and gurus in various massaging activities.

'Golly, it looks like we're in for the real ethnic experience here ladies,' said Alexandra.

We handed over our rupees to the aged Indian lady who was trying to make herself understood.

'Krpya mera peechha karen,' the old lady said with a head wobble.

'She's telling us to follow her,' I said.

We trooped into a room which drew astonished gasps. Dominating the space were four wooden benches resembling operating tables in a hospital theatre. Suspended over the head of each table was a frame which to my nervous, blinking gaze looked like the gallows on a platform used to hang people. Attached to the frame and dangling over the concave area for resting the head was a bronze bowl with a spout facing down towards the table. In one corner of the room was a wooden cabinet with front opening doors and a hole in the top for a head to poke through. In the other was a stainless steel sink unit with a two-hob electric burner, complete with pans containing bubbling hot oil. The room smelled of exotic lotions, potions and thousands of travellers.

'Oh dear,' said Betty. 'Where are the plush beds, fluffy towels, and complimentary slippers?'

We stood side by side like prisoners awaiting execution and exchanged nervous glances.

'Off, off, off,' the old lady gestured, showing that we should remove our blouses. She could have been one of the ancient ones depicted on the wall in the ante room, with her deep-lined leathery skin and long flowing, wild grey hair.

We folded our blouses on the chairs at the side of each table.

'Off, off, off.' We removed our trousers as instructed and stood in our bras and knickers.

'Off, off, off'

She wants us to take our bloody bras off. How embarrassing. Summer's not bothered, she's got hers off already. Alexandra's swinging her bra around in the air. Betty's more hesitant, though. Wey, howay man Jen, don't be so bloody uptight. Ye've all got the same.

We stood naked apart from our knickers. I covered myself with my crossed arms.

'Well ladies, this is jolly un-British,' said Alexandra, drawing giggles.

'Off, off, off,' the old lady cackled, her mouth gaped showing her one and only tooth, edged with tinges of a red paste.

I winced. My toes curled. My face, neck and ears burned.

Poor Betty couldn't stop coughing.

At last we stood side by side like sisters in arms, naked.

'Hang on lasses, I'll just get my camera,' I said. The hysterical laughter which followed swept away any vestige of the embarrassment hanging in the air.

* * *

THE HAGGARD OLD lady clapped her hands. The door opened and four young, delicate looking women in deep purple saris swept into the room and led us to sit on the stools by each bed. With graceful hand movements my masseuse poured hot oil from a spouted silver jug over the crown of my head. The creamy, woody bouquet of sandalwood coated my skull and flowed like a hot oil slick down the length of my hair.

'Aaah, that's wonderful,' I sighed, not expecting what happened next.

With the strength of an all-in-wrestler, my masseuse yanked at my hair. She tugged it up, down and from side to side, then pounded on my skull with her fist. I heard my neck crack. She dragged the oil through my hair until it was completely saturated and finished with a slap on my head. My scalp tingled. It felt good.

'Please, bed.' She gestured to the wooden operating table, and I climbed up, flashing my tuppence. I lay on my front, flinching from the chill of the shiny dark wood on my warm skin. In her hand she held a cloth bag which exuded aromas of citronella and lemongrass. She dunked the bag into the oil heating in the pan and pressed it onto my back. The intense heat seeped into my muscles and I felt them relax. When she'd finished working on my back, she smacked the bag and rubbed my arms and legs with her hot hand. The luxurious oil soaked into my skin, reaching into my deep muscles which softened under the pressure of her palms. With rhythmic strokes she rubbed, kneaded, squeezed and tapped ensuring a full body massage while I floated away to heaven. She repeated the treatment while I lay on my back, and I wasn't the slightest bit embarrassed when she gently rubbed oil into my breasts. Then it was time for her to pour oil onto my 'third eye' in the middle of my forehead. My masseuse filled the bronze bowl which hung from the gallows and placed a cloth over my eyes. The sumptuous oil oozed onto my forehead, flowed over the back of my skull, drenched my hair and trickled into the concave hollow in the head rest.

'Please, steam bath.' She pointed to the wooden box in the corner of the room. I was like a herring in a can. Oil dripped down my body from my hair and my feet were so slippy she had to help me walk across the floor. I sat on the stool inside the box. She closed the door, leaving my head poking out of the top where she plugged any gaps with towels to stop the steam from escaping. The hose on the floor pumped steam in the tiny space and after ten minutes, when I couldn't stand the heat any longer, she opened the doors.

While the others took their turn in the steam bath, my masseuse scrubbed my body with towels to remove as much of the oil as she could.

'Please, shower,' she said, pointing to the shower room.

I allowed the warm water to cascade over me. My skin was tingling, my joints were loose, my muscles flexible, my whole body had been detoxified. My mind, body and spirit were in harmony.

* * *

'OCH LASSIES, ye'r all glowing. Betty, yer skin's so bright,' said Fraser. He glanced at me. 'Ye look beautiful.' I smiled at him, knowing there was no ulterior motive behind his compliment.

We navigated our way across the chaotic road through rickshaws, tuk-tuks and cars and arrived at the entrance to the bazaar where we were pounced upon. Dressed in a long black kaftan and small white skull cap, the stranger followed us inside. He offered in a smooth voice to direct us to the 'best bargains in the whole of Calcutta.' The bazaar was a maze, bustling and busy with shops and stalls selling all items imaginable. Voices rang out from the vendors, initially in Hindi and then in English as they saw our approach. They were relentless in their attempts to interest us in their bright, sparkly bangles, bags or sandals. We turned a corner in the maze which brought us to clothing stalls with their wares hung on the outside and around their doors. The tempting wares of the bakeries and sweet shops filled the air with a delicious sweet aroma; fabric shops displayed rainbow-coloured silks and saris. The tantalising merchandise of the silver and gold sellers twinkled and shone from behind glass-covered shelves.

We turned corner after corner and the indoor scenery changed at every turn. The warren went on and on. Downstairs to another level then upstairs to another. We strolled through areas for household items; then a dimly lit butchery for meat where the sight of live chickens packed into small cages brought a lump to my throat. As we made our way around the stone-floored indoor warren, we tried to shake off our very attentive and unwelcome guide. As he tried to direct us one way, we deliberately set off in the opposite direction. Undeterred, he stuck to us like glue, determined to get his cut from any purchases we made from the sellers he directed us to.

'We jolly well may as well give in and tell him what we want to buy. He'll save us time.' We nodded in agreement at Alexandra's suggestion.

Every seller was our best friend, delighted to see us, wide smiles and sparkling eyes. Once we stepped over the threshold into their shop, they hit us with the hard sell. The proceedings were the same each time we showed a flicker of interest; they shoved items into our hands; we're not interested we'd say; they'd bring more and more items out and a crowd would gather round to watch the action. The pressure to buy was intense. Then in one shop I saw some very nice sandalwood carved items I wanted. As I wandered nonchalantly into the shop with, what I hoped was a bored look on my face, the vendor welcomed me as a long-lost friend. He laid out his wares on the counter and I touched and looked at everything, giving the least attention to my desired sandalwood pieces. I feigned interest in other items first then picked up the one I wanted and asked, 'how much?'

'One thousand two hundred rupees,' he said.

I calculated that was around fourteen pounds and fifty pence, and a bargain.

Now was the time for me to put on my Oscar winning performance I'd practiced at home for just this precise scenario. 'How much?' I exclaimed with a shocked look on my face. I paused for effect. 'I'll give you six hundred rupees.'

People in the near vicinity heard the exchange, smelled

a competition in the air and gathered round, joining our group to watch the drama playing out before them. The vendor and I faced each other like two gunmen at a duel. He expounded the attributes of the small piece I was holding in my hand; the many hours taken to perfect the hand-carving; the high quality wood, on and on he went. He knew I was interested and was laying it on thick.

'Give me one thousand rupees,' he said.

I wrinkled my nose, said I didn't really want the item and offered seven hundred rupees with the pretence of leaving the shop. A man in the crowd, probably the vendor's best mate, beseeched me to pay the one thousand rupees. It was getting hotter, I was sweating, the crowd was getting bigger, and the pressure intensified.

'Okay, okay,' came the vendor's voice from behind me as I shuffled to the exit, 'how about nine hundred rupees?'

I decided now was the stage in the proceedings to go for the kill. 'Eight hundred rupees, and that's my final offer.' I spoke with a voice I hoped would convey finality whilst holding out my hand in an invitation to settle the deal. He extended his hand, and we shook in agreement on the final figure.

I was exhilarated. Yes, I knew it wasn't the deal of the century, but the exchange had filled me with confidence. I could barter with these skilled Indian salesmen on their own terms, and for the next couple of hours I played my part in the exchanges with vigour.

'Och hen, at least they smile while they're ripping us off,' said Fraser as he clutched a painting he'd haggled for, showing the route of the Ganges.

We strolled towards the exit doors of the bazaar with our acquisitions under our arms, cheerful but exhausted by the hard haggling. Out of the corner of my eye I caught sight of something moving under the boarded floor of one stall. A head, with long whiskers attached, popped out and bright black eyes looked up at me. In a flash I took in the sight of a thick, long pink waving tail on the other end of the black furry body.

'Rat,' I screeched.

Our new friend the guide proudly exclaimed that we should come back at night when hundreds of rats would run around the floor of the bazaar. Our slow gait instantly increased as we fled into the street.

* * *

'CHARLIE AND SUMMER, you two sit here. Ivan, why don't you sit next to Vijay. Fra...'

Alexandra stopped mid-sentence as she caught sight of me scowling at her over the top of my glasses. It was our final meal together and Alexandra was bossing everyone around again.

'Oh, sorry everyone. I'm jolly well doing it again aren't I?' She looked around, contrite. 'Let's sit anywhere shall we?' she murmured.

We all said a resounding, good natured 'Yes,' and arranged ourselves around the table for our final evening meal of the trip.

The slight melancholic mood lifted as we ate and reminisced about our time in India. The unforgettable sights, sounds and experiences which we'd all take away with us. We agreed it had been our adventure of a lifetime. Vijay gave a speech where he thanked us for showing great respect for his country and said he hoped we would return someday.

I looked around the table at the people I now called my

friends. India had woven its magic and influenced each of us; Alexandra was reigning in her controlling habits; Fraser had released a pain he'd held inside for years; Charlie and Summer were falling in love; Ivan had satisfied his hunger for historical knowledge; and Derek and Betty had accomplished the huge challenge of visiting the country they'd longed to see before it was too late. As for me. My transformation was seismic.

* * *

LATER THAT EVENING, packing my bag for the flight home felt bittersweet. I was desperate to see Martin but I didn't want this trip to end. I had time to upload a final blog from India before heading downstairs for our last drink together in the hotel bar.

Ping, ping, ping, piiiiing. The counter at the top of the screen registered four thousand one hundred and twenty nine followers as the message headers popped onto the screen. A vision of me fighting for breath, on the brink of giving up my life, stuck in a deadly current in Rishikesh swam in front of my eyes.

That was when things began to change for you. Your friends chipping together to buy you a replacement camera was a decisive moment in this transformation you've undergone. Don't focus on the illness, Jen. Focus on your family and friends. Focus on the positives. You've got an interview for a great job when you get home. If you're successful that will be the last piece in this journey of discovery jigsaw.

'Coming Alexandra,' I shouted, forgetting to log out of my blog as I jumped off the bed to open my bedroom door.

It caught her eye the minute she entered the room.

'Oh, do you have a blog? You never mentioned it.' She picked up my laptop before I could stop her.

I'd not told anyone because I'd only intended to write the blog for my ten followers. Then when it took off I hadn't trusted that my articles were good enough. Alexandra was a book editor. I hadn't wanted her laughing at my efforts. But now things were different. Alexandra was the last person who would make fun of me. Of that I was certain.

'You can have a quick look if you want,' I said gruffly.

I finished my packing as she read through my uploads. 'You've a talent for writing and photography, Jen. I jolly well love your blog.' She paused. 'What a strange name. Who's Marra?'

I flung the blouse I was folding onto the bed and wrenched the laptop from Alexandra's hand. A shiver pulsed the length of my spine and the hair lifted on the back of my neck. I glared at the screen. It was the only word I could see. It taunted and challenged, daring me to open the lid and witness the malice contained inside.

'You've gone white, Jen. What the hell's going on?'

Click.

You should have taken my advice and come home. Now you deserve to lose him. Martin's going to leave you. Yours forever, Marra x

I handed the laptop to Alexandra. Her brow puckered. With raised eyebrows and a slight shake of her head she waited for an explanation.

'I'm being trolled. It started on the day we attended the Kumbh and has been going on ever since. Malevolent messages urging me to leave the trip and fly home because, according to Marra, Martin is having an affair while I'm out here.'

'Golly Jen, that's truly awful. Do you have any idea who it might be?'

'Oh, yes. A few months ago I had a serious row with a close friend. It ended our friendship. She's a right nasty piece of work, Alexandra. I've got every faith in Martin, he wouldn't cheat on me. When I get home, I'll be facing her down with this. She's not getting away with it.' We both started as the ringing of the telephone shattered the tension in the air. 'Fraser's waiting for us in the bar?' Alexandra nodded. 'Okay Fraser, see you in a few minutes. Yes okay, will do.' I replaced the receiver. 'He wants us to pick Summer up on the way downstairs.'

* * *

'I'll be there in one moment,' shouted Summer from somewhere inside the room. Alexandra pushed on the handle and the door creaked open.

'She's in the bathroom,' said Alexandra as we stepped inside.

I flopped down to sit on the bed and turned my head to the light flickering at the edge of my sight. There on the bedside table was Summer's iPad. A message, waiting to be sent.

> *Your trip is almost over. Just like your marriage. I did try to warn you! Your good friend, Marra x*

33

I sprang from the bed and grabbed the iPad to get a closer look. My thoughts rampaged, swirling so fast I found it difficult to follow them. *I don't understand, it can't be possible. There must be a reasonable explanation.* The ringing in my ears started a second before the spots appeared before my eyes. I was light-headed and swayed back and forth. 'Jen, Jen.' Alexandra's muffled voice echoed from afar. But I couldn't speak, a sense of paralysis freezing my muscles. I handed the iPad to Alexandra, her eyebrows furrowed as her mouth dropped open with an imperceptible gasp.

'Oh, you've let yourselves ...' Summer took a step back as she took in the scene. The flush of guilt flooded her face. I knew in that second it was futile for me to cling to my desperate desire for her to be innocent, and I wanted to throw up.

'It was you. All this time. You're Marra.' I didn't recognise my own voice, it bordered on animalistic and the air in the room crackled. Alexandra strode to my side and held me by the arm. 'Why have you sought to torture me day after day? What the hell have I ever done to you?'

She recovered quickly, a forced smile stretching her lips, her tone light and breezy, 'At last you've figured it out Jen. I wondered how long it would take you. Lighten up, it was just a game. I thought you would have sussed out it was me days ago, and appreciated the joke. '

I took a step forwards and the pressure on my arm from Alexandra's grip intensified. 'Don't you give me that. It was no joke and you know it. What drove you to this, Summer?' My voice shook as my fingernails bit into my palms.

'Jealousy. That's what,' said Alexandra. 'We could all see there was chemistry between Jen and Fraser. But I've watched you, Summer. I've seen the way you look at Fraser. I've also noticed your sideways glances of spite in Jen's direction whenever you've seen them together.'

Summer's cheerful demeanour faded and her lilac hair quivered as her chin dipped to her chest. She took a deep pained breath and closed her eyes. 'Yes, I admit I have feelings for Fraser. If you hadn't been here Jen, he may have looked in my direction.'

At that instant, images flashed in front of my eyes. Summer and those coincidental appearances at times when I was alone with Fraser; the village school after the dust storm as I comforted him; that morning in Varanasi when he and I nearly lost all control during those steamy sit ups. And the way she'd glanced back at me, gloating, as she skipped arm-in-arm with Fraser down the river bank to board our country boats.

'So you hid behind a false persona. You even went so far as to choose the Geordie word for *friend* as your username to throw me off the scent. My God, I can't believe the extent of your deception. What the hell did you think you would accomplish by doling out your special brand of malice? Did you hope to get me off the scene? Did you really believe I'd take fright and run home? Well, you failed to take one thing into consideration. I have faith in my husband.' My voice rose higher with every word.

Angered now by her admission, I screamed, 'You're sick, Summer. You need to get help.'

We didn't hear the door open.

'Hey, who the hell do you think you're shouting at, Jen?' roared Charlie. He stormed over to Summer and pulled her into a hug as she broke down. Her shoulders heaved as she sobbed onto his shoulder. 'Look at what you've done. How bloody dare you? Get out now before I throw you out,' he bellowed. Alexandra handed him the iPad. He glanced at it, mystified.

'Come on Jen, Fraser's waiting downstairs,' she said and I leaned against her as she led me from the room.

* * *

'YE TOOK YER TIME. Where's Summer and Charlie?' asked Fraser as we joined him, Derek and Betty, Ivan and Vijay at the bar.

'Oh, they'll be along jolly soon,' Alexandra said as she sipped her sparkling white wine.

We'd made a pact to keep the altercation with Summer a secret. The last thing I wanted was the group's last get-together to be ruined. 'It should be a celebration of group solidarity and friendship,' I'd said on our way downstairs, and Alexandra had agreed.

* * *

THEY ARRIVED FIFTEEN MINUTES LATER. While Summer chatted with Ivan, Charlie whispered in my ear, 'Can I have a word please, Jen?' I nodded and we moved to the corner of the bar. 'I owe you an apology. Summer's told me what she did. I can't believe she could do such a thing.' He shook his head. 'An internet troll.'

'Did she tell you why she did it?' I asked.

'Yes, she admitted she'd become fixated on Fraser.'

'Are you going to walk away from her, Charlie?'

'I don't know. I'll need to think about it when we get home. I'm in love with her, Jen. Maybe I can help her. Encourage her to get help.'

I patted his arm. 'You're one of the good guys. She's a lucky woman.'

Vijay shouted from the bar, 'Jen, Charlie please come. It's group photo time.'

* * *

LATER, on our way back to our rooms Alexandra and I paused at my door. 'May I ask you about something that's been bothering me, Jen? If you don't want to answer, just say so and I won't ask again.'

My bright reply belied my disquiet.

'I can't help thinking about that day during our sailing when we visited the village, and those kids were picking on that little girl.'

'Your reaction frightened me, Jen. It was so extreme. There was heartache and fear in your eyes that day. I can't get it out of my mind. I'm worried for you. Something is telling me it's not just fear of your illness that created such panic in you that day. What's happened to you to make you feel that way, Jen?'

You could send her away now, if you want to lose part of this new Jen you've found.

'Come in Alexandra and settle yourself on the bed while I make us a brew. It's a long story.'

34

After an eternity, my luggage emerged from the void behind the black plastic flaps and wobbled towards me. I steadied myself and with one heave landed the bag on the floor next to my feet. I was the last one of the group to retrieve my luggage from the conveyor belt of the New Delhi to London Heathrow flight baggage carousel. The others waited to say our final goodbyes. Betty wrapped her arms around me as I dropped my bag at my feet.

'It's been lovely getting to know you, Jen. Thanks for all your help,' she said.

Next it was Derek's turn to give me a bear hug.

'Thanks for finding me in Bombay, Julia,' he said.

I looked up into his smiling face and recognised his mischievous grin. With a wink he laughed, and everyone else joined in.

This was the real person, the man who was slipping away from Betty bit by bit. Tears glistened in her eyes. It was so sad that I'd only got to see glimpses of the man he must have been.

As I hugged Ivan, I thanked him for sharing his love of

history and bringing the places we'd visited to life through his knowledge.

Summer stood before me staring at the floor. When she looked up I detected shame in the depths of the brown eyes I'd once thought were beautiful. The self-assured woman had disappeared and in her place was someone full of remorse. 'Thank you for not telling the others, Jen. Will you ever be able to forgive me?'

There and then I decided I'd refuse to allow bitterness to take root inside me. I would need to harness every ounce of positivity I could muster in the near future. I would not allow the nasty episode with Summer to sap the strength India had instilled within me.

'If you want my forgiveness, you must promise me something.' She nodded. 'You need to get professional help, Summer. If you do that, then I can forgive you.'

'I will Jen, and Charlie's going to support me on that.' Charlie hugged her close to him, his love for her shining in his eyes.

The couple waved goodbye and strolled away hand in hand.

Fraser hugged me close then held me away from him at arm's length.

'Oh Fraser, if only things had been diff—'

'Shhh.' He placed a finger on my lips. 'No need for words. I know the score, hen. Let me know how yer surgery goes. I'm sure it'll be successful.' He kissed me on the cheek, spun on his heel and strolled away, disappearing amongst the throng.

'Well, this is jolly sad, saying goodbye for now, but this is the beginning not the end. As soon as you tell me the date for your surgery, I'll be coming up to Newcastle to help you recuperate. As long as Martin won't mind. I promise not to be too bossy when I'm helping you to recover. Oh golly Jen, don't cry. You'll start me off.'

We said tearful goodbyes and hugged. 'See you soon, Alexandra,' I shouted. She waved, and I turned and strode towards the exit.

I walked through the door pulling my luggage with heavy legs to be faced with a throng waiting to greet people arriving on the flight from New Delhi. I scanned the faces and placards showing unfamiliar surnames and then I saw Martin standing at the back of the crowd. Our eyes met. Any remaining shred of doubt about who I wanted to spend the rest of my life with, whether it be long or short, vaporised into thin air. There was my rock, my soulmate waiting to take me home. He waved, and I quickened my pace, running towards him. People jamming the door halted my progress. They created a bottleneck as they tried to push their way through the exit. From the short distance I could not tear my eyes from Martin's smiling face as I waited for my turn to move through the door. As I gazed, a warm tingling rose in the centre of my chest and spread outward. All I could see was that precious face, and I knew this was how love and happiness felt. At last the scrum at the door cleared, and I ran into Martin's arms.

'Welcome home,' he said as he hugged me tight and lifted me off my feet.

We stepped through the airport exit door into bright, chilly sunshine. Martin smiled, wrinkled his nose and grabbed his nostrils. 'You could do with a hot bath.'

EPILOGUE

The letter from Dr Khalid, the Urology Consultant, was propped up on the mantelpiece awaiting my return. I closed my eyes, took a calming breath and with trembling fingers tore at the envelope seal.

'He's arranged my surgery for April the twenty-sixth, Martin. Our wedding anniversary,' I said, swallowing hard.

Martin held me close. His heart thumped against my chest. 'Well, that's a lucky date, Jen. It's the date we got married.' He kissed the top of my head where it rested on his shoulder.

* * *

'I READ every one of your blogs.' Priti looked at me over the top of our monitors. 'Did you see the messages I wrote? Mam and Dad think you've got a talent for photography. They looked forward to reading your blog every day. It brought memories of home flooding back for them. Are you nervous about your interview tomorrow?'

'Nervous doesn't cover it, Priti. My feelings are flitting

between apprehension, ambition and excitement all rolled into one. I'm bound to be up against stiff competition.' As I spoke, my stomach fluttered with the wings of a thousand butterflies.

Martin had helped choose the best of my images for my portfolio. 'You've got to include these ones of the ladies performing their Morning Puja,' he'd said as we sifted through the prints. The panel will be drawn into these scenes. And, these ones of the Ganga Evening Aarti Ceremony at Rishikesh are so evocative, I can't help but smile when I look at them. I can hear the music and chanting.'

I'd practiced my presentation a million times. What questions would the panel ask? What questions should I ask them? Which countries did the cruises visit? What would be the start date? That thought jarred me back to the present.

* * *

THE FACES of the panel were inscrutable as they pored over my portfolio and asked questions about how I'd approached photographing strangers. That question was easy; India and my friends had shown me the way. The one-hour interview seemed to last but minutes. My presentation was word-perfect. I told them of my upcoming surgery and breathed a private sigh of relief when Dominic, the Head of the panel said, 'That's not a problem, Jen. Our current photographer is retiring in the summer and her end date is flexible. For the right person, we would be prepared to postpone the start date if necessary.'

I hoped the panel recognised the confidence and professionalism that had been growing in me every day. The tiny dot that was the real Jen wasn't so tiny any more. As I shook hands with Helen, the Company Entertainment Director, at the end of the interview she asked, 'What camera model did you use, Jen?' When I answered all three nodded, their faces gave nothing away. My chest tightened, my heart started to shrink. That's torn it. Every other candidate will have used top-end equipment. What on earth made me believe I could compete with a point-and-shoot camera?

* * *

IT WAS Thursday morning and before I headed over the Tyne Bridge to my yoga class, I logged onto my blog.

Ping, ping, ping, piiiiing.

'Eeeh Martin, look at this. Five thousand, six hundred and seventy followers. Where the hell are they all coming from? How are they finding my blog?'

'It's because your photos and writing are so compelling, Jen. Getting hit on the head by that raft must have knocked some talent into you as well as a bit of common sense.'

'Cheeky devil. I'm sorry the lens you spent a fortune on is languishing at the bottom of the Ganges somewhere,' I said.

> *Hi Jen, I started following your blog when the link to A Geordie Up The Ganges popped up in my Facebook newsfeed. I've loved following your adventures and I'm sad your trip to India has ended. You've evoked stories with your photos and got beneath the surface of the people you've met, to reveal their emotions. For me you've captured those special moments which tell the viewer what it is to be that person. Your images stay with me. I can't forget them. It's wonderful to find someone whose work isn't produced by the camera but is made by the photographer themselves along with their subjects. Look*

> *forward to following your work on your next adventure. Pete, Texas, USA*

> *Hello, I'm from India and I love the way you have written about my country, especially how you have described the Kumbh Mela. I was there too and your words bring my experiences back to life for me. Please continue to take us along with you on your next adventure. Thank you. Shalu.*

THERE WAS A PRIVATE MESSAGE HIGHLIGHTED, unopened at the bottom of the screen. The header said **Cruise Ship Photographer Interview.** I hesitated, holding my finger over the 'read' icon, reluctant to leave that space where anticipation spawned excitement.

I closed my eyes, lowered my finger and squinted at the screen when I heard the click.

> The words *delighted to offer you the position* were the first I saw, and as I read on: *We were very impressed with your portfolio which exuded that ineffable quality we are looking for in the work of our Cruise Ship Photographer. With your images we believe you will give our customers memories they will treasure long after their cruise has ended and will encourage them to cruise with us again. Your passion and enthusiasm shone through along with your talent made obvious by making evocative images with basic equipment.*

'Maaartin. I've got the job,' I yelled.

He wrapped his arms around my waist and lifted me off my feet.

* * *

After months of sub-zero temperatures, Newcastle had shed its winter woes. My spirits soared. Beams of sunlight bounced off the shimmering facade of The Shard concert hall as I drove over the Tyne Bridge to my yoga class in Gateshead. There was a sense of renewed optimism in the air. Even drivers on the Tyne Bridge were more disposed to kindness; giving way to other vehicles heading to and from the Toon. The river ran high, and there was a clean, damp smell riding on the whisper of the breeze after the brief morning shower.

The reaction from my fellow yoga practitioners as I stepped into the church hall took me by surprise as they crowded around me. I looked at their faces in astonishment. They were talking about my trip to India and my blog.

'Welcome back Jen, pet. I loved your blog,' said Gemma

'Aye me an all,' said Joy. 'I followed every one of your stories. Your photos are fantastic, you brought India to life for me.'

'Eeeh, you've made me want to go to India now, like,' said Anne.

They were firing excited questions at me and the clamour only died down when the singing from Emma's tingsha prayer bells announced that class had begun. From my mat at the back of the room, I could see the lady in the psychedelic leggings three mats away from me. I thought back to that fateful morning when she'd broken wind in my face.

It just goes to show. Everything in life can show you the way; be a signpost; a guide. Even the most unsavoury event can be a source of inspiration if you look at it in the right way. Even a fart.

As everyone filed out at the end of a relaxing ninety minutes, Emma took me to one side.

'You're aware I'm on the committee of the North East Yoga Association, Jen?'

I nodded.

'Your blog has impressed so many people. Everyone in the yoga community is talking about it. We'd like to invite you to present the story of your adventures in India at our Annual North East Convention in two weeks time. We'd love you to show your photos and talk to delegates about your experiences. Please say you'll do it.'

I could feel my mouth falling open. Butterfly wings fluttered in my belly.

'Eeeh Emma, no, I don't know enough about India to do that,' was all I could utter.

'It's your personal perspective on what you experienced there that people will want to hear, Jen. How the country and the people you met there have affected you. That's what's made your blog so compelling. Just be yourself and your presentation will be amazing.'

I knew that the old Jen would hide away. Well, I couldn't let that happen. Could I?

35

The bell rang, and I sprang from the sofa and bounced to the front door. I jerked the door open to see Alexandra sporting a huge smile, her shock of red hair flaming in bright sunlight. We stood hugging, swaying from side to side. She'd driven from Windsor to Newcastle to visit for the weekend, determined to see me before my operation.

I'd had my meeting with Mr Khalid where he'd told me I was to undergo a radical nephrectomy; major surgery to remove my right kidney. He could not confirm whether the cancer was restricted to my kidney. 'The scans we've conducted haven't indicated the cancer has spread to any of the organs nearby, but we won't know for certain until we open you up and take a look inside. The prognosis is uncertain at this stage. Recovery time is up to six weeks. After removal of a kidney the loss of kidney function is usually mild, and life span is normal. Most people with one kidney live healthy, normal lives. One healthy kidney can work as well as two,' he'd said.

Over the following days Martin and I had kept darkness

at bay by grabbing onto the positives. We'd refused to dwell on the unthinkable.

It was a breath of fresh air to see Alexandra, and after chatting over a coffee, Martin left us alone to catch up with our news and to reminisce. 'That wall hanging looks rather splendid in its frame. It's a jolly wonderful reminder of our time in India. This God with the elephant head is Ganesha, he's the remover of obstacles; this one's Shiva, the lord of dance and regeneration; this one with the blue skin is Krishna, he's the deity of love and compassion. What's the name of the monkey-faced God again, Jen?'

'That's Hanuman, the symbol of physical strength and perseverance. It's a gorgeous wall hanging, isn't it? It's so special to me. It's the present that Derek and Betty gave me in Calcutta.' I smiled at the memory.

'I got an e-mail from Betty yesterday,' I said. 'She said Derek's responding well to his medication. It seems to have slowed the advancement of the Alzheimer's down and increased the clarity in his mind. She said he's always talking about what a fantastic time they had in India.'

'I wonder if Summer and Charlie will stay together?' said Alexandra.

'Time will tell, I suppose. If she gets the help she needs then the relationship may stand a chance,' I said, not wanting to dwell on Summer any further, 'and did you hear? Fraser's going to open another fitness studio in Glasgow. His business is going from strength to strength.' As I said his name, my stomach fluttered at the thought of him. But now I knew it was the fleeting excitement to which thoughts of forbidden fruits can give rise.

'Oh, and Ivan e-mailed to say he'd signed up for a month-long trip around China,' I added.

'I was pleased to hear you'd been successful in your interview but there's something I want to talk to you about.'

I was curious. She looked excited.

'Have you considered a career in writing?'

'No, never.'

'I passed the link of your blog to one of the publishers I work with. She loved it, Jen. She said her company are welcoming new writers and that your story is just what they're looking for.'

'Eeeh, that's a shock, Alexandra. A writer!'

'I know it's a big decision to make Jen. Just promise me you'll think about what you really want in life.'

I looked into the earnest forest green eyes imploring me to be honest with myself and sensed a movement inside my being. Like a shoot, poking its way through soil, emerging from darkness into blinding light.

* * *

THE WEEKEND with Alexandra had been nourishing; the bonds that had blossomed in India had developed into a lifelong friendship. It had also been unsettling, and I needed to think. I drove to the place where I was always drawn to when I wanted to clear my mind. The place of my heart.

'Alreet Pet?' asked the woman pushing her stroller in the morning sun, her baby boy gurgling and waving his rattle.

'Aye. Aaam canny Pet. Yee alreet?'

'Aye Pet. Aaam canny. Tarra.'

'Tarra.'

On the quayside, life below the Sage was carrying on as normal.

I gazed at the ever-rolling water. The warm breeze fluttered on my face. The fog in my mind cleared, and I saw the way ahead. I knew I could trust my judgement.

* * *

THERE WERE record numbers at the Annual North East Yoga Convention. Two hundred and fifty people crammed into the tiered seating of the largest lecture hall at the local college. From where I stood behind the curtain, I inched the heavy grey velvet fabric open to peep through to the stage, and the audience beyond. My laptop was on a desk in the stage's centre. It was open and switched on in readiness, at the opening slide of my presentation. The microphone on the podium had been tested and the mammoth screen behind where I would stand flickered with impatience. I'd prepared to within an inch of my life, perfecting my slides, images and bullet points. A buzz filled the hall as people chatted with their neighbours, sipped from cans and bottles or devoured snacks from the college canteen. I searched the crowd for Martin. There he was, in the front row.

There was five minutes to go, and it felt like an eternity. I'd paced back and forth behind the curtain but that had only increased my dry mouth and nausea. I'd tried concentrating on the bulletin boards and the notices advising of lecture times. Studying the poster advertising local band Screech at the Black Swan every Saturday night for the millionth time didn't help either. The concerted effort to calm myself was starting a headache, not helped with the strong smell of floor cleaner stinging my nostrils.

I prised the fabric open an inch but, instead of Martin, my eyes settled on someone else, sitting in the middle row of seats. I knew that face. Where did I know her from? Was it work, was it the yoga class, was it from the shops around

Gosforth? No, I couldn't place her. It was when I noticed the woman sat next to her with the bright ginger, curly hair a memory stirred. The sounds whirred in my mind like a washing machine on the spin cycle. Nebulous and echoing from far away. Then the sounds formed into words. Words which now screamed in my face.

'Pigs love to eat shit. Here's yer dinner.' The face I recognised was Susan, the girl who had once been my best friend.

'Divvent come to play on our estate, Jenny Watson. We divvent want dirty pigs like ye near wor houses. Stay in yer pigsty.' The contorted, spiteful face of a little ginger-haired girl swam before my eyes.

The shock of seeing two of my childhood tormentors generated an electric current which pulsed up my spine. I froze, snapped the curtain shut and recoiled, covering my mouth with my hand. I was alone behind the curtain waiting for my introduction. In panic I turned round on the spot, twisting right then left, fighting the urge to run. A sudden explosion of freezing cold expanded in my stomach then crept upwards to spread icy fingers around my chest.

Why the hell had I let Emma talk me into this? I had to calm down. I slowed my breathing like I'd been taught and thought back to all I'd learned in India. I'd nearly died under a raft! Alexandra had staked her professional reputation on showing my work to a publisher. I breathed slow and deep into my abdomen until the pounding in my chest abated.

This was my moment. I'd show that never again would I let what happened to me in the past affect how I lived the rest of my life.

In front of the curtain I heard Emma's footsteps on the wooden boarded stage. A hush descended in the hall followed by three dull thumps in quick succession confirming the microphone was functional.

I took one huge breath as the curtain opened to a rapturous welcoming applause. I fixed my eyes on Martin and strode with head held high into the middle of the stage.

36

The day of our wedding anniversary arrived and we headed to the hospital at six o'clock in the morning. I'd fought with every ounce of my strength to prepare my heart and mind for this day. For me there was only one outcome. The surgery would be successful and I'd survive.

After the interminable round of form filling the nurse instructed that I remove all clothing and jewellery and get into the theatre gown. 'You'll need to remove this too.' She pointed to the raksha sutra wrapped around my left wrist.

'No, I'm leaving that on.' The priest had wrapped it around my wrist at the Evening Aarti Ceremony at Rishikesh, blessed me and said it would bring me luck. He told me it must be allowed to fall off itself when I no longer had need of it. They would have to chop my hand off to remove it from my wrist before I would undo that knot myself. My tone had demonstrated my determination and thankfully she didn't argue further.

Mr Khalid drew an arrow with a black marker pen on the right side of my abdomen. He read through the consent form and asked if I had any concerns. Suddenly I felt very scared but I knew how to conquer my body's reaction to the rising fear now, and called on the breathing techniques I'd practiced so often. Another tiny battle in the war was won, fear was banished and replaced with a feeling of calm determination. 'I feel I'm in very safe hands.' I looked up at him, he patted my arm and said he'd studied the scans carefully.

He left Martin and I alone. We held each other and made plans for our anniversary meal, to be celebrated a little later than we'd anticipated. When it was time the nurse came and led me towards theatre number seven. As the anaesthetist placed the mask over my nose and mouth and I breathed in the sweet, sickly gas I concentrated on every minute feature of the vision of Martin's beloved face now hovering in front of my eyes.

* * *

I WAS STOOD at the back of a brightly lit room. Martin and my friends were seated in rows of chairs facing the front with their backs to me. I walked over to the back corner of the room, opened a door in the wall and stepped through into darkness.

I found myself in a dim oak panelled corridor. Looking ahead the walls narrowed and converged to a black point which continued stretching on into infinity. I narrowed my eyes, straining to understand where the black point was leading to. But it was beyond my comprehension. I shivered.

Without warning I heard a loud creaking sound directly to my right and turned to see that one of the oak panels was slowly bulging out into the corridor. I watched with rising alarm as the bulge grew larger and the oak began to splinter.

The panelling split asunder with a deafening crash and before I could react a black wraith-like entity sprung from the gloom, landed on top of me and wrestled me to the floor. The weight of the thing was overpowering but something told me to resist with every ounce of my being. As I forced my way up to standing the creature grappled, trying to drag me back down again and we swayed back and forth locked in combat. It began to crook a finger, slyly beseeching. 'Come with me, come with me,' it kept repeating in a voice laced with poison.

Within the darkness I caught a glance of a huge hypodermic syringe in a black gloved hand advancing towards my neck. I grabbed at it with my free hand before it could make contact with my skin. I managed to prise my thumb under the plunger and push with all my might to prevent the needle from piercing my neck. As we grappled in the pitch black the mighty strength which flowed through my thumb forced the creature to abruptly release the needle which fell through the darkness to the floor. With an ever-increasing strength coursing through my body, I heaved the entity off my back. The shape was flung backwards, releasing me like a spring, and I crashed back through the door from whence I'd come. The startling bright light hurt my eyes. The people in the seats turned in surprise to look.

'Help me,' I screamed.

* * *

'How do you feel?' Mr Khalid stood at the bottom of my bed.

'Like I've just gone ten rounds with a heavy-weight wrestler,' I managed to garble, still groggy from the anaesthetic. Martin stroked my hand.

'It was a difficult operation,' said Mr Khalid. 'It took us nearly six hours to work on you. I tried to save your right kidney by performing a partial nephrectomy, just removing the tumour. Unfortunately it was situated very close to a blood vessel. I had no option other than to remove the whole kidney. I had to open you up wider that I thought. Sorry but you've a thirteen-inch scar across your abdomen. You've been in intensive care for two nights.' I studied his face, looking for clues as to what he was going to utter next. Watching for any twitch of his face. Searching for any slight change of expression in his eyes. 'I'm pleased to say there's no spread of the disease to other organs.'

The words exploded in my head. Martin and I inhaled a huge breath and squeezed each others hands. Mr Khalid continued. 'Recovery time will be about six weeks and as a precaution we'll need to scan you regularly for up to ten years, but I'm sure you'll make a full recovery.'

My head fell back and I stared at the ceiling, struggling to speak, to find the right words. I drew a long deep breath through my nose. The only words I could utter were, 'Thank you.'

Mr Khalid left Martin and I alone and we held each other's hands in a silence heavy with an all-consuming relief. My thoughts were ecstatic and hot tears ran down my cheeks. The only part of my body I could move without hurting was my left arm and I held it aloft. As I weakly began to wave my arm from side to side in celebration I caught a flash of movement out of the corner of my eye.

I looked down. There, lying on top of the bedclothes was my raksha sutra.

Its knot undone.

ABOUT THE AUTHOR

Nell Cook is an author, photographer, and Geordie Lass who writes stories about ordinary people in extraordinary situations.

Her debut novel, *A Geordie Up The Ganges*, was inspired by a life-changing trip to India that she undertook just five days after a shock cancer diagnosis.

Poignant and hilarious, Nell's novel celebrates the love, strength, humour and sheer determination to beat the odds we each have within us.

Nell was born and bred in Newcastle-Upon-Tyne and now lives in Blackpool. She is little but noisy, enjoys drinking coffee and loves witnessing the rising of the sun.

If you enjoyed *A Geordie Up The Ganges* please leave a review on Amazon as this helps other readers discover Nell's book.

Check out Nell's website below;

www.nellcookauthor.com

and connect with her on facebook and twitter.

facebook.com/nellcookauthor

twitter.com/AuthorNellC

INTERVIEW WITH NELL

Q: The inspiration for the story was your trip to India. Can you tell us more?

A: I'd discovered yoga five years before. It changed my life and my interest in yogic philosophy deepened when I studied the British Wheel of Yoga foundation course. That's when the compulsion to visit India was born. I needed to immerse myself in the country which had founded yoga over five thousand years before. After two years of planning my world was ripped apart when on my fifty-fifth birthday, just five days before my planned departure, I was given a bombshell diagnosis of kidney cancer. With support from my husband John and my family and permission from my Consultant I picked myself up, dusted myself off and boarded the flight for my adventure of a lifetime. My future was uncertain, so I was determined to make the most of any time I had left and face my treatment on my return home. I survived cancer and fell in love with India. I'm now cancer free.

Q: Why did you write a novel?

A: It all began when I set up a blog to document my adventure. The blog proved very popular and John instilled in me the belief that I had an amazing story to tell and a talent for writing to go with it. I decided against writing a memoir as I didn't want to be constrained by having to stick one hundred percent to the truth. I wanted to flex my creative muscle and give my readers a story that would entertain, surprise and inspire. That being said, I sprinkled the story with an element of truth, although the characters are pure fiction.

Q: What is the key theme and message in your book?

A: The theme is self-discovery with the message that your past need not dictate your future.

Q: What was the emotional impact for you as you were writing this book?

A: Writing A Geordie Up The Ganges unleashed emotions I didn't realise were stored away. I cried and my skin tingled when I reminisced. But I also laughed a lot.

Q: What do you hope your readers will take away from this book.

A: If my book inspires just one person or changes someone's life, then it would make everything that has gone before worthwhile.

Q: What is the future for your protagonist? Will there be a sequel?

A: Jennifer Barnes is a strong woman and I don't feel she will allow me to forget about her any time soon. I sense she has more adventures to come.

Q: What's your favourite quote?

A: "She believed she could, so she did". I have a large poster in a frame on the wall in my writing cave with these words. Such a profound and empowering quote. I gaze at the words often.

Q: What do you like to do when you're not writing?

A: Photography. My other obsession. Give me a beautiful landscape at the beginning or end of the day and I'm a happy bunny.

ACKNOWLEDGMENTS

My thanks to my Editors Claire Wingfield, who helped me to hone my narrative skills, and Susan Harrison, who encouraged me to test my writing mettle with fiction.

Jan Geddes, Jayne Timmins and Ted Cook my beta readers whose opinions were invaluable.

Rick, my hairdresser of many years, who planted the seed of me setting up a blog to record my Indian adventure during a cut and blow.

Katie Beavers my first yoga teacher, whose leaflet inviting me to her class dropped through my letterbox all those years ago, and led me to discover yoga. Debbie Farrar whose inspired yogic teaching instilled in me the desire to visit India.

Rosie Smith and Emma Smith who I worked with as a contributor on the production of a pilot television programme. Their belief in me and my story was the catalyst that galvanised me to return to finish my manuscript after it had been gathering dust for four years.

My girls Mam, Joanne and Freyja for listening to the many twists, turns and changes of mind in my plot points.

And extra special thanks to John, my husband, for his unshakable, total belief in me; for uplifting me on those unproductive days and for being the best editor, proof reader and most patient advisor any author could wish for.

Printed in Great Britain
by Amazon

58367369R00187